THE HUMAN BET

AN EQUILOAM ROMANCE
BOOK ONE

MONA HOWELL

Cover Designer: Melmul

Copy Editor: Joseph Perez

Sensitivity Reader: Shannon Clark

Author Photograph: Emily Winnie Photography

CONTENT WARNING

Content Warnings

The Human Bet is an adult interspecies fantasy romance novel. It contains adult themes, including Explicit Content, including a variety of Sexual Situations, Self Satisfaction, Non-Monogomous Intercourse, Sexual Exploitation, Sexual Violence, Bondage Fantasization, Non-human Genitalia, Vaginal Teeth, and Primal Play.

Some content may not be suitable for readers with sensitivities to Inter-family Conflict, Dysphoria, Alcohol use, Inference to Substance Use, Prejudice and Graphic Violent Descriptions of Death and Mutilation, and Arachnophobia.

For Jessica

Saetabis
Felt:Thalas
Smoghelm
Oar Curuhm
Wildomire
Equiloam Sea
Alfotdrath
Søgsund
Rookfall
Little Break
Big Break
Swi'loor
Th'myskóra
Brilansis

The Drowned Grimoire stood a few hundred yards away from the trade ports. Its sturdy limestone walls, and thatched roof were a welcome sight to visiting sailors and local Th'myskôrians alike. Everyone knew, day or night, if you could see the golden firelight flickering inside of its windows, you could stop in the Drowned Grim for an ale, and a hot meal. And Bridgid *always* kept the fires lit. Tonight the little tavern was teeming with visitors to the island. Bawdy music and raucous conversation shook its walls and spilled out onto the street.

Inside, Leeja squirmed against her wooden stool; she hadn't

mated in eight days, and the need welling up within her was becoming unbearable. She looked down at the ale trembling in her tankard. She was lightheaded. The sackbut and flutes rang out an unrelentingly cheery melody. Drunken revelers, called by the drums to the middle of the tavern, swirled and jumped, falling into each other's arms. The pounding feet of the dancers sent shockwaves through the floor and up into Leeja's aching core. Her swollen clit thumped mercilessly along with the music.

She tugged absentmindedly at her cote—the same dull shapeless brown dress she was wearing when she arrived on Th'myskôra all those months ago. The color was extremely unflattering, it made her inky green hair look muddy, and washed out her tawny complexion. And its loose fit almost completely obscured her powerful frame. Of course, no one cared about such things back home on Søgsund.

"Why did the goddess curse me with this orcish body?" she whined, finishing her pint and slamming her head down hard on the table.

"Technically," said Imogen, looking up from her pile of scrolls, "since you're of mixed parentage, your body is half human too."

"Yeah, too bad it's not the bottom half," Leeja whimpered, not bothering to lift her head. She let her long, heavily muscled arms hang limp in their sockets and grumbled an incomprehensible moan.

"I have had just about enough of this moping!" scolded Arlynn. "This place is *crawling* with guys."

"This place is crawling with *human* guys." Leeja looked around the Drowned Grimoire at all of the visiting sailors, "You know how I feel about humans."

Imogen looked up from her work again, eyes wide.

"I don't mean you two," Leeja soothed, patting Imogen's

soft arm. "I mean human *men*. I don't like them, and they definitely don't like me."

"I wouldn't be too sure about that," said Arlynn smugly, gesturing to a table across the room. "Those guys have been staring over here all night. Just walk up to one of them, say that you'd like to be rammed, please, and put us all out of our *fucking* misery."

Leeja squinted, struggling to see the men in the dim firelight from the hearth. The direct approach had always worked for her in the past; maybe it could be just as easy with humans. One of them did seem to be smiling at her.

Yes! Go! Fuck! Her body screamed.

"All right," she said, climbing down off her stool and smoothing her skirts, "tonight's the night I fuck a human. Desperate times and all that..."

Leeja's friends squealed with delight as she strode across the tavern.

"Excuse me," she said to the smallest of the men. He was swarthy and stout, not entirely unlike a dwarf in appearance, "I was hoping you'd let me borrow your dick for half an hour or so."

Conversation ceased. The swarthy man and all of his friends stared up at Leeja's towering countenance— stunned.

"You were smiling at me, so I just thought..."

"Oh! Oh, I see," the man stammered. "This is embarrassing. I was actually hoping to talk to your friend over there, the redhead? I'm so sorry for the confusion."

"Don't give it a second thought," Leeja said, green rushing to the surface of her walnut-colored cheeks. As she turned to walk away, she could hear the table of men erupt in laughter.

"Oy! Can you imagine going home with Big Bertha?" asked one of the men.

"She'd crush you to death," joked another.

"Crushed to death? I'd be worried about her ripping my balls off with those tusks," offered a third.

Leeja held her head high as each new insult rang in her ears.

Her eyes stung, and she forced her voice to remain flat as she reported to her girlfriends, "They were looking at you, Arlynn."

Of course they were.

Arlynn was beautiful. She was petite; men often joked about her small size as they hoisted her up above their heads, earning a torrent of giggles. Her silken, scarlet hair always lay in obedient waves, exactly where she wanted them to be. When Arlynn talked back to men, they called her "feisty". And when *she* blushed, timid peachy tones crept to the surface of her alabaster skin, mingling with cute, orange freckles.

Imogen, too, was gorgeous, perhaps even more so. Her wide hips, large breasts, and soft tummy were the exact proportions of the fertility goddess statue. Her skin was a rich bronze, and her honey-golden hair radiated out from her head in all directions like tightly wound spirals of sunshine. Her appearance dripped with lush, feminine abundance. When *she* refused men's advances, telling them she had a boyfriend and returning to her work, it made them want her more.

Leeja wasn't small, and she wasn't soft, but she could be injured. She needed to get out of this tavern before she started to cry.

"What a bunch of idiots!" said Arlynn; she'd seen the men erupt in laughter, and now the reaction made sense. "Do you want me to break their noses? Because I will walk right over there and—"

"No thanks," said Leeja, smiling despite herself. "I'm way too horny to enjoy a brawl at the moment."

"I guess they can live...for now," Arlynn scowled playfully. "Pull up a stool; we'll order another round!"

"Thanks, but I'm gonna get out of here." Leeja's friends frowned, "I'll be fine. I just really have to take care of this," she said, gesturing to her aching crotch. Arlynn opened her mouth to speak; thankfully, Imogen elected to interject at that moment.

"If an orc goes too long without mating, it can become a medical emergency. We really should let her go."

Arlynn huffed and folded her arms, "Fine, go home and rub one out or whatever. Just be safe."

Leeja nodded.

"Don't forget we have breakfast in the morning!" she heard Arlynn call as the tavern door swung closed behind her.

Finally alone on the street, in the privacy of the cool, dark night— Leeja cried. She wrapped herself up in her own strong arms and wept from a place deep in her chest. It wasn't just the rejection or the jokes at her expense. It was the looks her friends gave her. When Leeja returned to the table unsuccessful, her best friends' beautiful faces were marred with confusion and... pity. Clearly, they could not understand how any female could be denied sex from a whole table of human men. Leeja didn't understand it either, but she knew something was intrinsically wrong with her. After all, if she weren't somehow deficient, somehow wrong, she would have formed a horde by now.

Hells, if I weren't broken, he...that's enough self-pity. Leeja wiped her nose on her sleeve. *If I don't get laid soon, I'm going to lose my mind.*

As luck would have it, a large ogre stepped out onto the cobblestone street in the very next moment. He whipped his head around in her direction. A second later, his hand was on her lower back, his face inches from hers. He'd scented the desire pooling in her linen smallclothes.

The ogre was tall. Taller than Leeja. And he was properly green. He had a wide, flat nose and small tubular ears that stuck straight out from his head in either direction. He had broad, muscular shoulders and a thick, insulating layer of fat around his strong abdomen. His hips were a little narrow, and his legs scrawny, but if his thick neck and massive fingers were any indication, he'd get the job done.

"What's your name, love?" asked the ogre. His hot, earthy breath singed her nostrils; his ravenous stare singed her soul.

"Names don't matter tonight, big boy," Leeja said, smiling. She slid her hand over the sizable bulge at the front of his tights. She felt it throbbing, promising her relief. "How's about the three of us go back to your place?" She gave his growing erection a playful squeeze. The ogre let out a satisfied groan and led Leeja away.

Leeja and the ogre tumbled through his door, groping wildly at each other's bodies in the near-dark. The ogre tore his mouth from Leeja's neck and pushed her roughly onto the bed. A second later, he'd ripped off his tunic and threw his tartan tights across the room. Leeja looked up at his cock, transfixed. It was fully erect now. She could see a shimmering droplet of precum peeking out past the top of his forest-green foreskin. His dick was long and incredibly thick, even for an ogre.

Leeja smiled deviously, "Oh, this is going to work out just fine," she said, licking her lips.

The ogre charged at her, and a low rumble crawled up the back of his throat. He was making to pull off her dress.

"Not so fast, big boy," Leeja said, ducking out of the way and pinning him on the bed beneath her. "We're doing this my way."

"What did you have in mind, love?" The ogre asked, squirming and bucking at the mattress. Leeja was desperate for him to plunge inside of her, to feel him stretch her, but that didn't mean she was going to let him undress her.

Leeja slid off the bed and removed her smallclothes, the close-fitting knee breeches she wore under her skirts were soaked through. She tossed them aside and returned her attention to the fat ogre cock waiting for her on the bed. She slid her lips down his cockhead, gently pushing his foreskin back and tasting his bitter, viscous precum. It was thick, like honey. Leeja used her tongue to spread the precious drop across the roof of her mouth. To her delight, it stuck. A wide smile spread across her face as she closed her eyes, savoring the flavor and texture of him.

The ogre groaned, and Leeja licked frantically at the tip of his cock. She wanted so badly to coax out more of that earthy, ogre flavor.

Easy, girl. Make sure you get yourself off first. Otherwise, you'll be in this same mess again tomorrow night.

She hiked up her skirts and climbed on top of him, pinning his cock between his belly and her cunt. She slid back and forth along its length, grinding her clit against his swollen member. Leeja closed her eyes and chewed her bottom lip.

"Goddess, this is good!" She groaned, feeling her nipples tighten and her core clench.

The captive ogre reached up, groping at her large breasts. He was trying again to pull off her dress. Leeja's concentration was broken.

Damn, I'll have to start all over again.

She swatted his hand away and pulled her bodice back up, tying the little ribbon at the center in a tight double knot, obscuring her breasts.

"You just lay back and do as you're told."

"Yes, ma'am," the ogre's eager cock thumped hard against her.

Leeja readjusted herself and wrapped her hand around the base of his heavy cock. She sucked a sharp breath between her teeth when she realized it was too thick to close her fist around him.

"Big enough for you, love?" The ogre smirked up at her.

"No more talking!" Leeja said, smacking him lightly on the mouth. "It's time to cum." She adjusted them both so that the tip of his dick was pressed lightly against her opening.

Thank you, goddess, for this tremendous cock, Leeja thought as she slid herself carefully down its length.

The ogre let out a deep, guttural groan, and his hands flew up to squeeze the firm, muscular globes of her ass. The extra pressure was enough to send Leeja over the edge. Her breath caught, and her body was wracked with convulsions as the slick release of her orgasm slid down his shaft and pooled at its base.

Leeja opened her eyes. The ogre was smiling up at her, "I hope that wasn't the grand finale."

Leeja closed her eyes again, concentrating on the feeling of his cock inside her as she slowly rocked up and down its length. With each downward motion, she took a little more of him. Her inner walls strained to accommodate his girth, but the churning, vibrating hunger deep in her core demanded that she take more of him. It needed to be fed, needed to be full, needed this fat, green cock to split it open.

Finally, Leeja was about halfway down. She put her hands on the mattress, on either side of the ogre. She adjusted the angle of her hips, searching for her G-spot.

There you are.

Leeja let out a satisfied moan as she settled on a slow rhythm, massaging herself with the ogre's deliciously bulbous cock-head. She could feel the pressure building again. She was close.

Beneath her, the ogre was getting impatient. He dug his fingers into her hips and slammed her down, simultaneously thrusting up to meet her.

Leeja growled in pleasure as his pelvis crashed into her ass. The ogre was holding her hips in place and fucking up into her in short, quick strokes. His balls bounced off her ass each time he buried himself in her, and little flecks of her cum sprayed off in all directions every time their bodies made contact. Leeja's cunt was tensing,

This is going to be a big one.

"I'm cumming!" shouted the ogre, and Leeja sat up straight, forcing his cock deep inside her and holding it there. She felt his balls tense under her ass and his cock jerk wildly inside her. That's when her own orgasm rocketed through her. As her inner muscles fluttered, the quick contractions radiated outward through her entire body. Her arms and legs shook so violently that she had to brace herself on the wall behind the bed. But she refused to give up even an inch of that fantastic cock. She pushed hard against the wall, forcing herself down against the ogre.

Leeja's senses were returning to her slowly. The ogre's sloppy green cock was still twitching inside her.

"I want it all," she panted. "You're going to give me every last drop of cum." Leeja rocked back on her haunches and clenched around the ogre's dick as hard as she could. Then she slid up his shaft, dragging his cock forward as she worked. Just before she reached the tip, she relaxed her pussy and slammed back down to the base to start the process all over again. She fell back into her slow, pounding rhythm, and the ogre cursed as he came inside her again.

Leeja felt his fat cock jumping and sputtering and lurching inside her as she kept up her slow, merciless rhythm. The evidence of their pleasure leaked out of her and slid down his shaft and balls, dripping on the mattress beneath them.

"You're incredible," he groaned, pulling her hips down and grinding against her clit.

"You're godsdammed right I am."

TWO

The sun was still low in the East as Norrin pulled his long, narrow boat out of the water and settled it into the golden sand. The turquoise waters around Th'myskôra were the best anywhere in the Three Realms for small-craft racing. But that was just one of the many reasons Norrin was proud to call this place his home.

Th'myskôra sat in a perfectly centralized position in the Equiloam Sea; almost exactly the same distance from the outermost edge of each of the realms. As a condition of The Peace, it was decided that this place would become a neutral city state, controlled by no kingdom or realm. Th'myskôra would serve as an example for the rest of the world of what could be accomplished through cooperation instead of war.

Norrin looked out over the water at his young students, children born right here on Th'myskôra, as he had been. Children who would live the rest of their lives knowing nothing of war.

"All right, Zet," he said to a small goblin boy hopping eagerly up and down next to his boat, "it's time for you to go out alone. If you think you're ready, of course…"

"I'm ready! I'm ready!" Zet's pointed, green ears wiggled excitedly as he tugged the boat back out toward the water.

"Not so fast, little man," Norrin tried hard to hide his smile, but he was especially proud of Zet's progress over the past few weeks. "What are the three most important rules of Norrin's racing school?"

Zet stood up straight and recited, "Keep your knees soft…"

"Good…"

"Don't go past the breakers in a single-man craft…"

"And?"

"And? …and have fun!" Zet's serious expression was quickly replaced with one of elation. The little goblin pulled the boat a third of the way into the waves before scrambling inside. Norrin pushed the boat the rest of the way out and stood on the shore, beaming like a proud manticore.

"Look at me, Norrin! Look at me!" Myrtle, a bright young lizardman girl was leaning back in her boat and flicking her long, yellow tail in the water, causing her boat to pop up out of the water and come crashing down onto the waves, making a tremendous splash.

"Great job, Myrtle!" Norrin shouted back, "Way to use that tail!" She'd been one of his very first students. When his mother suggested that Norrin start teaching boating as a companion to her children's swimming class, Norrin was less than keen. It sounded an awful lot like responsibility and work, but now, a year into it, he couldn't think of anything he'd rather spend his

Saturday mornings doing. When Myrtle first showed up on the beach a year ago, she was so timid that she would barely make eye-contact with him. She kept her tail tucked behind her, like she was trying to hide it from the other kids.

Look at her now.

Now Myrtle wasn't afraid of any kid on the beach. She loved to peacock, and she'd earned the right.

"I went so high, Norrin!" she shouted, "I bet it was four feet!"

"I bet it was six!" Norrin shouted back to her, "Definitely a new record!"

Qipan the githyanki sailed up next to her and stuck out his long pointed tongue, "Sure you've got some tricks, but I'm still faster!"

"You are not, Qipan! Norrin said *I'm* the fastest," Myrtle fired back.

"Kids, kids!" Norrin refereed from the shore, "What's the rule about arguing?"

Both of the children answered Norrin together, "Never argue when a race will settle things!"

"That's right!" Norrin shouted, "Now get out to the southern rocks and let's find out who's really the fastest."

Myrtle and Qipan made for the southern rocks, exchanging barbs the whole way.

With all of the kids happily practicing out on the water, Norrin settled into a comfortable pile of sand to watch them and enjoy a little breakfast.

He shoved a chunk of hard cheese into his mouth and stretched his long limbs out in the sand. Norrin closed his eyes and relished the feeling of the sun and the salt baking him. He liked to imagine he could feel his tan deepening and his hair bleaching to an even lighter shade of blond.

He looked around at the other boaters on the beach; there

were humans: inventive, curious and tenacious, creatures from the Magical Realm: small, cunning, known for their extreme magical prowess, and the inhabitants of Titan: large, strong, honest, and brave...they all lived peacefully on Th'myskôra. All committed to building a better world for those who would follow them.

Half a dozen humans were on the beach today; like Norrin, they were tall, lanky, and tan. But there were plenty of other creatures, too. Just from where he was sitting Norrin could see Phlip, the dragonborn who used his powerful golden tail to facilitate sharp turns and sudden bursts of speed out on the water. And there was Martel, who was a manticore, *no a griffin...* Norrin could never remember the difference. Martel was which-ever had an eagle in the front and a lion in the back. It didn't really matter much to Norrin which was which. The beach had an ever-changing cast of characters, and all the locals got along.

Norrin was from a long line of shipwrights. Either he or his father had made many of the racing boats in circulation today. When Norrin opened his class, his father came up with a special, smaller boat for the children to use. Of course, plenty of people in the community made their own boats, too. Old timers like Kurt and Oisín, a pair of grey humans, had been tinkering with their own designs for as long as Norrin could remember.

The Bulwark twins, a couple of little tieflings with the cutest lilac horns you've ever seen, were explaining the recent adjustments to their bow and how it improved their hydrody-namic performance to a human girl Norrin didn't recognize.

"You plannin' on taking another crack at those two?" The voice that spoke was rich, and gravelly, but had a practiced evenness meant to give the impression of a rational actor, like the crackling embers hidden deep within last night's campfire. Norrin would recognize that voice anywhere.

"I'm sure I have no idea what you're talking about," Norrin didn't bother turning his head.

"If you're going to keep snatching up all of our women," the voice bristled, "could you at least do it one at a time?"

"*Your* women?" Norrin asked, "I didn't realize you'd staked a claim."

"What? No, I haven't..." stammered Thorne, the tall, well-built cyclops, "but someone's got to stop you taking all the uninformed, magical women of Th'myskôra." Flecks of sea water sparkled on Thorne's rust-colored skin. Norrin was rarely thrilled to see Thorne at the beach, but today even his horn seemed smug.

"Who's taking?" asked Norrin, beaming up into Thorne's one huge, cornflower blue eye, "I always put them right back where I found them."

A nearby human joined in the conversation, "You didn't really sleep with *both* of them, did you?"

"What kind of a guy would split up such an efficient team?" Norrin answered, getting to his feet as a small group of males gathered around, eager to hear the salacious tales of his inter-species exploits. Thorne was smoldering, and Norrin couldn't pass up the opportunity to pester him just a little.

Let's see if I can't get that bald head steaming.

"What's it like?" asked Pytr, an awkward young human Norrin was used to seeing on the beach and around the docks, "Sleeping with a... a *you know...*"

Thorne rolled his eye and Phlip's feathers ruffled. The humans didn't notice.

"Now, Pytr, a gentleman never kisses and tells" he whispered, leaning in close and looking straight into Thorne's devilish blue eye, "so all I'll say is that those tails aren't just for show..."

The other human let out a long, low whistle as his eyes bulged in their sockets.

"Do...do you think you could introduce me?" Pytr asked, "You know, put in a good word?"

Norrin never answered. In fact he stopped listening the moment a tall, emerald-haired beauty strode into view. The second he saw her, Pytr's libido (and Thorne's grudge) faded into nothing. Norrin was transfixed.

She kept her head locked in its forward position, clearly focused on her destination. Her long, well-muscled legs propelled her with unrelenting speed. The sleeves of her dress strained around the peaks of her biceps. Norrin could tell from the bounce and sway of her large breasts that she wore no bindings. Her skin was walnut-brown everywhere he could see, except for her cheeks, where she had the slightest hint of a mint-green sunburn.

"I wonder what else is green," Norrin said. His eyes were transfixed on her. Norrin couldn't look away. His head tracked her movement, and without realizing what was happening, he had started taking slow, wobbly steps through the soft sand toward her.

"What do you mean green?" Asked Pytr, "we were talking about prehensile tails!"

Norrin hardly heard him—there was an angel storming up the esplanade, after all. Two long, curved tusks flowed up from her jaw and framed her exquisite face. Her long, dark-green hair was tangled and messy in a way that screamed 'sex' to Norrin and made his loins stir.

"Watch the kids for me a minute, will ya', Martel..." he said, never taking his eyes off her, and bounded away without waiting for a reply.

"Lovely morning for a walk," Norrin said as he scrambled up to the esplanade.

She ignored him, her gait steady.

Norrin easily matched her pace. He was only an inch or so shorter than she, and his legs, while not as developed as hers, were deceptively strong.

"Looks like someone had an exciting night," he said, smiling broadly.

"Ermph."

"I'd love to get you some breakfast, and you could tell me all about it."

No reply.

"Don't like a big meal early in the morning? I know exactly how you feel. Maybe just a nice cup of tea, then? Or we could meet for dinner tonight; my mother makes the most fantastic cabbage stew you've ever had..."

"Look, human," she said, stopping so suddenly that Norrin almost ran into her back. He felt the heat radiating off of her body and wanted to bury himself in it. "I don't know what game it is that you're playing, but I'm not in the mood. So you can just jog back down to the beach and tell all your little friends that the big, scary orc isn't biting".

"You don't look so big to me." Norrin said, sliding around to face her, "And to be perfectly frank, it takes more than a little biting to scare *me* off." She scowled at him, breathing heavily through flared nostrils.

Is she scenting me?

That's when Norrin really saw her eyes for the first time. They were the darkest green he'd ever seen, like the secret lakes in the forest on Swi'loor, deep and teeming with unseen life. "W...o...w," he whispered, taking a small step towards her.

The orc looked confused.

Or was she offended?

Before Norrin could decide, she shoved past him.

"Hey, wait!" Norrin called after her, "You can't just leave!"

He was practically running now, but somehow her pace kept quickening. Her beauty was challenging and unparalleled; and besides, he couldn't remember the last time a woman from any of the Three Realms had rejected him. Norrin had to have her.

"If you can be Frank, than I can do whatever I damn well please! Kindly keep your human nonsense to yourself!" she shouted over her shoulder.

"My name's not Frank!" he called after her; Norrin had nearly caught up again.

"Stop following me, Frank!" she shouted as she crested a small hill and then disappeared from view.

In a daze, Norrin stumbled back down to his friends on the beach.

"Fellas, I have just met the most incredible woman."

Thorne and Phlip threw their heads back, laughing. Fire shot out of Phlip's nose, and a gleeful tear pooled in the corner of Thorne's eye.

"Who?! *Her?!* Good luck," Thorne barked, "Leeja hates humans!"

"Leeja? That's her name, the orc?"

Leeja...

Norrin let the sound of her name dance around his mind, enjoying the musicality of it before tucking it away in his memory for safekeeping.

Leeja, her name, his new treasure.

"So you know her? What's she like?"

"*Half*-orc," Phlip corrected, "and we know 'er all right. Works down on the docks with the rest of us Titans, unloading cargo ships for Bowen."

"Bowen? Bowen... he's the satyr who manages the Red Fleet, isn't he?"

"Yeah, that's him."

"The same Red Fleet that's had a freighter in dry dock for half a year?"

"What of it?" Thorne asked.

"Alright, kids! Time to pack it in for today!" Norrin shouted to those children still out on the water. "I've got to go see a man about a ship."

CHAPTER

THREE

The Leeja who turned up for breakfast at the Drowned
Grimoire was a different woman than the one who'd
stumbled out of its doors the night before. Last night,
she was weak, desperate, sweaty, and overcome with a debilitating need to orgasm. This morning, she was confident and
clear-headed, freshly bathed and freshly fucked.

"You two look like several hells," she said, sauntering up to
her friends who were already seated at a low table in the darkest, quietest corner of the tavern. "Exactly how much did you
end up drinking last night?"

"Too much," grumbled Arlynn.

20

"Do you think you could keep your voice down, please?" Imogen asked meekly from behind several disheveled stacks of correspondences and academic tomes. Her normally pleasant, round face was puffy and grey.

"Not you too, Imogen!" Leeja laughed, settling into a heavy wooden chair. "You're usually back in bed with Keneth before last call."

"I was," Imogen whimpered, "I just couldn't get any rest. I've been having these...*disquieting* dreams."

Before anyone could press for details, Brigid, the stout dwarfess who ran the Drowned Grim, bustled up to the table.

"And what'll you be havin' this mornin', deary?" she asked Leeja through a thick dwarfish accent, twirling a short finger in her waist-length, marmalade-colored beard.

"Whatever they're having," Leeja said, "and three dried figs if you've got 'em."

"Atta' girl!" Brigid barked, slapping Leeja hard on the shoulder before hurrying off to the kitchen.

"Dried figs, eh?" asked Arlynn, perking up. "Is there something you'd like to share with the group?"

"Now that you mention it," said Leeja smugly, "I did end up getting that ramming last night."

"Um, yeah. We figured that out," said Imogen impatiently

"It's not like anyone eats dried figs for fun," Arlynn teased.

"And while we're both very happy that you're taking your family planning so seriously," Imogen continued. "We *would* like details, please."

"Well..." Leeja teased, dragging out the suspense as long as she could, "I went home with an ogre last night."

"An *ogre*!?" the girls squealed.

"How was it? I mean *he*? Who am I kidding...I mean *it*!"

"Green," said Leeja, grinning, "and *meaty*."

Excited squeals and laughter erupted from the table, earning the group dirty looks from several tavern patrons.

"All right, all right," said Arlynn, "We all love a huge cock, but did he know how to use it?"

"Well, I came four times last night...and three this morning, so he must have been doing *something* right."

"Seven orgasms?" Imogen asked, picking her jaw up off the table. "I didn't know that was possible."

"Oh, Imogen," Arlynn said, patting the back of her hand, "we are going to have to sit that boyfriend of yours down one of these days and have a very serious talk."

"You don't mean that *you've* had seven orgasms in a row before too?"

"Remember that illithid I was seeing last month?" Arlynn said, leaning in and lowering her voice, "On our second date, he dragged me down to his undersea grotto and fucked me for thirty hours straight. I stopped counting orgasms after we hit twenty-three."

Imogen clapped her hand over her mouth, and Leeja laughed. It was always funny to her that angelic Imogen and adventurous Arlynn should be such close friends.

"So *that's* where you disappeared to," Leeja said, eating the first of her newly arrived figs.

"Caspian was a very skilled lover," Arlynn said, placing her hand above her heart and adopting a somber tone, "and his many face-tentacles will be missed...but we are talking about *your* ogre right now. What's his name? Where is he from? When are you seeing him again?"

"I don't know. I don't know. And never." Leeja said, taking a deep swig from her mug.

"Gah! Water?" She sputtered, "You two ordered water? Last night really *must have* gotten out of hand."

"Don't change the subject, Leeja," Imogen said. "We want to know why you never see any of these males more than once."

"Oh, *we* do, do we?" Leeja asked, looking from Imogen to Arlynn and back again. "I wasn't aware the council was mandating monogamy now." She could feel the hairs standing up on the back of her neck.

No one tells an orc what to do.

"I didn't mean it like that," said Imogen timidly.

"And no one's saying you have to marry the guy," Arlynn interjected, "but being in a relationship, even a brief one, *does* come with some perks."

"Imagine having someone to go to dances with or to help you carry in your packages." Added Imogen.

"I can carry my own bags. Leeja's hackles relaxed; Arlynn and Imogen clearly didn't want to do battle. Still, their lecturing was becoming tiresome.

"Of course, you *can*," Imogen continued. "But it's nice when someone carries it *for you*. It's nice when he opens your door... and when he learns about your hobbies."

"Not to mention getting to have sex at predictable intervals," Arlynn chimed in.

"And then you get to do a bunch of nice little things for him too," said Imogen, "and it's all just very..."

"Nice?" Leeja finished, sarcasm eking out of every pour. "I'd expect these kinds of apologetics from Imogen but not our resident libertine." She turned her attention back on Arlynn.

"The difference between *my* sleeping around and *your* sleeping around," said Arlynn, "is that I've actually been in relationships. Loads of them. And I'm choosing to pursue other opportunities at present. You, my friend, have never so much as slept with the same man twice."

"Ha! You're wrong; I fucked the ogre last night and again this morning. And remember last winter, when the storms were so bad we had to close the port? I bunked up with that troll, Whatshisname. We had sex every day for a week."

"I think you know that's not what I mean."

There's that smug human tone.

"I'm talking about sex on non-consecutive days. I mean that you've never met a man, slept with him, and liked him enough to meet up with him again at some future date."

"What a bunch of human nonsense!" Leeja interrupted the lecture, "I'm not going to see the ogre again because I don't want to see the ogre again. There wasn't anything special about him. Nothing worth pursuing further."

"You see!" Arlynn barreled on, "You're doing it again. For all you know, this ogre is a great guy, the love of your life. You're avoiding even the most basic levels of emotional intimacy. From where I'm sitting, that's cowardice." Arlynn stuffed a heaping spoonful of stew into her delicate mouth to accentuate her point.

Leeja's lip curled, and her grip tightened around her tankard, denting the tin. "Don't call me a coward."

"Prove me wrong then." Arlynn was smirking now, "After all, didn't you say you moved to Th'myskôra to learn how other people live? Well, humans are people too! So...try dating like a human...unless you're incapable of meeting my challenge, of course..."

"Name your terms, human." Leeja slammed her fist down on the table. Imogen jumped and let out a little shriek, but Arlynn was used to these sorts of theatrics. If Leeja hadn't known better, she might have thought that Arlynn was intentionally riling her up.

"I'll believe you're not a coward if you can learn a man's name, where he was born, and at least one thing he's passionate about *before* you fuck him," said Arlynn grinning.

"Easy." Leeja spat back across the table.

"I wasn't finished," Arlynn continued, waving around her spoon dismissively. "You also have to have sex with him on two non-consecutive days *and* go on at least three *real* dates. And… and you have to find out at least one thing the two of you have in common."

"Is that all?" Leeja asked impatiently.

"No! You also have to —"

"To tell him something private!" Imogen interrupted. "Something we don't even know about you."

"Why would I ever do that?" Leeja barked.

"A man can never love you if you won't let him get to know you," Imogen stated matter of factly.

"Accepted," Leeja said, taking Arlynn's forearm in her firm grip. They shook once, sealing the bargain, and returned their attention to breakfast. As Leeja's rage simmered down, another emotion rose in her.

"What if," she said quietly into her stew, "what if no man wants to do those things with me?"

"Gods, Leeja," Imogen said, throwing an arm around her and squeezing as tightly as she could in their awkward orientation, "I am so, so sorry about last night. Those guys were horrible. There are plenty of men, Titans, imps, and yes, even humans who would give their right arms to get to spend time with you."

"If you find yourself having trouble locating one," said Arlynn, "Imogen and I will find you a suitable match."

Leeja rolled her eyes and smiled weakly over at her friend, "Like the guys you found last night?"

"I know," said Arlynn, "I'm sorry, but I swear I'm a much better matchmaker when I'm sober."

"Speaking of human men," said Imogen, "that tall blond over there has definitely been peeking over his shoulder at us since he sat down."

All three women craned their necks to see two lanky human men, one blond, in his middle thirties, the other grey-haired, much shorter, and in his late fifties or early sixties. The two men were so alike in appearance and mannerism that they could only be father and son. Sitting with them was a very familiar rotund, brown satyr: Bowen, Leeja's manager.

"He's not so tall," Leeja huffed.

"I'd say he's at least six foot three." Arlynn was sizing him up, chewing absentmindedly on her wooden spoon.

Leeja rolled her eyes.

If there's a man around, you can be sure Arlynn will start praising his looks.

This time though, she had a point. Leeja had tried not to look at the human earlier, but now that she was staring directly at him, his beauty was hard to ignore. He had a sharp, square jawline, golden hair, and soft looking lips that he frequently pulled up into a very inviting smile.

A little on the scrawny side, but not every member of a horde has to swing a broad sword...

"What in three hells is Frank doing with Bowen in the Drowned Grim on a Saturday morning?"

"Frank?" Both of her friends said together.

"You know him?" asked Arlynn.

"What sort of a name is Frank?" Imogen asked.

"His name isn't really Frank," said Leeja, "he followed me down the esplanade when I was coming home from the ogre's this morning."

"Scary followed *or*..."

"I just wasn't in the mood to suffer humans first thing in the morning," Leeja said, bristling. "Truth be told, I was probably still a little angry about last night."

"Not scary...so he's a candidate!" Imogen said brightly, ignoring the dig at her entire species.

Leeja breathed deeply though her nose and was filled with the same scent she'd encountered on the esplanade that morning. It was a warm, musky, smell with hints of the sea. It was simultaneously familiar and threatening, and it made her loins stir.

Stop it, Leeja. Human men are too dangerous, even to fantasize about.

"No humans. Especially not *that* human... I don't like the smell of him." Leeja said, "Besides, I'd be much more interested to learn what business he's got with the Red Fleet..."

"No!" Arlynn interrupted. "No work talk today. It's bad enough that *this one* drags those dusty old books around everywhere we go."

"This research project is vital," Imogen said, "why, the interactions we're discovering between impish and titan magic could—"

"'Could improve the lives of millions or even change our very understanding of the natural world,'"Arlynn recited impatiently, "yes, we know." "But today is not a workday; therefore, your vital discoveries can wait. And you, Ms. Leeja," she said, turning her focus, "already spend more time down at that dock than any other longshoreman. You break your back for that satyr for six straight hours, three days a week. What enchantment has Bowen placed over you to keep you there day after grueling day?"

"I don't do it for *him*," Leeja said, smiling. She loved being able to confound Arlynn. "I do it for the simple pleasure of lifting heavy crates."

"I refuse to believe that sweating and straining in the hot sun is pleasurable."

"I haven't been in a single raiding party in the whole time I've been on Th'myskôra."

"Raiding was forbidden on the island as a term of The Peace," said Imogen.

"Exactly," said Leeja, smiling broadly enough to show off a good number of her razor-sharp teeth, "I haven't felt the hot spray of a man's entrails across my face in almost a year. I've got to do *something* to clear my head."

"Well, your head will have to stay muddled today. No work. And no *reading*." Arlynn slammed Imogen's book closed. "And no letters. Today, we're going to have fun, godsdammit!"

Arlynn was breathing heavily and starting to sweat. Leeja and Imogen shared a conspiratorial look before devolving into wild laughter. A moment later, Arlynn joined them, and all three friends cackled as they finished their stew and water.

FOUR

It had been three days since Norrin saw her walking down the esplanade, since he first heard her laugh at the Drowned Grimoire. It was a bright, clear laugh, almost girlish. The moment Norrin heard it, he knew there was more to her than her gruff exterior. Somewhere, under all those muscles, was a vulnerable and sensual woman. Now Norrin, standing with his father at the dry docks, knew he had to convince her to let her guard down.

"Hells, Bowen!" Leeja shouted as the satyr shooed her toward the ship, towards *him*. "I know less than nothing about shipbuilding. Why am I here?"

"Because," Bowen answered, his voice echoing between the towering ships all around them. "there is currently a two-year wait for ship repair, and they're skipping me in the line if I lend them a pair of strong hands."

"What about Hupurt? Or Thad? He's got *three* strong hands!"

"It's got to be you, Leeja," said Bowen dismissively, "It's only for a few days, and if this works out, and I can put the ship back in circulation, I'll owe you one."

"A big one," Leeja grumbled.

"Good morning, gentlemen," Bowen said, nodding to the smiling humans standing in front of the Flannery. "This is Leeja; she's going to be helping you fellas out with the repairs."

"It's a pleasure to meet you," Norrin said, rushing up to kiss the back of her hand. When he'd seen her before, she wore a heavy wool dress with long, flowing sleeves. She'd been dressed modestly in the style often worn by new arrivals to the island, but today, she wore skin-tight leather britches tucked into calf-length leather boots. Every time she took a step or shifted her weight, Norrin could see the muscles roll and twitch in her thick legs. Above that, she wore tight-laced, heavy leather stays, that lifted her ample breasts, allowing Norrin occasional glimpses of her bosom through her thin, linen tunic.

"I'm Norrin, and this is my father, Aengus."

"So I've heard," Leeja said, retrieving her hand and shooting Bowen a dirty look.

"I'll just leave the three of you to it then," said Bowen. Then, taking Aengus' hand in both of his, he added, "I really can't thank you enough for this." Then he was clip-clopping away.

"Well, Leeja," Aengus started, hooking his thumbs into his leather tool belt, "I'm told this will be your first repair job."

"That's right, sir." He looked exactly like his son, except he was about a foot shorter and had a tight-cropped silver beard.

"Oh, please, call me Aengus," he said, smiling approvingly at her. He put his arm gently around her shoulder, and Leeja's body relaxed. "And there's no need to worry about a lack of experience; Norrin's a great teacher. If you're willing to put in the work, you'll practically be an expert in no time at all."

"Let's get to it then," Leeja smiled half-heartedly and followed Aengus toward the massive ship. Norrin hung back a few paces so he could admire the view.

"She took quite the beating," Aengus ran his hand along the Flannery, assessing the damage.

"Sure did," said Leeja somberly, "a freak storm off the coast of Rookfall had her pinned against the rocks for days. It's only by the grace of the goddess that she returned to us at all."

"Then by the grace of the goddess, and with your help, she'll sail again," said Norrin grinning, putting his arm around her shoulder. Leeja didn't swat it away, she didn't even flinch or snarl. Norrin's heart quickened, and his pants tightened.

This is going to be easier than I thought! Those guys down on the beach don't know what they're talking about. I bet she doesn't even hate humans at all!

"This hole here on the portside is the biggest; we'll have to strip her down to the bilge stringer, cut out the damage, put in a couple new pieces, and reinforce the patch." Aengus dragged his fingers absentmindedly through his beard. "If we're lucky, we won't have to replace any frames, and we can just go straight to patching the planks, but we won't really know how bad it is until we get into the ballast stores," Aengus said, mostly to himself, jotting down notes on a large piece of parchment.

"And exactly how do we get into the ballast stores?" Leeja asked cocking an eyebrow. Her face was even more beautiful when she was incredulous.

"Lady's choice," said Norrin, sidling up to her, a saw in one hand and a sledgehammer in the other.

"Ship-mending might not be so bad after all!" Leeja said,

happily taking the sledgehammer and swinging away at the rough edges of the hole.

Bits of wood splintered off and flew through the air, showering Norrin's face and sticking in his hair. Leeja was terrific to watch. She pounded away at the hull in a steady, unrelenting rhythm, never slowing even as droplets of sweat formed on her temples and slid down her sculpted neck, disappearing into her tunic.

"Last I checked, Frank," Leeja shouted over her shoulder, still not missing a beat, "we were on a job site. How's about you grab a hammer and help me?"

"Yes, ma'am!" Norrin eagerly snatched up a nearby hammer and joined in on the smashing. Now that they were standing shoulder to shoulder, Norrin could feel the heat radiating off of her again, just like that morning at the beach. Her smell permeated his senses; it was sweet, musky, and unlike anything he'd ever smelled before. His balls twitched in his smallclothes, and his nipples hardened under his tunic. He felt electrified. "There's something special about you, Miss Leeja."

Norrin was hoping for some witty banter or perhaps a giggle in response. He expected her to smile at the very least, but Leeja furrowed her brow instead.

"Special? Yeah, I'm six-foot-eight, and I've got giant tusks jutting up from my bottom lip," she said sourly, "thanks for noticing."

Alright, this might be a little *difficult after all.*

Norrin and Leeja worked together in silence for a few more agonizing minutes before Aengus came back, sending them inside the hull and putting Norrin out of his misery,

"How are those frames looking, son?" he called from the dock.

"First one's fine!" Norrin shouted as he and Leeja explored the inside of the hull. His eyes were used to the dark guts of a ship's belly, but Leeja's clearly were not. She moved slowly, knees bent, right foot in front of her left, taking small, awkward crab steps and feeling her way down the narrow corridor two steps behind him. The feeling of her warm body so close to his was exhilarating.

"I want to show you something, Leeja," he said over his shoulder, "this frame, just up ahead here."

Leeja squeezed up next to him, and her soft breasts brushed against his chest. His cock stirred; Norrin wasn't sure if he wanted her to notice or not. He took her hand and slowly moved it up to touch the nearest frame. She didn't yank it away. "If you touch right here," he said, leading her hand along the smooth length of the frame, "you can feel this crack."

Leeja drew in a ragged breath, "Was this caused by the crash?" Her voice was softer now in the cool, dark of the ship's guts. She seemed more willing to be led by him, to be taught by him.

"Probably," Norrin said, his hand still resting on hers, "but cracks like this can also occur as part of normal wear and tear. It's a horizontal crack against the grain of the wood," he dragged the pad of his middle finger gently across the back of her hand.

Leeja closed her eyes and let her head loll back slightly.

"So, we can get away with bracing it. But if we find a vertical crack..." Norrin said dragging his finger up her forearm. Leeja let out a soft moan before finishing his sentence, "...we'll have to replace the whole section to make sure it doesn't spread."

Beautiful, powerful, and *a quick study.*

"Precisely," said Norrin. Their faces were inches apart now. Even in the dim light of the ship's belly, he could see into those glittering green eyes. She was smiling. Norrin leaned in closer; he could feel her breath on his mouth.

This is it. All I have to do is lean forward and I'll feel those tempting green lips against mine.

Norrin moved his other hand slowly, carefully up and placed it gently on Leeja's hip. Her leather britches were cold under his hand, but he could feel her flesh, warm and ready under the surface.

He closed his eyes and leaned in toward her.

"I want to check the next one!" Leeja grunted, squirming past him and rushing away, into the deep blackness of the hull. Norrin was chasing after her again, at least he got to feel her thigh brush across his crotch this time.

"Godsdamn," he grumbled on a shaky breath.

"What's that?" Leeja asked brightly, apparently unaware of his growing...excitement.

"Nothing. You're just...you're doing a great job!"

They spent the rest of the morning crawling over each other in the cramped, muggy hull of the Flannery. Leeja's perfect ass had been within grabbing range at least a dozen times, but Norrin had managed to keep his hands to himself.

If I mess up today, I could lose my chance...or my arm...

When they found an imperfection, Norrin would call out to his father on the dock, who would make a note on the long list of necessary repairs.

Finally, every inch of infrastructure had been examined, and Norrin and Leeja crawled out of their hole and out into the blinding light of midday.

Aengus was looking over a list of supplies, "So that's three frames that need bracing, a seven-foot section of bilge stringer, and a floorboard that needs to be replaced, and this impressive hole in the planking on the portside, and a four-foot hole in the planking on the starboard side?"

"That sounds like all of it," said Norrin.

"Great!" Leeja said, snatching up the sledgehammer again, "What do we smash next?"

"I'm afraid there's no more smashing to be done today," Aengus said, laughing softly, "as a matter of fact, I've got to go put in the orders for this lumber, so that's quitting time. You kids go have some fun." Then he winked at Norrin and went on his way.

"You can't really be done with work for the day, can you?" Leeja actually looked disappointed. She had her bottom lip jutted out. It was adorable.

"Don't worry," Norrin said, running a soothing hand over her shoulder and down her back. She didn't pull away.

So back rubs aren't off the table...

"We'll have plenty of work tomorrow. In the meantime, would you mind helping me with *that*?" He indicated a large, lidded basket on the ground nearby.

Leeja shrugged, dropping the sledgehammer unceremoniously on the ground and picking up the basket.

"Where to, Frank?"

"Just up here, Miss Leeja." Norrin beamed.

I've only known her four days and she's already given me a nickname, that's gotta be a good sign.

The two of them walked away from the dry docks and up a secluded dirt path. The longer they walked, the steeper the path became until they were practically hiking. The landscape was changing too, the higher they climbed. Now, the path was flanked with gnarled live oak trees and dry scrub. They were both sweating. Norrin kept looking nervously over his shoulder to gauge Leeja's expression. At least twice, he was fairly certain that she was checking him out.

"It's not much further now," he said after he thought he saw the hint of a frown creeping onto her face, "It's just around the next bend."

The trees opened up to reveal a small, grassy meadow on a cliff. Norrin rushed forward to the cliff's edge and clambered onto a large, flat rock. "Come on, Leeja! You've got to see this!" He extended his hand to help her up.

Leeja dropped the basket on the rock and climbed up, without accepting his hand.

"This is the best view anywhere on the island. To the north, you can see as far as Croygate Harbor, and to the south, the Elmholm Covert. And if you look straight out, on a clear day, you can just make out the skyline of the human city Little Break."

"Do you miss it?" Leeja asked, "I mean, is that why you come up here? To feel close to home?"

"*This* is my home; I was born here on Th'myskôra." Norrin smiled at her. "I come up here to feel the wind, smell the sea, and clear my head. Hardly anyone knows about this place; it's a great spot to come and be alone."

"Then why'd you bring *me* here?" Leeja's nostrils flared.

There's that gruff incredulity again. I'm going to kiss that frown right off of her pretty face.

"Sometimes it's nice to have a little company when you're alone." Norrin took a small step towards her. They were face to face again. There was no one around for miles. Up here, there was no Aengus to interrupt them. There was no sunless ship for her to disappear into. The attraction between them was so strong that Norrin hadn't been able to think of anything else since he first laid eyes on her down on the esplanade. Leeja had to feel it too. It wasn't his imagination; she really had been sneaking looks his way. She really had trembled with delight when he caressed her hand.

This is it; they always fall for the romantic view. She'll be all over me in three, two, one...

"Aren't those your friends down there?" Leeja snapped her face away, to observe the tiny figures down on the beach.

"What?" It took Norrin a long second to recover from his trance. "Yeah, those are some of them. You should come race with us sometime; I get the feeling you'd be really good at it."

"Ha! The only time I've been on the water was the ferry ride over here from Titan."

"Why did *you* leave?" Norrin started unpacking the basket, carefully laying out the sensual and aphrodisiacal foods he'd prepared for them to share. "If you don't mind my asking, that is."

Leeja sat down beside him, "I just...I didn't fit in there." She ran her finger absent-mindedly along the curve of an overripe peach. Norrin couldn't help but picture her strong digit penetrating its supple, juicy flesh.

"By the time a female orc reaches sexual maturity, she should be leading her own horde."

"Let me guess," Norrin beamed at her, "you couldn't get on board with the idea of all those big, muscle-bound lovers pawing at you all the time? Too much of a free spirit to be bogged down in a serious relationship?"

Leeja coughed a dry, humorless laugh, "I wish it were that simple." She stared off across the horizon, almost as if she could see Søgsund from here. "I tried to form a horde; for almost a decade, I slept with every eligible male I could. I really tried to be a good orc, but it never worked for me. There's a bond, like a chemical bond, when a male joins a horde…I was never able to stimulate it."

"Oh, I… I'm sorry, I had no idea that orc hordes were so… biological." Norrin scooted closer to Leeja on the rock and slid his hand behind her.

I could hug her now. A shoulder to cry on could lead to a very exciting night. Of course, she could also rip my arm out of its socket… better play it cool.

"Did you try going to a healer?"

"And have the whole countryside pitying my dysfunction? No thanks." Leeja scooted angrily away from him on the rock.

"But if it's a medical issue, maybe…"

"The medical issue," she shouted suddenly, "is that I'm half-human. I will never get to live a normal orc life because I'm not a normal orc!"

"I'm sorry, I didn't mean to upset you." Norrin spoke gently. He wanted Leeja to know she was going to be alright, that things rarely turn out as badly as we imagine they will. "So… why come all the way to Th'myskôra? Couldn't you have stayed with your mother's horde? I'm sure there's a lot you have to offer."

"If two sexually mature females are in the same mating territory, things can get…*heated*."

Norrin cocked his head. He was very confused but grateful that Leeja had stopped yelling at him.

"Apparently, I'm functional enough to secrete the orc mating scents…without a horde, I have no one to protect my territory, no way to maintain borders. I have no army to lead into battle." Leeja picked up the peach again; she lifted it to her nose and inhaled deeply. "If another, more established female caught me in her territory, we would have to fight to the death. That *includes* my mother."

"Oh, I had no idea. I can't imagine fighting with my father; we've always been so close…"

"It's not personal. When the mating frenzy takes over, there's almost nothing you can do to stop it." Leeja rolled the peach gently between her massive hands. "We had a pretty bad brawl just before I came here. She spared my life, but I could tell it took all of her willpower not to crush my skull."

Leeja sank her teeth into the yielding flesh of the peach. Its sticky, sweet juice spilling down her chin. "There are so many different kinds of creatures living here on Th'myskôra, I thought maybe…I don't know what I thought."

"Th'myskôra is a wonderful place," he said, scooting closer to her again. "There's something here for everyone."

Leeja closed her eyes and chuckled, "Goddess knows why I'm telling you all this."

"Maybe you just like me."

"Don't flatter yourself, human!"

Norrin whimpered, feigning emotional injury, "And here, I thought we were getting along!"

"Okay," she said, chuckling. "I'll admit it, you *may* not be as bad as other human men." Leeja smiled and raised the peach to her mouth again. She took another bite, this time sending syrup dripping down her forearm and onto her tunic. She closed her eyes, and a soft moan of pleasure escaped her lips.

"We don't have fruit like this back in Søgsund."

Norrin scooted closer to her on the rock. He was transfixed by the viscous fluid glistening on her tawny skin. He wanted to lick it off her. To taste the thick nectar mixed with the flavors of her skin. He wanted to press his mouth against hers, to gently part his lips and find her tongue eager and waiting for him, bathed in the flavor of that heavenly peach.

He scooted closer to her on the rock. Close enough now that their hands were practically touching.

If I brushed my finger against her hand, would she tremble again like she did in the Flannery?

"There are many delights available here on Th'myskôra that you can't get anywhere else in the Three Realms. It would be my pleasure to introduce them to you."

Leeja punched Norrin hard in the shoulder and laughed, "Alright, human! You can be my new buddy."

CHAPTER
FIVE

The next morning, Leeja woke up before the sun and was immediately aware of a persistent pounding in her core, "What in three hells is going on down there? It's too early for the frenzy again..."

She forced her throbbing desire out of her mind and was able to get dressed for work and gobble down some dried fruit and hard cheese before making her way out the door. Leeja was often awake before the rest of the island, she liked the privacy. In the cold, damp morning she could walk as slowly as she wanted without being rushed by the regular, bustling crowd.

On Main Street, she could peruse all of the new window displays. She could climb up and down the giant stone stairs of the troll temple. When she was up especially early (like she was today), she got to see the last of the nightjars settling in for the day. Their huge pink mouths practically splitting their heads in two as they yawned and nestled into their hiding places like tiny, plump dragons.

Eventually, Leeja's early morning meanderings led her to the boater's beach. The beach where she'd met Norrin a few short days before, "...I must have boats on the brain," she mused, smiling to herself; and then tromped happily down the esplanade to the dry docks.

"Demolition day! You promised! Today, I get to smash!" Leeja called out as she bounded up to Aengus and Norrin.

"As promised, madame," Aengus said, affecting a slight bow and presenting her with a large saw.

"I've been dreaming about you all night, beautiful," she said to the saw, grinning. Norrin let out an impertinent huff and Leeja turned to face him, "I'm sure there's more than one..."

Aengus had set up a workbench; there were stacks of papers covered in measurements and calculations. Nearby was the cart, full to bursting with all manner of wood and tools.

"What's all this then?" she asked, picking up and inspecting various colored chunks of wood, bladed instruments, and pots of foul-smelling substances. Some of the instruments she recognized, like the various calipers and planes, but others seemed exotic and inviting. Leeja was drawn to a collection of what looked like modified axes. Each one had a large, flat head...like a duckbill. Leeja ran her hand over the cool, smooth metal.

"That's a shipwright's adze!" said Norrin. Leeja dropped the thing immediately. How long had he been watching her? And why was his shirt off? "I can show you how to use it sometime if you want."

"There'll be plenty of time for that later," Aengus said. "For now, I'm going to recheck these measurements while you two get to work removing the damaged sections of wood."

"Aye, aye!" Leeja answered, perhaps a little too eagerly, and she quickly made her way over to the Flannery.

She and Norrin were supposed to be sawing away at the ragged edges of the hole they'd smashed the day before. It was hard work; even in the early morning sun, Norrin had already begun to sweat...and to smell. Leeja struggled to concentrate on her work; his constant, invasive scent was very distracting. He was tangy and briny and somehow familiar, even though Leeja was sure she'd never experienced anything like this smell before. If that weren't bad enough, she kept looking at him too! The svelte musculature of his back and shoulders shifted as he plunged the saw into the wood and dragged it out again. A bead of sweat rolled down his long, tapered back and disappeared into his britches.

"Goddess, help me," Leeja muttered as her guts wrenched and her cunt throbbed. *It's only been four days since I was mated; the craving shouldn't be this intense.*

"It's only demolition day," Norrin said, straightening; he smiled at her, and her core clenched. Leeja wanted to knock him off his feet, to tackle him and bury her face in his chest. She wanted to roll around the dock with him until she'd pinned him and she was covered in his scent. "I don't think we'll need divine intervention just yet."

Leeja's stance widened instinctively; her tusks were bared, her mouth was watering, and she was preparing to pounce. Then she remembered the saw in her hand.

Get ahold of yourself, Leeja. He is a human, and you are at work, and it isn't even sex day yet.

Nervously, Leeja returned her attention to the ship and started to saw. It was hard work, and as the sun rose higher and higher, the shimmering air emanating from the ship became oppressive. Leeja had never sawed anything before, and she struggled to control her strokes.

"Like this," Norrin said; he'd come up behind her to place his hand on hers, guiding it easily back and forth. He was pressed against her ass, and she could feel her desire pooling. "You're working too hard; let gravity help you with that."

"Thanks," she muttered and shrugged him off of her.

Thank the goddess that human noses are so underdeveloped.

They spent the next couple of hours preparing holes of varying sizes to be patched. When they were nearly done, Leeja sneaked away from Norrin to catch her breath (and clear her head) in the shadow of a nearby freighter.

Alright, Leeja. Just a couple more hours to go, then you can get out of here and figure out what's going on in your pants.

"Great work today, Leeja," Aengus said, handing her a water bladder.

"I'm sure you're just saying that," she said, blushing.

"Not at all! A job like this would have taken Norrin and me at least twice as long if we were doing it on our own. Have you ever thought of joining a shoring crew?"

"Can't say that I have," she said smiling, "I've never considered myself handy."

"Well, mull it over," Aengus said. "If you're interested in improving your carpentry skills, it's a great way to learn. Plus you get to travel all over, be a part of a ship's crew...get a great tan."

"Hey Dad, don't go chasing off my apprentice," Norrin said, joining them in the shade.

"Sorry," Aengus said, smiling slyly, "but when I see natural talent, I just have to say something."

"Well, there are plenty of opportunities for craftsmen right here on the island," Norrin said turning to Leeja, smiling, "if you're interested in construction, I'm sure we could get you an apprenticeship with Rakka."

"Rakka?" Leeja was beside herself, "*The* Rakka? The famous troll architect?"

"You've heard of him?" Aengus asked.

"The masonry works of the great Rakka are legendary. His work is revered all across Titan. Even among orcs."

"In that case, we'll set you up with a meeting as soon as possible," said Norrin, grinning, "won't we, Dad?"

Aengus ran his fingers through his beard, "I suppose that could be arranged...maybe he could take you on a walking tour of the island. Point out some of the notable buildings..."

"I..." Leeja was overrun with emotion. One day of work and she was being offered the opportunity to meet one of her artistic heroes.

"Sounds great!" Norrin interrupted, "I bet the two of you will get along great. He loves smashing things too."

Leeja blushed.

"I bet he offers you an apprenticeship," Norrin had that stupid, earnest, enticing smile on his face again, "and then *you* can become one of Th'myskôra's premier builders and you'll live here forever."

"I um...for now," Leeja said, blushing a deeper green, "I think I'll stick to fixing just this one ship."

"Well, in that case," said Norrin, "There are a couple big sections I need your help with inside the hull."

"Great." Said Aengus. "While you two finish that up, I'll make my last few cuts. Then we can call it a day."

THERE WAS dim sunlight creeping in where Norrin and Leeja had sawed holes. She could see more of the structures of the hull today. Leeja stepped gingerly between the planks and timbers and ducked under the thwart, careful not to trip. She ran her fingers along the carvel planking, admiring the precise angles to which they'd been sanded and the delicate curves of the s-bottom hull they achieved when fitted tightly together. The further she got into the ship, the harder it became to see. By the time Leeja reached the large sections of wood, presumably cut free by Norrin, she was groping around in the darkness again.

"Can you help me with this big one?" Norrin called out from

somewhere in the cramped darkness. "It's an awkward lift for one person."

"Where are you?" she asked, her heart rate rising. "There's something I have to come clean about, Frank." Leeja's voice shook and cracked, "Orcs don't exactly have great night vision."

"I never would have guessed!" Norrin laughed.

"Yeah, we rely much more on our hearing and sense of smell when we need to make our way in the dark."

"Then just keep smelling for me!" Norrin teased, "I'm about ten feet in front of you. Just keep coming forward. You're doing great."

Leeja stumbled trough the hull, it seemed to get darker with each step she took. The ceiling was low, and the floor was uneven. She tried to take careful steps along the keelson, but every few feet there would be a floorboard or frame she'd have to step over.

"This is definitely my least favorite part of ship shoring."

"You'll get used to it!" A jovial voice answered from somewhere in the void.

Leeja swore as she stubbed her toe.

At least I'm not thinking about sliding Norrin's cock in my mouth.

"Goddess, dammit!"

"What happened?" Norrin asked, "Are you alright?"

Now all *I'm thinking about is sliding his cock in my mouth,*

"I'm fine! Don't worry about m—Hells!" Leeja shouted as she tripped over a loose two-by-four, her face plummeting toward the floor.

"I got cha'," Norrin said softly in her ear. Her face was pressed against his bare chest, and his long, wiry arms were wrapped firmly around her. Norrin was fully supporting her weight.

That smell.

"You're a lot stronger than you look, Frank," she stammered, "I never would have thought a human could—"

"Handle you?" He smirked. "I'm much more resilient than I look."

She wanted to rip off his britches and slam him against the hull. She wanted him to thrust himself inside of her right there.

"W-where's this wood you need my help with?" she asked, choking on her words and forcing herself out of his embrace.

"If you mean the lumber we're meant to be carrying, it's over here."

Leeja felt her cheeks burning, and for the first time, she was grateful for the dark.

A few minutes later, after Leeja and Norrin had wrestled the unwieldy piece of timber out of the hole, they were both sweaty and breathless. Leeja was bright green. She dropped her end of the wood the second they were both out in the sun and practically ran away from Norrin.

"Hey, Aengus, I just remembered I have something to take care of. If it's all the same, I'd like to head home early."

"No problem. You did great today, kid."

"Thanks," she said and started her escape from the dry dock.

"Hey, wait!" Norrin called out, running after her. "There's still like... six pieces of wood in there."

"Don't you worry about that, Leeja," Aengus interrupted, "Norrin and I can finish up here. You just be back bright and early tomorrow morning," he leaned toward her conspiratorially and winked, "We're going to use *the adhesive* tomorrow."

"I can't wait!!" she said, resuming her retreat.

"But I wanted to take you down to the beach after work and show you my racing boat." Norrin was still walking towards her with that stupid, charming, sexy smile on his dumb, handsome face.

"Tomorrow, I promise!" Leeja called out without looking over her shoulder.

Please, goddess, don't let him follow me. Please, goddess, don't let him follow me. Please, goddess, don't let him follow me. She prayed all the way home.

CHAPTER
SIX

Leeja rushed up the shallow, dusty, limestone steps taking them two at a time. She flung open the creaking old wooden door that led to their shared living space. Inside, Arlynn was lounging on a bench, on the shady side of the room, shielded from the midday sun. Her long, red braids were draped across her, and pooled on the floor, and one leather slipper hung precariously from her big toe. She didn't bother to look up from her book, when Leeja burst into their apartment.

"I think I'm going insane!"

"And a good afternoon to you, too," Arlynn said smugly, putting down her book, *'The Unauthorized Biography of Bacchus'*.

"I'm serious, Lynn. This is an emergency." Leeja was pacing frantically around, opening drawers and slamming them closed again, as if the solution to her problem must be contained inside one of them.

"Leeja," Arlynn said, guiding her gently down on the bench beside her. "Whatever the problem is, I'll help you figure it out, but you have to tell me what's going on."

"I don't know," Leeja eeked out between labored breaths. "Something is changing. I thought I had this all figured out. As long as I got a really thorough nailing once a week or so, I'd be able to exist in relative peace, but my body is rebelling. It's only been four days since that ogre had me twisted up like a pretzel, and I'm already crawling out of my skin."

"Let me get this straight," said Arlynn suspiciously, "all this thrashing around is because you're *horny*?"

"Not horny. *Orc* horny. I need to be mated, or I'll be staring down a full-blown breeding frenzy!"

"Huh…" Arlynn considered her, "So *right after* we make a bet that you're too chicken to actually date someone, your sexual needs quadruple? That's very convenient."

"Calling me a liar, human?" Leeja saw red. In a flash, her razor-sharp tusks were pressed against Arlynn's throat.

"What in three hells, Leeja?"

The sound of Arlynn's voice snapped Leeja out of her rage. Horrified at her own behavior, she released her friend and slinked across the room.

"I'm so sorry, Lynn," Leeja struggled to explain herself, but how could a human ever understand the frenzy? "I don't want to hurt you, I would never. It's…it's the frenzy; I can't control myself when I'm like this."

"You're assuming I don't want you to bite my neck…" Arlynn

teased, "but you know it wouldn't count, our bet is for you to date a man."

"I'm not welching," Leeja said, relieved that Arlynn was taking her outburst so well. "But you can't possibly expect me to make good relationship decisions in my present state. Goddess knows, I practically mauled Norrin today."

Arlynn gave her a quizzical look.

"Frank. The human from the Drowned Grim?"

"Oh, he's cute," Arlynn said, crossing one slender leg over the other and twisting an alabaster finger through her copper-colored hair.

A savage growl ripped through Leeja. Arlynn was within striking range; in a second, her pretty head could be rolling around on the floor.

"Not for *me!*" Arlynn said, resting a hand on Leeja's shoulder. "He's cute for *you*. Tall, blonde, and earnest? Sounds like a perfect starter boyfriend. Why don't you just fuck *him?*"

"No humans!"

"Leeja," Arlynn said, employing her serious tone, "If you insist on living your life by these arbitrary rules, you're going to miss out on a lot of...*living*." Leeja rolled her eyes, but Arlynn pressed on, "I know you like him...'practically mauled him on the job site,' eh?" Arlynn started elbowing her friend lightly in the ribs, trying to get her to laugh or smile, but Leeja's expression became more grave.

"Of course I like him." Leeja sighed. "The problem with human men is...they never like me back."

"But this one clearly does," Arlynn was practically pleading with her friend to see reason. "He followed you down the esplanade that morning...and you keep going on and on about how nice he's being to you at work...how he's going out of his way to teach you things..."

Leeja shook her head, "He's teaching me so that he can get

better work out of me; I'm nothing but a big, strong body to him...Norrin's interest in me stops at the edge of the dry dock."

"But if you would just go *talk* to him..."

Leeja growled, "No! Not him. I agreed to your scheme, but I never agreed to be humiliated.

"I will meet your challenge, Arlynn. I will date and hold hands and tell secrets and whatever other human nonsense is required, *after* I get my head cleared. But not with Norrin and not right now. Right now, I need a cock inside of me. This is an emergency. If I don't have penetrative intercourse within the hour, I can't be held responsible for my actions."

Leeja's breathing quickened. Without realizing it, she was back on her feet, pacing around the apartment again.

Why is Arlynn being so difficult?

"Since I would very much prefer not to take this apartment down to its frame and be permanently exiled from Th'myskôra," she growled, "I am asking for your support. So, are you going to help me or are you going to sit on that bench looking smug all day?"

"You mean, am I going to drop everything on a Wednesday afternoon to act as my friend's personal penis broker? Of course I am. Go put on a dress."

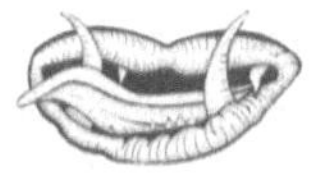

Twenty minutes later, Arlynn was leading Leeja down an empty alleyway.

"I've never been to this part of the island before," Leeja said, marveling at the decaying stone buildings.

"I don't see why you would have," Arlynn said, "these are the ruins of the old Stronghold, troll-made. It's generally understood that if you're in the Stronghold, you're up to something untoward."

"You make it sound like we're going to kill a guy; it's just sex."

"*Just* sex? I was under the impression this was an emergency orc crotch thrashing," Arlynn teased.

Leeja just growled.

"Look, this is the best place on the island for rough, anonymous sex. We'll get your brains plowed out today, and then it's back to the bet. No more excuses."

They stopped in front of a round tower that stretched up taller than any other surrounding structure. It had a steeply pitched roof topped with a golden spire. Compared to all the other buildings in the area, this one was remarkably well-maintained.

"Can you imagine building something as beautiful as this?" Leeja was so enamored with the troll craftsmanship that she almost forgot the aching desire between her legs. Almost.

"This is The Keep," Arlynn said, pushing open a heavy wooden door covered in ornate trollish ironwork.

The air in The Keep was thick with opium and magic. Leeja's head spun, "All the smells in this place...they blur together."

Arlynn guided her up to a handsome blackscale who stood in a corner, sucking on a long, iridescent tube. He was tall, muscular, and nearly nude. His thick, glistening black tail undulated slowly on the floor around him. Every time he took a long drag from his pipe, the bright red flesh under his chin swelled into a round sack which flattened again with his exhale. As the girls neared him, his eyes flashed gold and the spiny sail on the top of his head stood at attention.

"That's Galdur," she whispered to Leeja. "He is well versed in all of the sensual arts."

Galdur opened his mouth slightly, and a long, thin, forked tongue flicked out, tasting the air. "Do my senses deceive me, or has the ambrosial Arlynn of Little Break returned to once again grace my bed with her singular...*tang*?" Galdur smiled as two plumes of glittering pink smoke poured out of his nostrils and swirled around Leeja and Arlynn, engulfing them.

"Hello, Galdur," Arlynn said, kissing him warmly on the cheek. "Today, I'm here on behalf of my poor friend, Leeja. She's in a bad way, and I told her you'd be able to ease her suffering." Arlynn relinquished her friend to the lizardman and sauntered across the room to talk to a tabaxi who had been eying her from beneath his heavy woolen hood. Leeja watched him suspiciously.

I don't know who he thinks he's fooling with that cloak and dagger act, I can smell his feline odor from here.

Galdur stepped close to Leeja, burying his nose in her hair and inhaling deeply.

Arlynn is a big girl, she'll be fine.

He slid a heavy, reptilian hand around her waist and brushed her ear gently with his velveteen lips, his long, agile tongue was fluttering along her neck. Leeja shuttered and swayed on the spot.

If he keeps this up, I'm going to cum right here in front of all these people.

"From the smell of you, I'd say you're ripe and ready to pop, Leeja," he rumbled, and the words rolled around inside his mouth. It was the first time she'd been aroused by the sound of her own name. "Would you like to come upstairs to my apartments, Leeja?"

She nodded slowly, and Galdur tightened his fingers into her hip as he led her through a small doorway and onto a narrow, spiral staircase. The door had barely closed behind them when Galdur hoisted up her skirts and plunged the right head of his forked cock into her eager pussy.

Leeja's vision whited out, and her desperate moans ricocheted all around them in the stone stairwell. Her aching pussy clenched around Galdur's serpentine member, and she orgasmed immediately. She struggled to catch her breath; the blackscale still writhing, his cock inside of her, "More," she whispered in between ragged breaths.

"Oh, we're just getting started," Galdur said, hoisting Leeja's limp body up over his shoulder and dragging her up the stairs.

CHAPTER

SEVEN

The next morning, Leeja happily trotted down the road toward the dry docks, savoring not only her figs but their necessity. Galdur had performed his duty admirably; he'd fucked the sense back into her. Now, Leeja was very much looking forward to getting back to work on the Flannery with a clear head.

When she arrived, Aengus was nowhere in sight; neither was his workbench, lumber, or the cart. In fact, the only thing on the dry dock was Norrin, his sparkling white human smile beaming at her. He had a long, slim, single-passenger boat next

57

to him, and he was dressed in nothing but a very thin pair of cotton britches.

Leeja's nipples tightened, and her skin prickled all over. "Seven hells." she muttered.

I should not be this horny already! I can still feel Galdur dripping out of me.

"What's the big idea, Frank? Where's Aengus?" Leeja tried desperately to appear unaffected.

"I gave Dad the day off," Norrin said, smiling, "because you promised to let me teach you how to race today."

"A promise is a promise," Leeja grumbled.

The pair of them hoisted the little boat onto their shoulders and started down to the beach. Norrin insisted that she go first. Leeja could feel his eyes on her the whole time. Whenever she shifted the boat slightly on her shoulder, she was sure the massive muscles of her back were bulging under her tunic. With each step along the dry, rocky terrain, she felt her hamstrings and glutes flex and twinge. She was sure Norrin saw all of it, all of her unsightly orcish body through her tight leather britches. Leeja was mortified thinking of him scrutinizing her, but also inexplicably aroused, knowing his eyes were on her.

On the beach, dozens of bathers and boating enthusiasts scampered around in various states of undress. Most of the women wore nothing but their smallclothes, chest bindings and short braies cut up so high over the hip, that Leeja blushed. Most of them were humans. There were a few non-human women were present, but they were all imps and fae...delicate, graceful creatures. The kinds of women that human men *wanted* to see sunbathing.

"Beautiful!" Norrin called out, stopping abruptly, pulling the boat and Leeja to a halt.

"Which one?" Leeja tuned to see Norrin's raised eyebrow, and head cocked to one side. He looked utterly confused.

"This is a beautiful spot for us to practice!" Norrin set the boat down and was orienting it in the sand. "You're gonna want to strip down."

"Right," Leeja mumbled, "people strip on the beach..."

She looked around the beach to see that no one was staring at her. Leeja took a steadying breath and quickly removed her leather britches, boots, and stays. She stacked them in a neat pile in the sand and kept her gaze focused on the boat. Leeja kept her tunic on over her chest bindings and smallclothes.

No need to make any more of a spectacle of myself than this.

"If you fall in, that thing is going to make it pretty difficult to swim back to the shore." Norrin teased, tugging at the edge of her tunic.

"You'd better make sure I don't fall in then, hadn't you?" she teased, hoping her face didn't look as green as it felt.

"I'll do my best," Norrin said, climbing into the boat and offering his hand. When his skin touched hers, electricity ran through her body.

Not now. This situation is uncomfortable enough.

"Usually," Norrin instructed, "you'd pilot one of these racing boats alone, but we'll ride tandem until you get the hang of it."

"Alright," Leeja said, "struggling to ignore the growing ache in her groin. "What do I have to do?"

"The first thing to do is get used to standing on the boat without falling out, then we'll work on operating the sail." Leeja tried not to stare at Norrin's beautiful body, but the line of wispy blond hairs that started at his navel and trailed down his pelvis to his waistband, was extremely distracting.

Leeja adopted a stance similar to the ones she'd seen other

racers employing, left foot forward, right foot back, both hands gripped firmly around the boom.

Norrin stomped down hard on the starboard gunwale, shifting his weight, and Leeja went tumbling out hard onto the sand.

"Cute."

"If you think that was intense, wait until the ocean gets ahold of you," he smiled down at her. "Now, let's try that again."

When Norrin bent down to help her up, Leeja's nostrils flared. She couldn't control herself, she had to fill herself with the wonderful smell of him.

"Are you…" Norrin asked, beaming down at her, "are you scenting me?"

Leeja flushed. She was sure she was bright green now. "I… um…you…"

"What do I smell like?" His smile sparkled.

"You smell…human" Leeja grumbled, resuming her stance inside the boat. Norrin slid up behind her, moving her left hand from the boom to the mast.

"Now," he said, "the trick is to keep your knees loose. You're not going to overpower the ocean, so you've got to try and roll along with her." Norrin rocked the boat gently back and forth in the sand, and Leeja's eyes fluttered closed. She felt like liquid with Norrin pressed against her. His crotch made frequent contact with her ass, and it wasn't just arousing; it was… comfortable. She almost let herself imagine she belonged there, wrapped in his arms.

"I don't believe my lyin' eye!" A voice boomed out across the beach, wrenching Leeja back into the present moment. It was Thorne the cyclops standing there with Phlip, Thad, and a couple other Titans she didn't recognize. "Is our resident human-hating, half-orc actually consorting with the blond barnacle?"

"What are you, the brute squad?" Leeja crouched, prepared to tackle him.

Thorne snarled at her.

Everyone was silent, waiting to see which of them would strike first.

Leeja leaped out of the boat and flung her arms around Thorne's neck.

Before anyone could act, his hands were around her waist. The pair laughed wildly as he swung her around in a circle. As exasperating as he was, Thorne was always a welcome sight. Leeja knew how to act around him...like any other member of the freight crew. When Thorne was around, Leeja was just another one of the guys.

"I guess this explains where you've been all week," Thorne said, placing her back gently on the sand. "Having a vacation while the rest of us are stuck lugging cargo in the hot sun."

"Something like that," Leeja answered, "Bowen lent me out to help repair the Flannery."

"Is this what passes for shipwrightery these days?" he asked, raising his singular eyebrow.

"Last I checked, a lady has the prerogative to have a boating lesson if she wants to," said Norrin.

Thorne ignored him, "You just watch yourself, girly. That human's a real heartbreaker."

"Yeah, yeah, yeah," she said, waving him off.

"See you at the Grim tonight?" Thorne asked.

"*We'll* be there," Norrin shouted as the whole group of Titans turned to leave.

"Now that our distraction is gone," he said, grinning at Leeja again, "what do you say we try this on the water?"

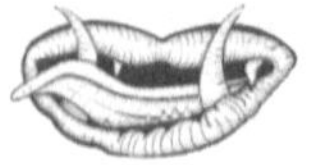

THE SAIL WAS FOLDED flat against the boat, and Leeja sat cramped to one side of the bow seat, gripping the thwart with all her might.

"Try to relax!" Norrin called out from behind her. He was soaked up to his thighs, pushing the craft further and further out into the ocean. "If you fall in, I'll dive in after you and drag you back to shore!"

It's not drowning I'm worried about.

With every step, the lapping ocean crept further and further up Norrin's thin linen britches. They were becoming transparent and clinging to his body. Leeja was mortified. She couldn't stop imagining what she might see when the water finally swallowed up his waistline. She could already make out the outline of his hefty package, and his britches were growing more transparent every second.

I was fine when I was talking to Thorne. He literally swept me up off my feet. He spun me around and I didn't even start hyperventilating a little bit. What is wrong with me?

The boat rocked back and forth, and flecks of icy salt water sprayed across Leeja's hot skin. Norrin was in the boat, standing behind her.

"Now comes the fun part...you gotta stand up so we can extend the sail."

Leeja wobbled to her feet, "Goddess, this is difficult," she said, working hard to stabilize herself. "I don't think I've ever worked so hard just to stand up!"

"How do you think I got to be so incredibly strong?" Norrin said, with a swagger so evident Leeja could've sworn that she *heard* him wink.

"Strong for *a human*, you mean."

Together, they raised and secured the sail, "Alright," Norrin said, "Just like we practiced." He placed her left hand on the mast. He gently guided the boom, helping her feel the subtle changes in the wind's direction and bracing her against the rocking of the sea with his taught muscular body. Norrin held her tightly against himself. He was pressed hard into her ass... for stability, of course. If Leeja hadn't known better, she might have convinced herself that his penis was stiffening for her.

The pair spent the rest of the afternoon making wide, lazy circles and figure-eights off the coast. Leeja spent the rest of the afternoon fighting the urge to grind her ass against Norrin's heavy cock.

Sunburnt and ravenously hungry, Leeja and Norrin sat at the bar in the Drowned Grimoire. Each time one of them reached for their tankard or shoved their lamb shank into their mouths, caked-on sand flaked off their bodies and sprinkled down around them. Norrin watched Leeja sucking the marrow from a lamb bone, and his cock was instantly hard.

"Leeja," he said gently, "I had a really great time with you today."

"Me too," she answered, blushing.

All right, this is your chance. Tell her how you feel and make it official.

"To be honest, Frank, I've been having a wonderful time all week." Leeja's expression grew serious. "I want to tell you something, Norrin, something I've never really told anyone before. Is that alright?"

"Of course, I'd be honored."

Gods, is she going to ask me? *This day could not possibly be going any better.*

"Well," she said, running a finger lightly around the rim of her tankard, "I know I was unfair to you when we first met, but there *is* a reason."

Because you're madly in love with me,

"Mmhmm?"

"You're a human, and...and I've never felt like I was good enough around human men. Whenever I'm with them, they insult me; it's like every human man I've ever met has gone out of his way to make me feel small...Maybe that's my fault for being so big..." Leeja's eyes were starting to mist over.

"Don't talk like that," he said, taking her calloused hand in both of his. "As far as I'm concerned, you, Miss Leeja, are exactly the right size."

She laughed and pulled her hand away to dab at her eye, "I know you're not like those other humans. You and Aengus have been so kind this week; I never once felt out of place with the two of you."

"Well, we Galanou men certainly aim to please," Norrin said, winking as he lifted his ale.

"As far as I'm concerned, you're doing a first-rate job." Leeja clinked her tankard against his in the air, and they both drank.

"Can I tell you another secret?" she asked, leaning in conspiratorially.

"Anytime."

"I've always sort of had this secret fantasy..."

of bedding a beautiful, blond human man?

"That someday I'd be sort of ...adopted by a dad...like Aengus."

Norrin choked on his ale.

"I know it's stupid..." Leeja said, looking down at her plate, "But back in the horde...well, all they ever did was break things. I guess I've always thought of humans as being the opposite of orcs. When I think of humans, I think of builders. I guess that's why I like Aengus so much; no one's ever taught me how to build anything before I met him."

"That's not stupid at all," Norrin said, "And speaking of Aengus, he set up that meeting with Rakka for you."

"Really?" Leeja roared in delight.

"In four days, it's all set."

"No one's ever done a favor like that for me before! I don't even know how to act. How do you thank a person for something like that?"

"Well, he sure likes you a lot, Leeja. I already know what he'll say, 'Forget it! Forget it!'"

Leeja laughed, "you sound just like him!"

"As far as dads go, you could do worse. Aengus is great for *all kinds* of dad stuff...He can teach you how to fish, drive a carriage, or woo a lusty maid, all of your basic human skills. I'd be happy to let you borrow him anytime."

"Speaking of wooing," Leeja smiled,

Finally, let's get this conversation back on topic.

"...look who's on the dance floor!"

There was a group of human women, from the look of their attire, all newly arrived from Little Break.

"We gotta get you laid!" Leeja shouted. And before he could protest, Norrin had been dragged out onto the floor.

Hot, sweaty bodies whirled and spun all around her. Leeja had been dancing (and drinking) for what seemed like hours. The band played loudly. She hopped and skipped and happily allowed any willing hand to grab her body and shove her around the dance floor. But when the next hand holding hers was Norrin's, that churning desire that had been plaguing her all week was back.

"Come get another drink with me," he shouted into her ear before leading her back to the bar.

Goddess, protect me from my libido. Please don't let me fuck this up.

In a room packed with sweaty bodies, all she could smell was him.

"See anybody you'd like to take home?" she asked, praying that he couldn't somehow detect how much she wanted him.

"That's actually what I wanted to talk to you about—"

"Leeja!" A familiar voice cut through the crowd. It was Thorne, her favorite hard-headed cyclops.

Thank the goddess.

Leeja could position him in between Norrin and herself.

She'd still be able to smell him, but maybe Thorne could serve as an unwitting chaperone.

"How was it out on the water today?" Thorne asked, clapping a powerful hand down on each of their shoulders.

"Not nearly as terrifying as I thought it would be," she said, smiling, "Norrin is an outstanding teacher."

"Well, now that you know the basics, you should let a real man take you for a ride," Thorne said. He was unbelievably tall; even before you accounted for the horn, he towered over Leeja, which was an accomplishment. "I could show you all kinds of tricks."

"You wanna give us a minute here, Thorne?" Norrin asked, stepping in front of him. Thorne snarled, but Norrin was still smiling. Norrin was always smiling, "Leeja and I were having a private conversation."

The thought of doing anything private with Norrin made Leeja quiver.

"That's right!" Leeja said, "We were just trying to decide which of these lusty wenches Norrin would deign to bed tonight." Leeja held her breath and looked around the room. She was too terrified to make eye contact with Norrin.

"How about her?" Leeja indicated a cute, slender human dancing with her friends on the other side of the tavern.

"I don't think she's quite Norrin's type," Thorne said. There was the hint of a threat in his voice, but Leeja chose to ignore it.

"And how is it that you know Norrin's type?" Leeja asked, turning further away from Norrin. It wasn't any good, though. She could still smell him.

"Ol' Norrin and I go way back," Thorne said grinning and shaking Norrin's shoulder.

Norrin rolled his eyes, "You don't know me as well as you think you do, old friend."

"See!" Leeja piped up, "He *does* like cute human girls!" She pulled on his sleeve, trying to get Norrin back out onto the dance floor. "She's blond and gorgeous, *you're* blond and gorgeous... it's a perfect match."

"Leeja, please..."

"Don't make the lady beg," Thorne said, taking Norrin by the shoulders, "go over there and get your dick wet!" Thorne shoved Norrin out onto the dance floor, and he was enveloped by the crowd.

"Thank the goddess," Leeja mumbled, slumping over the bar.

"Speaking of getting wet," Thorne said, sliding up close to her, "What do you say the two of us get out of here?"

"If you'd asked me on any other day, I'd have been delighted, but I've got this stupid bet going with Arlynn..."

"Pity," Thorne said, turning to go. "Guess I'll have to ask again some other day."

"Some other day, Thorne," Leeja turned back to the bar, ready to order another drink, when a sudden realization hit her. "Thorne? *Thorne!*" Leeja reached out and grabbed his arm. "Wait a second, I know your name."

"I should hope so," he smiled down at her.

"You wouldn't, by chance, be interested in fucking me on two non-consecutive days, would you?"

CHAPTER

EIGHT

"Oooouch!" Norrin groaned as he rolled over off of his stiff cock. He'd been dreaming of Leeja again. He slid the sheet down, letting the crisp morning wind caress him. His heavy balls recoiled at the sudden cold. Yesterday he'd had her in his arms, nearly naked and pressed against his aching body.

Norrin ran his fingertips along the impressive length of his shaft, making himself twitch every time he brushed along a particularly sensitive spot.

He'd been so close on the beach, he thought for sure she'd be in his bed this morning.

But then there was all that weirdness in the Grim. She started treating me like her buddy! I probably could have still salvaged the

69

night if Thorne hadn't shown up and started all that human *talk again.*

"What's everybody got against humans all of a sudden, anyway?"

Earlier in the week, in the warm dark of the hull, she'd brushed her ass against his crotch. She had to know what she was doing to him. She had to want him too.

Norrin's cock throbbed at the thought of Leeja's pert ass pressed up against it, and he took a steady grip around the thing.

She was so beautiful in the tavern last night. When she danced, raising her hands above her head, twisting her wrists, and snapping her fingers in a syncopated rhythm against the music, the tendons in her forearms rippled. When she leapt and spun, those glorious breasts bounced like they were trying to escape her tunic. Like they needed to be in his hands. In his mouth.

Norrin dragged his fist up and down his cock in firm, even strokes.

But then she ran away.

She always ran away. Leeja was the most challenging woman he'd ever met. But she couldn't run in his dreams. In his dreams, she was tied to this very bed, naked and spread for him. Thick leather straps held her strong wrists and shapely ankles, tethered to the bedposts.

Norrin's pace quickened. His cock was bucking now.

In Norrin's imagination, Leeja's face flushed bright green, and her breasts rose and fell with her quick, shallow breaths. In Norrin's dream, her nipples were bright pink. He sucked one gently into his mouth as he slid a hand down her abs. Did she have a four-pack? Or was it six? In his dream, she always had deep, tapered grooves framing her torso, directing him downward to the promised land.

Norrin's strokes were faster now, more erratic.

In the dream, he dragged two fingers over her mound, lingering in what he imagined was a thick tuft of green pubic hair.

Norrin's balls clenched and drew up close to his body. He was close.

In the dream, he slammed two fingers into Leeja's wet, waiting cunt. Her back arched, and she screamed out in pleasure.

In his bedroom, Norrin came in thick, milky white ropes that lashed against his belly over and over again. Finally, his balls were nearly empty, and the last of the hot fluid dribbled down over his knuckles.

His breathing steadied, and his consciousness slowly returned to the present moment.

"Why can't the real Leeja just be easy like dream Leeja," he asked, groping around for a rag to clean himself with. He hoisted himself out of bed and looked around for a pair of britches.

"Rest day today. Teaching tomorrow. Rest day the day after that. That means no more Leeja until Monday." Norrin tied his leather sandals at the ankles.

And then he had a thought he'd never had before in his life, "...what if I don't wait to bump into her again? What if I go and find her today? It shouldn't be too hard." Norrin stood up and paced excitedly around the room. "She eats breakfast at the Drowned Grim almost every day." He threw open his wooden storage chest and put on his best looking linen tunic before racing down the stairs and into town.

"As the gods witness me, I'm going to find that woman today. There's no reason I should spend another night alone. I'm going to walk right up to her, and then I'll...I'll hint harder than I've ever hinted before!"

. . .

Leeja, Imogen, and Arlynn all sat at their favorite table in the Drowned Grimoire, blinking the sleep out of their eyes.

"Tree bowls a' porridge, tree ales, and tree orders a' *dried figs!*" Bridgid crowed as she unloaded her tray and bustled back to the kitchens.

"Okay ladies, spill it!" Imogen said excitedly, snatching up her figs.

"You first," said Leeja.

"Oh, my story isn't exciting at all," Imogen said, blushing a bit.

"It's at least a little exciting," Arlynn pressed her. "I can't remember the last time we saw *you* eating figs on a Friday!"

"Alright," Imogen said, taking a steadying breath, "you know those...*upsetting* dreams I've been having?"

Her friends raised their eyebrows.

"Well," Imogen continued, "they weren't exactly nightmares. I've been having..." she leaned in and whispered "...*erotic dreams...*"

"Imogen!"

"About a man who *isn't* Keneth...and, well, Keneth and I haven't really been *intimate* since they started."

"Thank the gods!" Arlynn cut in. "That boyfriend of yours

leaves a lot to be desired. I've been counting down the days until you send him packing."

"But we *were* intimate last night," Imogen said firmly, knitting her brows. "I put those dreams out of my head and reaffirmed my commitment to Keneth."

"How was it?" Leeja asked, around a mouthful of porridge.

"Nice," said Imogen, nodding. "Really nice. Comfortable, you know?"

"I prefer my sex *un*comfortable, personally," Arlynn laughed.

"Alright," said Imogen, pouting, "tell us all about *your* amazing sexcapades then."

"I thought you'd never ask!" Arlynn squealed. "As you know, I've been seeing these two men for a while now, and yesterday, I finally made love to *both* of them!"

"At the same time?" Imogen blushed.

"That *does* sound uncomfortable," Leeja chuckled.

"No," Arlynn said smiling, and waggling her spoon back and forth. "I met one of them for a little afternoon delight and the other for an evening gala...although now that you mention it, that's not a half bad idea."

Arlynn and Imogen laughed. "What about you, Miss Relationship?" Imogen teased.

"As a matter of fact..." Leeja said, setting her spoon down in her porridge and leaning in conspiratorially—

WHAM!

The doors to the Grim flew open and standing between them, silhouetted by the brilliant morning sun, was Norrin. Tight and lean and tan and smelling wonderful.

Leeja was transfixed.

The sun glinted off of his incorrigible blond hair, and his perfect white smile gleamed at her. As he strode across the tavern, Leeja could hear his heart beating stronger and faster. Or was that her own heart pounding in her chest?

Arlynn and Imogen giggled and Leeja was snapped back to reality. Suddenly aware that she and Norrin weren't alone. She blushed and forced her giddy smile back down into what she hoped was a neutral expression.

"Good morning, ladies," Norrin said, taking a seat across the table from Leeja. They both had unusually long legs, and when he slid into place, his shin brushed against her knee.

"Good morning, Norrin," Arlynn and Imogen sang out in unison like a couple of bratty little kids.

"What are you doing here, Frank?" Leeja asked, fumbling with her spoon.

"I came here to see you." Norrin's stupid, beautiful, human eyes were smiling at her. Inviting her to...to what, she couldn't tell. "I wanted to let you know that I had a really great time with you last night."

Oh, that's it. He's here to boast about bedding one of those blonde humans from last night.

"Yeah, I guess we make a pretty good team, Frank." Leeja felt hot tears burning the backs of her eyes.

Get it together, Leeja. You don't have any right to be jealous anyway...it's not like you slept in your own bed last night either.

"I'm glad you think so," Norrin took Leeja's hand in his and gently ran his thumb across the pronounced veins on the back of her hand. "I thought, maybe...if you don't have other plans, that you might want to team up with me again today?"

"Gee, Frank," Leeja said pulling her hand away.

I'd rather be eviscerated by a giant boar than help to send him home with another woman today.

"I'd love to, but...but" Leeja looked around the table, desperate for an out, "but we're having a girls' day!"

"I'm sure the girls wouldn't mind if I borrowed you for an hour or two this evening?"

Leeja looked at her friends, Imogen was smiling so hard it looked like her cheeks might burst. Arlynn's eyes narrowed fiendishly and she opened her mouth to speak.

"It's not up to them, I'm afraid," Leeja said, "I made a promise. It's impossible for an orc to break a promise...you know...orc code." Leeja scanned the faces smiling at her around the table.

"Another time," Norrin flashed his dashing smile again before rising from the table. "Ladies," he said, nodding at Imogen and Arlynn before swaggering back out of the tavern.

As the doors closed behind him, Arlynn and Imogen erupted in a flurry of squeals and giggles. Leeja looked down, hiding her face and pretending to stir her porridge.

"I can't believe you didn't tell us right away that you were dating Norrin," Arlynn said.

"The two of you do seem to be an optimal pairing," Imogen grinned.

"So?" Arlynn prodded, "How was it? We want details!"

Leeja looked up from her breakfast, "I went home with Thorne last night," she said flatly.

"*Thorne*?" the girls chorused.

"Yes," Leeja continued. "And we have plans to mate again tonight." Leeja's friends looked concerned, so she quickly added, "*After* he takes me to eat at the Spiced Goat. It's a *date*, as they say."

"That's a great first step, but...Thorne?" Arlynn asked.

"What's wrong with Thorne?" Leeja could hear a slight growl sneaking into her own voice.

"Nothing's *wrong* with him," Arlynn answered. "We were just expecting..."

Imogen blurted out, "Norrin's obviously crazy about you and..."

"No," Leeja said, stiffening. "No humans, especially not *that* human."

"Then what was all of that about?" demanded Arlynn. "He had a great time with you? He can't wait to do it again?"

"We went out drinking last night," Leeja grumbled, "I helped get him laid."

"Oh," Imogen said, a slight frown spreading across her full lips. "So, what are you wearing on your big date?"

"I don't know," Leeja said, looking down at her tattered, shapeless brown cote, "This?"

"Absolutely not!" Arlynn said. "As soon as we're done with breakfast, we're taking you to the dressmaker!"

"And the apothecary?" asked Imogen eagerly.

"Don't you have equations to bewitch or whatever it is you do all day?" teased Arlynn.

"Not when there are makeovers to be had!" Imogen was practically giddy.

"You don't mean that I should wear one of those tight-fitting, sparkly gowns the two of you always wear?" Leeja had been admiring the fine garments worn by the residents of Th'myskôra since she arrived. "They seem terribly impractical. I bet you can't even raise a broad sword over your head in one of those!"

"I've never tried," Arlynn said, rolling her eyes and taking a sip from her tankard. When she raised her arm, the fine amethyst beadwork along the edge of her sleeve glittered in the sunlight.

Those little stones would pop off the moment hand to hand combat began. And look at how tight her bodice is! You can see every curve of her body! And that low-cut neckline! Her breasts are practically bursting out of it. She looks ridiculous. If I were back in Søgsund, I'd be laughed off the battlefield...but I'm not in Søgsund anymore.

"Look," Arlynn said raising an eyebrow, "you already told Norrin you were having a girls' day with us, so unless you're planning on becoming a liar, you pretty much *have* to come with us."

"Fine." Leeja said, setting her jaw, "We can go into town, and I'll let you doll me up."

Imogen and Arlynn cheered bouncing up and down in their seats. And after a few moments, Leeja let herself giggle too.

NINE

Out on the water, Norrin was unstoppable. The master of his own destiny. He grabbed the boom with both hands and pulled it hard until it was at a sharp ninety-degree angle with the canoe. A mighty gust of wind blew up from behind him. He threw his weight back, thrusting the stern into the air. In the next moment, Norrin was airborne.

"Whoo-hoo!"

Sea air rushed past his face, whipping his thick, blonde hair around fiercely. For a moment, he hung suspended in the air. Then his body fell faster than his guts, and he felt a familiar and thrilling sensation like his testicles had jumped up into his stomach and plopped back down. He landed back in the water with an impressive splash.

Norrin was utterly at home on the water. Experiencing his own competence lit a fire in him.

I was incredible back there! I wouldn't have believed I could be so suave if I hadn't seen it myself. Leeja and I are meant to be together. I know she can feel it too.

He beached his little boat and hopped out.

She wants me, it couldn't have been more obvious this morning at the Grim. I'll give her the rest of the day to stew about it and then tomorrow...I might just happen *to run into her again. We'll be making love in no time.*

Norrin trudged through the sand, pulling his racing boat behind him.

"Niccce air!" Hissed Phlip, the dragonborn as Norrin passed a small group of seaside regulars.

"Nothing compared to *your* recent ride, though, eh, Thorne?" Martel said coyly, rustling his feathers excitedly and nudging the cyclops in the ribs.

"Orc women aren't for inexperienced lovers," Thorne laughed, "but I escaped mostly unharmed...I even still have all my teeth!"

Son of a bitch!

"You bedded an orc woman last night, huh? The only orc I know of on Th'myskôra is Leeja." Norrin advanced on Thorne. "You wanna, maybe elaborate a little on that?"

"With pleasure," Thorne snarled, "After you struck out at the Grim, I took Leeja home and fucked her senseless."

Norrin's face was suddenly very hot. His hands clenched into fists, and his vision hazed over red.

How could she? And with Thorne of all people!

"You're lying! Leeja wouldn't!"

"Oh yes, she would, and she did. Apparently, her friends bet her she couldn't go out on three human-style dates with the same male, so I'm taking her to the Spiced Goat tonight. *And* we'll mate at least two more times; it's part of the bet! It's almost like she *has to* sleep with me again! Who knows, if I play my cards right, maybe I'll be the first inductee to her horde."

Norrin could barely make out the conversation. He was so angry. The words of the other boaters sounded far away and tinny.

"You wouldn't seriously join a horde, would you?" asked Martel, cocking his avian head to the side and blinking his huge blank eyes, "You don't strike me as the type."

"You mean leave all this behind," Thorne said, gesturing around them at the crowded beach, "to spend all day plea-suring my queen and separating her enemies from their heads?" Thorne smiled devilishly directly at Norrin. "I could be convinced."

"Even knowing that she was also bedding every other male in the horde?" Martel asked, watching Norrin's face closely.

"We cyclops are more progressive than griffins in our thinking around relations," said Thorne, sliding a finger along his horn. "We don't mind sharing, especially when there's so much to go around."

"Well, I *do*." Norrin huffed, and he dragged his boat off the beach while Thorne and Phlip laughed, clapping each other on the back.

THE MERCANTILE DISTRICT was on the northeastern tip of the island. The imps built it during their rule over Th'myskôra, so it was near their old docks, the closest to Felft'halas. They were the first inhabitants of the island to use it as a trading hub and the tradition was alive and well here among the shops and dusty stalls.

Many new businesses, run by many kinds of creatures, had been created in the centuries since impish rule ended on the island. Walking down Zeluk Row, one could surmise the entire history of the island just by observing the many varied architectural styles.

"This is wonderful," Leeja marveled breathlessly, "I can't believe you've never taken me here before."

"We didn't think you were very interested in clothes," Arlynn shrugged, indicating Leeja's old brown cote. The same dress she'd been wearing when they first met her, the only one she owned.

"Clothes?" Leeja was baffled, "I've never seen so many interesting buildings!"

There were stick-built structures mortared together with ancient clay and bits of straw, sporting thatched roofs lining the principal boulevard in neat rows. There were also low mounds of earth and stone. From the outside, they seemed pretty unremarkable. Still, each had a set of subterranean stairs, which led to unseen structures. Taller, spindly brick structures, each with several high, narrow chimneys jutting out at odd angles, seemed to have been wedged into any remaining real estate. And, of course, there were the many hastily constructed wooden stalls erected and deconstructed daily by humans to tread out their wares.

Leeja could have spent the entire afternoon marveling at the architecture, "Hey, you don't think any of these shopkeepers have the original blueprints, do you?"

"Please stay focused," Imogen admonished her. "We're here to get glamorous today!"

The streets were packed. Creatures of every conceivable race shuffled about, bumping into each other and haggling loudly. A group of school-aged blackscales and dragonborns fighting over a bag of candied dragonflies ran between Imogen and Leeja separating her from the group.

A little blue imp strode by with each of his short arms outstretched and loaded down with glittering amulets made of every known precious stone, each one hanging from either a thick golden chain or a fine leather strap,

"Charms, totems, spells!" he called out as he walked up the street. "If you've got a barter, I've got the cure to what ales you! Protection! Bravery! Love spells!" If Leeja didn't know better, she would have sworn that he winked at her.

Bewildered, she looked around for her friends.

How did they get so far away so fast?

Before she could take a step in any direction, a lanky human slipped out of a ceramics studio and nearly walked right into Leeja.

Norrin?

Her heart leapt.

How is it that he turns up everywhere I am?

But it wasn't Norrin. Just some strange human who smelled wrong. Leeja started to notice how uncomfortable she felt in the crowd. And how alone she seemed when she couldn't smell Norrin's cool briny musk.

She looked around and found her friends in the crowd. Arlynn was quite at home, no surprise there...but even bashful Imogen seemed energized by this place. Maybe some lingering magic in the air would rub off on Leeja. She took a deep, steadying breath.

Time to start living like a Th'myskôran.

She forced her shoulders down and gently rolled her head around, loosening her neck muscles.

"This is it!" Imogen cried as she grabbed Leeja by the arm and dragged her toward one of those unassuming-looking little mounds of clay. The sign above the little door read "Stitch-Craft." Leeja had to crouch down and duck her head to avoid smacking into it. The little door led to a cramped, narrow stairway. At the top, the stairs were made mainly of limestone, but as they descended, the rock gave way to sturdy wood planks strategically placed to keep the cool, dark earth at bay. Leeja had to brace her hands on both walls to keep from tumbling down on top of her friends.

Deeper and deeper into the earth, Leeja lost count of the steps as she stumbled down behind her friends. Still, she figured they must have been at least forty feet below the earth's surface when the staircase finally opened to reveal a large, inviting showroom. The floor and walls were made of warm oak, the ceiling was high and vaulted, and delicate oil lamps and ornate mirrors hung from almost every surface. Along the walls were countless bolts of fabrics in every imaginable shade, texture, and pattern. In the center of the room was a little round stage, about six inches off the floor. There were dozens of dress forms scattered about the place, presumably one for each sort of creature that had frequented the shop over the years.

Arlynn skipped up to the counter and rang the little brass bell sitting on it. "Jagluk, come out!" she said, "It's your favorite customers!"

Not a moment later, a soft puff of translucent glitter exploded and then dissipated behind the counter, revealing a slender, blue, diminutive man.

"And what can I do for my favorite humans today?" Jagluk

smiled, kissing each of their hands in turn. His voice cascaded over Leeja's fingers and filled the room like perfumed honey.

"This is our friend, Leeja," Arlynn said. "She's new to the island, and she has a crucial date tonight."

"Can you believe she's never once had a gown custom-made for her?" Imogen asked.

Jagluk stepped out from behind the counter and assessed Leeja's drab, threadbare dress. "Yes, I can," he said, ushering her onto the little stage. "Fear not, dearest Leeja, for now you are a patron of Jagluk the Magnificent. You'll never want for fabulous gowns again."

Jagluk closed his eyes and drew in a serene breath. A moment later, Leeja's faded brown cote began to float up off of her shoulders and into the air. She cast nervous glances around at her friends and tugged futilely at her dress.

"Don't fight it." whispered Arlynn loudly.

"This is the fun part," added Imogen, smiling, "trust us."

Leeja stopped struggling. She lifted her arms above her head and allowed her dress to be whisked away. She was in the middle of the room, wearing only her thin chemise. Leeja started to cross her arms around her mid-drift, but before she could cover herself, unseen hands drew her arms straight out from both shoulders. A tape measure bobbed over through the air and began taking her measurements.

Jagluk watched approvingly as a nearby scroll began to display Leeja's measurements in a tidy, even script.

"Now," said Jagluk, turning his attention back to his patron, "how would you like to *feel* on this date tonight? Describe to me your ideal emotional landscape".

"I dunno..." Leeja struggled, "I guess I just want to feel... comfortable?"

Imogen broke into the conversation. "This is a *first date*,

Leeja! You should feel excited and hopeful and a little bit scared.”

“I have no idea what’s gotten into her,” said Arlynn, “but she’s right. You should feel desired and desirous. On a first date, you know very little about the person sitting across from you, except that they’re sexy and that they think you’re sexy. But every first date holds the possibility that the other person is someone you could form a fundamental emotional bond with.”

“But I do know him. My date is with Thorne from work. Does it have to be so complicated to count as human dating?”

“Well, no,” said Imogen, “but on a *first* date, you don’t know what you’re getting yourself into. You’re about to gaze into the emotional depths of someone you’ve only ever considered a friend. Who knows, you and Thorne could make a true love connection tonight! You should feel like you’re on a sexy, tingly adventure.”

“You’ve said too much already,” Jagluk interrupted, the words rolled off his tongue. “I know exactly what to do.”

Bolts of raw silk and fine satin in various shades of pink and red floated out from their unseen resting places around the room. They circled Leeja slowly, bobbing up and down in the air, allowing Jagluk to compare each color to Leeja’s complexion.

“This one is perfect.” he muttered, focused on the task at hand and waving away the excess bolts. “Come back in four hours; it’ll be ready.”

Leeja shrugged her old brown dress on as Imogen tugged at her wrist, and Arlynn pushed her incessantly from behind.

“That’ll give us plenty of time to get our girl ready for the big night!” called Imogen over her shoulder.

“Get me ready?” Leeja was beginning to panic. “We already got the dress, what else could you two sprites possibly do to me?”

Imogen giggled deviously, as she tugged Leeja's wrist harder and harder in the direction of the stairs.

"See you in a few hours, Jagluk! You're the best," Arlynn added, gently shoving Leeja up the stairs.

TEN

Norrin had been pacing up and down the block outside the Spiced Goat for what felt like hours. He didn't know what time Leeja was supposed to meet Thorne. Norrin didn't know what he would say to her once she got there. The only thing he knew was that if he didn't say something to her, if he didn't act now, he'd regret it for the rest of his life.

Maybe I heard the name wrong.

Maybe it's not tonight.

Maybe they're already inside. I should go in and ask somebody.

Every time someone walked by or a lizard rustled through the refuse barrels, Norrin *knew* it was Leeja appearing in the corner of his eye.

What if there never was a date? What if Thorne made this whole thing up to get under my skin?

The sun had set, and the gas lamps were flickering magically to life. Norrin was about to give up and go home...when he saw her.

Leeja was walking down the cobblestone street. She looked...*different*. For starters, she was dressed in an elegant, deep pink silk gown. Its bodice was tightly fitted, showing off her incredible figure. The neckline was square and dangerously low, and her ample dugs teased that they might free themselves with every step she took. Leeja's gown had flowing bell sleeves and was accentuated at the hips with a girdle belt, embroidered with an intricate pattern in emerald and gold, and accented with delicate saltwater pearls. The same embroidered design accented her hem, cuffs, and bust line.

Her wild, dark hair was plaited and wrapped in gold ribbons. Two long braids swayed enticingly along with her thighs. As Leeja drew closer, Norrin could smell a sweet, intoxicating perfume wafting off of her.

She stepped closer still, and he could see that her already enchanting facial features had been enhanced with cosmetics. Her sparkling emerald green eyes were haloed in glimmering shadows of maroon and coral-pink and framed with thick curtains of luxurious jet-black lashes. Her high cheekbones were painted a soft, mint green...an even more obvious nod to her orcish beauty than her natural, subtler green blush. And her plump, curvaceous lips were painted a deep, inviting pastel green. Her tusks, elegant and dangerous, were capped with delicate gold filigree.

And then there was the apparent change in attitude. Leeja looked light, optimistic, and eager.

...Eager for her date with Thorne.

"Dear gods," Norrin said when she was only a foot or so away.

Leeja stopped in her tracks and looked around, puzzled, for the source of the sound.

"Norrin?" she finally asked when her eyes focused on his face.

Just tell her. Tell her that she's the most incredible woman you've ever met, and you want to be in a committed relationship with her.

"Good evening, Leeja," he croaked out. "I know what you're doing, and I'm here to stop you."

That didn't come out right.

"The hells you are!" she said setting her fists on her hips and raising an eyebrow.

"Look, Thorne isn't right for you," Norrin said, trying desperately to diffuse her anger. "He's so big and grumpy and aggressive, and he's always on the verge of getting into a fist fight. He's totally emotionally repressed."

Okay, if we're being honest, I'm a little emotionally stunted too. But I want to get unstunted with her.

Leeja rolled her eyes.

"And besides, he's got some serious daddy issues," Norrin continued. "It's really annoying how he brings it up all the time."

Leeja let out a low, grumbling growl and made to shove past Norrin and into the restaurant. "I get it, you don't like Titans."

"No! What I mean is..."

I wish I were the one taking you to dinner tonight. I wish you'd spent all day getting ready for an evening with me.

"...don't do him," Norrin blurted out. "That didn't come out right...what I mean is...do *me*?"

"Norrin, I don't *do* humans, you know that." Leeja was rejecting him, but she didn't look angry anymore. She looked down at her shoes and wrapped her arms around her middle.

Is that pity or guilt on her face?

"Leeja, I want you." he said, "I've wanted you since that first morning I saw you on the esplanade."

"Goddess," Leeja groaned, rubbing her temple. Norrin thought his heart was going to fall out onto the street. "So what? You saw me charging down the street and thought, 'I bet that monster is a real challenge in the sack'? Are you trying to take me to bed so you'll have something to brag to your human friends about?"

"No, Leeja," Norrin pleaded, "it isn't anything like that."

"What am I to you? This week's adventure? Another community service project?" Leeja's eyes were starting to water. "While that's very flattering, Norrin, I'm trying to be...*better* than that. I'm tired of sleeping with a different guy every week."

Leeja had stopped yelling. Norrin wanted to wrap his arms around her. He wanted to make her understand how special she was to him, but he didn't have the words. He'd never had to talk anyone into liking him before.

"Right, the bet. Thorne told me. You know you don't have to change yourself to fit in with your friends." Norrin gestured vaguely at her appearance, "You don't need all...this."

Leeja squeezed her arms even more tightly around herself and fired back at him, "I want *this*. I like this dress. I like feeling beautiful. And I like my friends! If I wanted to stay the same, I would have stayed in Søgsund. I moved to Th'myskôra to live a different kind of life...to be a different kind of me."

A single tear sneaked out of Leeja's eye and rolled down her face.

Great job, jackass.

"That's not what I meant, Leeja." He stepped closer and tried to make eye contact.

She refused.

"You look fantastic, and you're allowed to look however you

want and do whatever you want." Leeja's body relaxed a little, and she met his gaze. "But you don't have to settle for their kind of relationship."

"Yeah, spending every day with the same male...learning every intimate detail about each other and fostering each other's talents...being each other's family...sounds terrible..." Leeja rolled her eyes again, "I *want* their kind of relationship."

"Okay, sure...I guess I can see how that could be appealing... but why Thorne? I've known him a long time, and he's so... *Thorne.*"

"I like straightforward people," said Leeja, "they don't make you play guessing games."

"I do too!" Norrin shouted nervously, "I mean, that's one of the things I like about you. It's just...if you're going to try dating, maybe it would work out better if you went for someone a little more laid back. You know, 'opposites attract' and all that..."

"I have heard people say that," said Leeja, "But I've got to start somewhere, and Thorne asked me. And besides, at least he's not..."

"Human?" Leeja didn't answer, but her face told Norrin everything he needed to know.

"Look, Leeja," Norrin said, taking a steadying breath, "I know you've had some unpleasant experiences with humans, but I'm not those guys." Norrin took her hand, gently running his thumb across her prominent veins and tendons. "I've never really done this before either, but I want to date you. I didn't realize how much I wanted you until I thought I might lose you. I don't know if I'm the right guy for you, Leeja, but I'd never be able to forgive myself if I didn't find out. I want to try *real* dating with you. Whatever you say that means, I'll do it. I want us to share our feelings. I—I want to meet your parents."

Norrin held his breath. He desperately searched Leeja's face for a sign that he hadn't been wrong about her. Any tiny indication on her face that she was even the slightest bit interested in him.

Leeja's eyes softened, she took a deep breath and Norrin was sure he saw the hint of a smile creep into the corner of her mouth.

He leaned in close to her and tilted his head up.

Leeja's lips parted. Her perfumed breath was warm and sweet. Norrin knew he'd be tasting it soon.

And then, Leeja slid her hand out of his. "I've gotta go, Norrin."

"I know," he said, watching her leave, "Just please think about it, okay?"

"Broiling over a low flame is fine," Thorne smacked through a mouthful of mutton, "Don't get me wrong, but if you want a *really* tender goat, you've got to eat it raw. Still warm, fresh from the kill? You can't beat that!"

"Mmhmm," Leeja hummed. Thorne had been talking about eating raw game for several uninterrupted minutes, and he didn't seem to notice that she'd stopped paying attention. How was she supposed to focus on goat talk when Norrin had ambushed her like that? The moment she recognized his scent on the street, her thoughts were hijacked. She kept replaying the reverent look on his face as he took her in. And then there was the tender way he'd caressed her hand, the closeness of his mouth to her ear in the tavern last night...when she felt his breath on her skin, she quivered. And last week, in the ship's hull, when she'd had to brush past him, she'd felt his erection on her ass then. She wouldn't mind feeling that cock again now.

I guess it wasn't *all in my head. But why would he want* me? *What human could ever love...this? Look at me, "Big Bertha," that's what they call me. But not him. Not Norrin.*

What about Aengus? If Norrin and I fuck, even if we do go on a couple of dates about it, when he's done with me, I'll lose Aengus, too. We won't become best friends who go fishing on the weekends. I'll never get to work on another ship, and I might as well say goodbye to ever getting on a shoring crew without a master shipwright's recommendation.

Who am I kidding? Once the Flannery is fixed, I'll never see Aengus again. He doesn't actually like me; he's only being encouraging on the job site so that I'll work harder.

So, really...what do I have to lose?

What do I have to gain? Incredible sex with my first-ever human? Probably. He'd certainly be the prettiest man I've ever bedded. A deep and fulfilling lifelong romantic relationship that confirms my humanity and heals every psychic wound I've ever suffered? Not likely...although he did show me his favorite place...and he said he wants feelings...

"...once you got your claws securely gripped in there, you gotta twist your wrist real quick to the side. Like this," Thorne's fingers were flexed into a sort of rounded cage, and he flicked his wrist hard, ninety degrees, demonstrating the technique, "You gotta make sure you do it fast. Otherwise, the animal suffers."

"Thorne?" Leeja asked, "What's your position on feelings?"

"C'mon, Leeja," he said, smirking at her, "that's human talk. We're Titans; we don't have to worry about feelings."

Leeja bit her lip. "I happen to be very interested in feelings; besides my challenge is to go on three *human* dates. Human dates include feelings."

"Alright," Thorne said, "before we sat down to eat, I felt hungry. Having finished my meal, I feel fed. And when I look at you in that sparkly dress, I feel...*lustful*."

"What about excited to learn more about me? Or optimistic about our future together? Or...or a little scared that everything might go wrong?" Leeja searched Thorne's face for some of the passion she'd seen on Norrin's earlier.

"Leeja, you are an invigorating lay, and your company does not displease me."

Leeja searched her own feelings and had to admit that Thorne's scent didn't send waves of pleasure racing toward her sex. His touch didn't thrill her. She didn't find his detailed explanations of bare-handed hunting endearing. She didn't yearn to find in him a safe harbor to confess her oldest wounds. And she certainly wasn't afraid of what her life might look like if Thorne were suddenly absent from it.

"Thorne," she said, looking him straight in the eye, "I think we should see other people."

CHAPTER

ELEVEN

Norrin sat on the wide, flat rock in the clearing that looked out over his favorite view on all of Th'myskôra. The sky was moonless and clear. A million beautiful stars burned hot white in the endless black of the night sky. Each one was reflected perfectly in the rolling surface of the ocean. Every star had its perfect match. In all the cosmos, only Norrin was alone.

"Thorne? How could she have chosen *Thorne?*" Norrin asked aloud.

"Sure, he's seven feet tall, he's built like an ox, and he fucks like a jackrabbit...but he can't race for a damn, and he's always got something stuck in his teeth. And I'm...well, I'm *me!*" Norrin threw a rock off the cliff and waited, as if the pitiful splash of

95

one little stone could be heard over the relentless crashing of the sea.

"He *asked* her?"

Norrin kicked at the dirt.

"I hinted *all week!* I've never had to *ask* anyone before. They always just walk up and start kissing me. It's like Dad always says, 'You'll know if a girl wants you when her mouth is on your —' oh, never mind, *her* mouth is on Thorne now."

Norrin stood up and walked slowly around the rock. The rock where a few short days ago, he'd sat next to one of the most powerful and impressive women he'd ever known.

"But Leeja *does* want me. She's been giggling and blushing at me all week. She wants me, but she's with *him*."

Norrin sighed and raked his fingers through his shaggy blond hair.

"He's probably watching her with his eye. And *she's* loving him with that body...I just know it!"

"Um, Norrin?" A female voice asked.

He spun around, "Leeja!"

He'd been so consumed by his ruminations that he hadn't heard her approach. "Where's Thorne? Did you two come here to make out in front of me?" As happy as he was to see her, he was still wounded.

"I left him at the Spiced Goat."

A smile spread across Norrin's face, "I knew it! You *do* want me too!" Leeja blushed that beautiful deep green, "Admit it. Please, Leeja, I need to hear you say it."

"I want you, Norrin."

He rounded the huge rock and stood facing her: his beautiful, glittering prize. This powerful, statuesque goddess stood before him, caressed by moonlight, waiting for him. Wanting him.

"Since when?"

Leeja cocked her head slightly and raised an eyebrow.

"When did you start wanting me? Was it when I stopped you in front of the Spiced Goat? When I held you during our sailing lesson?"

Leeja turned her head away, presenting Norrin with her noble, moonlit profile,

"On the esplanade," she said quietly. Her voice was gentle and clear. Her words cascaded through him. "I smelled you running up the sand toward me, and I knew I wanted you then."

Norrin rushed up to her and wrapped himself around her eagerly. Every part of her body was hard and strong, every part but those gigantic, soft breasts. He buried his face in the warmth of her neck and breathed in her scent, a rich mixture of hair oils, perfumes, and natural musk. He touched his lips to the shell of her ear and dragged them down to her earlobe.

"I've been wanting to do this for a very long time," he whispered before gently sucking her earlobe into his mouth and nibbling it.

Leeja moaned softly, bucking her hips against his crotch.

Oh, gods, she's ready.

Then she stopped. She wriggled out of his mouth and pushed his chest so that they were, once again, standing much too far apart.

"Wait, Norrin," she said, her hand resting on his chest. "I want to be sure I'm not making a mistake. I...I've never done *this* before."

Norrin raised a hand and cupped Leeja's face.

"I've never done this before, either."

He'd never worked so hard to get a woman's attention. He'd never cared if a girl chose him over any other guy. He'd never taught a girl how to swing a hammer. He'd never before looked into someone's eyes and felt an overwhelming need to protect them. He'd never wanted, no, needed to have a lover all to himself.

"But we won't mess it up, not as long as we do it together."

"Promise?" Leeja asked.

"I promise," Norrin ran his thumb up her long, sharp tusk, and Leeja melted in his arms. Norrin guided her face close to his. Leeja shivered, and he pressed his warm mouth to the soft, green pillows of her lips. "You are going to win that bet."

Leeja's mouth worked eagerly against his. She sucked and nipped at his upper lip. All of her hesitations seemed to have vanished. She wrapped her arms around his waist, pulling him into her, positioning his hip against her crotch. She ground against him, letting soft moans escape into his waiting mouth.

"Gods," Norrin creaked out as his cock throbbed in his smallclothes. He groped blindly at the lacings on the back of Leeja's bodice.

Leeja's hands raced from his back down to his ass and back up again. She kept pulling him into her as if he could fuck her through her clothes.

Once Leeja's laces were loose, she tore her face away from Norrin's just long enough to pull her gown off over her head. The second it landed on the ground they were kissing wildly again. Norrin tore off his tunic as Leeja worked to quickly untie and remove her stays.

Norrin grabbed Leeja by the hand, leading her to a soft patch of grass as he hobbled along, kicking off his leather booties. He pulled off his britches and smallclothes, and Leeja's smallclothes joined them in a heap on the ground.

Now she was standing in front of him in nothing but one thin, white underdress. Norrin could see her imposing, powerful silhouette through it.

Leeja pushed Norrin down on the ground and mounted his naked body. Her pussy was warm and wet against his crotch, and he ached to be inside her.

Norrin reached up, grabbing her chemise. Leeja stopped grinding on him. She gripped the hem of her skirt in place at hip level.

"It's a little late to start playing hard to get," Norrin teased, tugging at her chemise again.

"It's not a game," Leeja muttered, suddenly serious, and she climbed off him.

Norrin sat up next to her, "You haven't changed your mind, have you? I mean, it's fine if you did, but...*did* you?"

Godsdammit, Norrin, what have you done now?

"No, I still want to mate," Leeja struggled, "It's just that I, um...I always...I've never been *naked* with a man before." She looked down at her hands, worrying the embroidered hem of her white chemise.

"We're *supposed* to be doing things we've never done before, aren't we?"

Leeja nodded, refusing to meet his gaze.

"Then do this with me." Norrin lifted her chin and kissed her softly on the mouth. "Trust me. Please?"

"Alright." Leeja took a deep breath and loosed her grip. Norrin slid the chemise up over her head. He rocked back to see all of her.

"Leeja," he said, "you look..."

"Gigantic."

"Perfect."

He wrapped her up in his embrace and held her tightly until her breathing evened out again.

"Thank you for sharing this with me." He laid her down in the grass and admired her well-sculpted body in the faint starlight. Norrin could have looked at that robust and feminine body all night, but Leeja started to shiver and squirm. He threw his warm body on top of hers and kissed her deeply.

His cock was rock hard now. Leeja bucked against him, pressing his length with her body. Desire was leaking out of him.

"If I'm not careful, I'm going to make a mess all over this situation."

Leeja was sucking and biting at his neck. Her fingers were dug into his ass cheeks, pulling him rhythmically down to meet her.

"I want you, Norrin," Leeja growled in his ear. "I need it now!" Her grunts were growing louder, her thrusting more insistent.

Norrin steadied her. Pressing her shoulders firmly into the soft, wet earth. He licked her from the spot just under her ear, down to her erect nipple. He slowly traced his tongue over its ridges, and Leeja howled.

"Green," he muttered, "they're mint green."

His hands flew to her breasts, kneading the supple flesh, and his tongue continued down over her abs.

"Six pack," he whispered as he kissed each one. Leeja wriggled and let out a little squeak each time he kissed her.

Her hands were in his hair. The gentle tugging sensation made Norrin's eyes roll back in his head.

He moved his mouth further down, applying more pressure now. The closer he got to her throbbing cunt, the harder it was for him to control himself. His mouth reached the soft mound of her lower pelvis, and Norrin lost himself. He bit her. Leeja's back arched, and she cried out in pleasure.

So soft, so warm,

"All for me."

He moved his face further down, burying his nose in her thick, green pubic hair.

"Oh, fuck," he muttered against her clit, breathing her in. Her scent was warm and earthy, like rare spices. He breathed her in, then tasted her, and then proceeded to suck and devour her. She was perfect, a goddess of sex, so she would be worshipped properly.

Norrin hummed against Leeja's clit. She shivered under his mouth.

He moved down a little further so he could fully explore her. Norrin slid his tongue out from between his lips and through hers. He again found her swollen, pulsating clit, and sucked it gently. Leeja screamed again and fisted her hands in his hair. Norrin's cock dripped a steady stream of precum that reached from the tip of his cock to the dewy ground beneath them.

Norrin went right back to work, lapping at her cunt. Leeja moaned and bucked. With one hand, Norrin pressed gently down on her pelvis; he used the other to slide a finger inside her.

Leeja groaned again. She was struggling and gasping for air. *She's close.*

Norrin kept suckling at her clit, applying gentle pressure, and working his finger in and out of her quickly.

She was grunting and bucking and tugging wildly at his hair, but Norrin was diligent.

You've got a job to do.

He could feel her pussy tightening around his finger. The pressure was building. And then it happened.

She went silent; her back arched. Her strong fingers dug into the earth on either side of her. Her pussy was pulsating around his finger, sending shockwaves out through her whole body. Leeja convulsed, and a cascade of warm fluid rushed out into Norrin's mouth. Her taste was fresh now, sweeter...more tangy. Norrin knew he'd made her cum, and he exploded all over them both.

Norrin laid down on the grass beside her, and Leeja rolled over on her side, nuzzling her head on his chest.

"No one's ever done that to me before," she managed after a few minutes. Norrin smoothed her loose hairs back into place and kissed her on the forehead.

"We're going to have a lot of firsts, I think."

TWELVE

A tremendous lilac tent had been erected in the middle of a large, flat field. The summer festival was in full swing, and half of the island was there, milling around, trading wares at temporary wooden stalls, playing carnival games, and enjoying street food from cuisines across the Three Realms. Leeja stood in a long, winding line in between a group of rowdy, inter-species adolescents and a wizened old troll woman holding her small granddaughter by the hand. It was late in the morning, and the weather was starting to heat up.

Jagluk had decided to build Leeja a linen kirtle in addition to her silken evening gown. This dress was honey-peach colored. It had shorter sleeves and fewer adornments than the silk gown she'd worn the night before. Leeja felt very pretty in it. She reached up to feel that her elaborate braids were still secured inside Imogen's snood. The girls had helped her with it this morning. Leeja still wasn't entirely comfortable in all of this finery.

"A *lizard* for m'lady." Norrin bounded up next to her with two filfola lizards on skewers, battered and deep fried.

"Oh! This is wonderful!" Leeja crunched out through a healthy bite of lizard. "I can't believe I've been living on the island all this time, and I've never been here before."

"Don't be too hard on yourself," said Norrin. "The Periwinkle Prestidigitator only comes once a year for the summer festival; you picked the best possible time to start exploring the Olde Magic Core. Well...the winter festival is pretty great, too. And during the fall festival, the best brewers from all over the Three Realms come here to participate in the annual cider contest."

"Sounds like a lot to keep track of," Leeja said, inching toward the tent's opening with the rest of the line.

"Don't worry, you've got the best tour guide on the whole island. It'll be my honor to show you all of the pleasures Th'myskôra has to offer." Norrin took Leeja's free hand in his own, and that familiar, sexual thrill raced up her arm, spread through her chest, warming it, and raced down into her crotch, setting it ablaze.

"Goddess, help me." she muttered.

"What was that?" Norrin asked.

"Nothing. Sorry."

Is this going to be my life now? Constantly teetering on the edge of orgasm?

"So, what kinds of festivals did you have back in Titan?" Norrin asked, still holding her hand.

"I don't know about all of Titan," said Leeja, polishing off her filfola, "but orcs can only really get together in big crowds like this once a year."

"Right, because you're nomadic. The logistics of getting everybody in the same place at the same time must be next to impossible." They were near the tent's opening now, and Norrin dropped her hand to fish around in his pocket for their tickets.

"Oh, it's not that," Leeja said as they ducked slightly and entered the darkened tent.

The performance space was immense: a huge open area of dirt under a thin layer of straw, and in the middle, several octagonal platforms of varying sizes and heights, the largest and tallest of which was in the exact center of the tent. Along five of the tent's walls were wooden bleachers that climbed at least twenty feet into the air.

"Winter is the only time it's *safe* for orcs to gather in big groups of multiple hordes." Norrin had located their seats and was leading the way over to them.

"Why's that?" he asked, offering his hand to help Leeja climb the narrow stairs between benches.

"Orcs don't have a mating frenzy in the winter." They were carefully sidling past audience members already seated and juggling popcorn, programs, and crying children. "Normally, if two sexually mature females can smell each other...there's a terrible battle. The winner leaves with every available male in the area, and the loser is killed...or at least maimed."

The image of another female tossing Norrin's lean body over her shoulder and racing off with him flashed across Leeja's mind. She snarled and scented the air for a fight.

"I didn't realize orc males were in such short supply," Norrin said, settling into his seat.

"What?" Leeja shook her head.

There are no other orcs on this island. No one is going to take this human…except for me. As soon as we're done at this fair, I'm going to find some bushes, and take him and his meaty, pink cock.

"Orc males," Norrin said, "I didn't realize they were an endangered species…"

"Oh, they aren't," said Leeja, taking her seat beside him. "Orc women need to be serviced many times throughout the day. The older and larger an orc female becomes, the more… *demanding* the love making."

A smirk creeped across Norrin's mouth.

"This is nothing to smile at, human." Leeja continued, "sexual encounters often result in soft tissue damage or even broken bones, so male orcs have a pretty long refractory period. That's why our hordes are structured the way they are, with a dozen or so males to every female. A single male would likely die trying to service a female alone."

The goblin woman with the young child coughed loudly.

That was directed at me, wasn't it?

"Should I be worried?" Norrin joked.

He's grinning. Humans are braver than I gave them credit for. I wonder if he'll still be smiling when I'm grinding his bare ass into the dirt for round four of afternoon lovemaking.

"I think you'll be alright. I am only a half-orc, after all." Norrin stretched up and kissed her on the cheek.

"How does that work? With the kids, I mean. If multiple males are…*servicing* the female every day, how do you know which baby belongs to which dad?"

"We don't," said Leeja, "All of the fathers take equal responsibility for all of the children in the horde, unless…unless there's something…*different* about a particular kid that would cause the horde not to want her…it…them?"

The troll woman in the next row coughed loudly again, this time looking over her shoulder at Leeja.

That was definitely *for me.*

"The show's starting!" said Norrin, squeezing Leeja's hand as the lamps around the tent dimmed. The troll turned back around in her seat.

"Titans, Fey Folk, and Humans," boomed a male voice from some unseen location as spotlights darted and spun across the stage, tent walls, and grinning faces of audience members, "... Please put your hands together for the Periwinkle Prestidigitator!"

Unmanned horns, drums, and tambourines floated above their heads and began playing bawdy music.

The spotlights all went black at once, and a drum roll was heard from every corner of the tent.

Norrin gripped Leeja's thigh and whispered, "Keep your eyes open; this is going to be great."

Leeja's thigh went liquid where he held it. A warm, rippling sensation moved through and up both of her thighs and up into her molten core. Leeja's eyelids drew closed as she savored the feeling.

BOOM!

An explosion of purple flame burst through the tent. Leeja's attention was wrenched back to the center platform where a handsome human woman was now standing.

The Periwinkle Prestidigitator was an older woman with silver hair, cropped tight along the back and sides of her head and scooped up into a glittering pompadour on top. She was dressed in leather britches, boots, cloak, and gloves, all in varying shades of purple. The music swelled, and she took off her cloak, swinging it over her head. The crowd cheered, waving their arms, trying to convince her to throw it to them.

"Stand up," said Norrin. "Get ready to catch."

Leeja stayed in her seat.

She isn't going to throw it to me.

The Periwinkle Prestidigitator sent the cloak soaring over the crowd. Mid-flight, it transformed into hundreds of purple roses flinging out in all directions. And Leeja's worries about the day burst into pieces right along with it. She wasn't worried about the opinions of old trolls, or anyone else who might see her with a human. She wasn't worried about her hair, or her fancy new dress. She wasn't even worried about the bet or proving Arlynn wrong. When Leeja saw those roses explode out of nowhere, she decided to give into the simple pleasure of spending a summer day with a beautiful man.

Everyone laughed and cheered as they scrambled to get their hands on one of the flowers.

Norrin plucked one out of the air and slid it into Leeja's braid behind her ear. Leeja blushed and laughed,

"I think I like your festival, human."

AFTER THE SHOW, Norrin and Leeja walked around the fairgrounds. Leeja was different. Even less guarded then she was last night. She was light on her feet...*happy* even?

There's nothing like a little sleight of hand to get the ladies in the mood. By the end of this date, I'll have her walking on air!

Leeja skipped happily from booth to booth, dragging Norrin along by the arm everywhere she went. One moment, they were sampling bambinella tarts. The next, they were admiring delicate lace garments crafted on Spider Island.

"Ohh," said Leeja, picking up a shimmering blue snood covered with tiny sapphires. "Imogen would love this!" She looked around the table and found two more identical hairnets, "There's one for each of us! Arlynn, Imogen, and I can all go out matching! What do you want for them?" She asked the spider behind the table.

The spider smiled at Norrin, "I owe the Galanou family a great deal. Consider them a gift from me."

"Thank you!" Leeja hugged her treasures tightly to her chest before sliding them safely inside her bag.

"I've never seen you grin before," Norrin said admiring Leeja's dazzling smile. "I wasn't sure orcs were capable."

"Well, you've never given me a gift before, or are humans incapable?" Leeja stuck out her tongue.

"Give your father my respects," the spider said, rolling all eight of her eyes before Norrin and Leeja hurried along to the next booth.

It was an archery game; several large hay bales were set up with increasingly small bullseyes painted on them. In front of them was a tiny toy bow and three arrows.

"Hit a bullseye, win a prize." hissed the dragonborn manning the booth. "The sssssmaller the bullseye, the bigger the prize!"

A grin spread across Norrin's face. Leeja's enthusiasm was infectious. He wanted to keep her smiling forever.

I am going to win Leeja the biggest prize she's ever seen.

He picked up the little bow and pulled back the first miniature arrow.

THAWK!

He hit the largest bullseye. The dragonborn behind the booth looked up from his newspaper just long enough to mumble, "Congratulations, winner! Choose your prize or press your luck."

"Wow, Frank," Leeja said, squeezing his arm and staring intently at the target. "You weren't kidding. You really *are* a crack shot!"

There was no way Norrin could miss such an easy shot, but he played up the drama of the moment for Leeja's benefit.

"Whad'a'ya think?" he asked her, winking, "Should we try for the second one?"

Leeja looked at the prizes; on the left was a large pile of hand-sewn velvet dolls with buttons for eyes. Next to that was an equally impressive pile of stuffed dolls twice as large and more complex; these wore little lace dresses. The last pile of prizes was composed of large stuffed dolls, bigger than her head! They all had intricately embroidered faces and complicated, multi-piece outfits.

"Can you make it?"

Norrin chuckled and drew back the second arrow. "Watch this," he let loose the bowstring.

THAWK!

Another bullseye!

Leeja squealed with delight, "I want this one," she said, reaching for a horned doll in a blue dress from the middle pile.

"We still have one shot left," said Norrin, stilling her hand, "Don't you think we should try for the big one?"

"You can't hit that bullseye! I can barely even see it! It can't be much bigger than an Etruscan shrew!"

"If you'd rather give up..." Norrin put down the bow and made an exaggerated show of walking away, turning slowly to look into Leeja's eyes and shrugging his shoulders.

The dragonborn groaned and rolled his eyes. Little wisps of smoke rolled out of his nostrils.

"No!" Leeja called out, grabbing Norrin by the sleeve. "Orcs never give up!"

"If it's *imperative*, I suppose I could try." Norrin lifted the little bow and the last of the arrows. In his estimation, the target was at least as wide as one and a half Etruscan shrews; he'd shot enough of them over the years, he ought to know.

"Alright," Norrin teased, "Don't. Breathe."

Leeja sucked in a sharp breath, and the dragonborn shook out his newspaper.

THAWK!

Norrin hit the tiny bullseye!

"You did it!" Leeja squeezed Norrin tightly around the middle, nearly knocking the air out of him, before snatching up a stuffed harpy doll in a pink satin dress. "I'm going to call you Rampart," she said to the doll, and then turned back to Norrin, "That's an incredible talent you got there, Frank!"

"Yeah, thanks," Norrin said, running a hand through his hair, "My dad used to take me out hunting every weekend."

Leeja hugged the effigy with both arms.

Gotta be careful not to brag too much.

"With fourteen dads, I bet you learned how to do all sorts of impressive things."

"Actually," said Leeja, hugging the stuffed harpy tighter, "The fathers never wanted much to do with me...since I'm..." she made a sweeping gesture, indicating her body.

Norrin just stared at her. He had less than no idea what she was trying to imply.

"Half-human," Leeja said.

"Oh, I didn't realize that sort of thing was such a big deal in Søgsund."

Leeja didn't speak. She just shifted her weight back and forth in the dirt.

"Well, at least you had your human dad, right?" Said Norrin, desperately trying to get their day back on track. "One dad's not as good as fourteen, but it sure beats none!"

"What's that over there?" Leeja asked, wandering off to a large pen wherein several unusual and remarkable animals from across the Three Realms were being displayed. There were a bunch of children feeding millet to a massive three-headed ram.

"Look, Norrin! They let you pick your own dinner!" Leeja's stance widened, her nostrils flared, and she bared her tusks.

"Not so fast, m'lady." Norrin stepped in front of his snarling date. "This is a petting zoo. We feed the animals; we don't eat them." Then leaning in conspiratorially, running his lips along the shell of her ear he whispered, "But you can pounce on me later."

Leeja smiled, her eyes burned a dangerous emerald and she placed her strong hand on the small of his back, pulling him toward her.

Norrin closed his eyes, savoring the feeling of her large, soft breasts against him. It took a great deal of restraint to keep from burying his face between them.

Someday soon, I'm going to let this woman lose control all over me. But not today.

Norrin wriggled out of her grip. "I'll be right back with some ram food," he said, "and then you can feed them too!"

A moment later, Norrin presented Leeja with an overflowing fistful of salvia selvaggia. Her eyes went wide at the sight of a thousand tiny purple and indigo blooms, and she buried her face in them, breathing deeply.

"This is wonderful!"

Norrin sighed, "I'm not sure if you're sexier when you're smiling or snarling."

"They smell like...like iris and violets and...*melons*?"

Leeja wasn't the only one enjoying the intoxicating flowers.

The largest of the rams had caught the scent and was grunting and butting the short wooden fence that separated it from the rest of the fair with both of its heads.

"Alright, you noisy thing," Leeja said playfully, leaning down to offer the ram some of her salvia. The head on the right got to the food first and happily chomped away. When the head on the left noticed, it tried to rip the flowers away. The scuffle caught Leeja off guard. She started to tumble over the fence and into the mud. Norrin raced up, grabbing her by the hips and steadying her...by pressing his pelvis into her rump.

"Three Hells," she muttered, and Norrin shifted, rubbing her ass gently back and forth against his crotch. It was a risky move; they were in public; after all, she could reprimand him, but Leeja moaned softly, settling into his grip and rocking her ass back into him.

"Leeja, please," Norrin managed, "You're gonna wake my cock all the way up, and then we'll be in trouble."

Leeja relinquished the remaining salvia to the greedy ram and straightened up. She spun around to face him. Now his hands were boring into her ass.

"I saw some big bushes over by the leather mug maker's tent," Leeja said, smiling devilishly, "Let's go have sex behind them." Norrin was stunned into silence, "Rampert can be our lookout," she added, waiving the stuffed effigy in the air.

Norrin kissed her deeply, and Rampert hit the ground. Leeja's hands tugged at his hair. There was no way he could mask his excitement now.

"Okay, yeah," he breathed, and Leeja wasted no time dragging him behind the bushes. The blood rushed from Norrin's head so quickly that his vision blurred. He controlled his breathing and blinked Leeja back into focus; she was kneeling in the dirt, tugging at the laces of his trousers.

"Wait, stop," Norrin forced himself to say.

"What's wrong?" Leeja asked, her fingers still eager to free his manhood.

"What were the exact terms of your bet again?"

Leeja rolled her eyes, "I have to learn a man's name, where he was born, and at least one thing he's passionate about. Your name is Norrin. You were born here on Th'myskôra. And you are passionate about both shipwrighting and ship racing. I'm also supposed to have sex with you on two nonconsecutive days and go on three dates with you."

"Well," said Norrin, helping Leeja to her feet, "I'd say this definitely counts as a date, but I think we'd better not fuck in the dirt right now...that would be consecutive, after all."

Leeja grabbed his bulging manhood and ran her thumb across its length, "Your human cruelty is truly unmatched," she said, pouting.

"And shouldn't I learn a thing or two about you? That seems only fair," Norrin said, taking her breasts in both hands. He rubbed her hard nipples with his thumbs, and it was Leeja's turn to suffer. She closed her eyes and trembled in his hands.

"What do you want to know, human?" Leeja growled into the crook of his neck.

"What..." Norrin struggled to think of something other than his turgid member sliding into her mouth, "What is your favorite thing about Th'myskôra so far?"

"The people," she rumbled, then nibbled at his neck.

"What about the people exactly?"

"The relationships they form...friendships, families, trade partners." Leeja was rubbing Norrin's cock through his britches. "The relationships on Th'myskôra are meant to last. People don't throw each other away so easily here."

"That's really beautiful," Norrin slid his fingers into Leeja's hair. He tightened them, pulling slightly, and she moaned.

"Can I fuck you *now*, human?"

"It's got to be nonconsecutive, Leeja," he pleaded, "Be a good girl today. I promise you'll be rewarded tomorrow if you do."

"Fine," she said, stepping back and smiling at him, "but I'm not going to make it easy on you." Leeja readjusted her hand on his cock. Stroking it, she leaned in close to him. She nestled the sharp edge of her tusk against his neck and dragged her wet mouth slowly up to his ear.

"Let's go back and enjoy the festival." She gave his dick one more squeeze and danced back toward the lights and music.

THIRTEEN

Early the following day, Leeja stood on the piling docks among various small pleasure craft. The sun had just risen, and the marine fog still hung thick in the air. Leeja filled her lungs.

"I will never get tired of that smell," she said.

She was wearing a loose-fitting, lightweight tunic, comfortable knee-length britches, and well-worn leather booties. Norrin had hinted that they would be on the water today, and she had no intention of stripping down in front of strangers.

"Ahoy, Leeja!" Norrin called from a sailboat that had

bumped up against the dock. This boat was larger than his racer; it could have sat five or six people.

"Ahoy, yourself," Leeja said, smiling as she helped Norrin tie the boat to the dock. "How many boats do you own anyway?"

"This one is on loan from my father," he said, extending a hand and helping her aboard, "You should come by the workshop sometime. We're always working on at least half a dozen or so. Sometimes, Dad even has a new experimental design he's trying out."

Leeja was surprised by his strength every time he held her. *Where does someone so lean get off feeling so steady and safe?*

"Is this one of Aengus' prototypes?" she asked, settling in next to a large basket, presumably full of a packed lunch.

"Bertha?" Norrin asked, shoving off from the dock.

Leeja cringed at the name.

"Naw, this old girl has been around forever; she was the first ship I ever sailed solo!"

Norrin had begun lazily paddling north.

"I take it we're not having another racing lesson today, so where are you taking me?"

"I'm so glad you asked," Norrin smirked over his shoulder as he raised the sail. "Today, we are going to my favorite spot in all of Th'myskôra."

"By my count, this is your fourth most favorite spot," Leeja teased.

Norrin grinned back at her as he adjusted the sail. "Well, *this* favorite spot is really something special. We're going to Swi'loor, the lesser island." Norrin's voice adopted a mysterious air, and he raised both eyebrows at her.

"Isn't it dangerous there? I've heard terrible stories of mangled ships and whole villages being leveled in a single night!"

"If you get frightened," Norrin said, leaning in close to Leeja's ear, "Just grab onto me;

I swear to keep you safe!" He leaned even closer and kissed her behind the ear.

Leeja trembled at the feeling of his skin on hers, but she commanded her eyes to stay open. She didn't want him thinking she was afraid.

"I'm going to take that to mean the legends are highly... *exaggerated*," Leeja said, casually brushing the back of her hand across his crotch.

Norrin stepped back, evading her, "There's only one way to find out."

Bertha slid onto the beach, gently parting the carpet of small, smooth, grey stones as her advance slowed and eventually stopped. The sea lapped at her stern, and Norrin hopped overboard to secure a docking rope to a large, black rock jutting out of the pebbles.

Leeja carefully dismounted. The pebbles shifted under her feet, making it hard to keep her balance. This beach was so different from the ones she'd been to on Th'myskôra. Instead of the fine, golden sand she was used to, there were these damned slippery pebbles. They were impossible to walk through. Was she moving more slowly here?

The air feels like it is pushing against me...no it's the rocks. It's got to be the rocks.

The further she slogged away from the water, the larger the stones got. Out where Norrin was now working, they were practically boulders. Beyond that was no esplanade dotted with charming cottages. No lizardmen pushing carts full of snacks, ringing their little bells to attract hungry beachgoers. There were no *beachgoers*. Try as she might, Leeja couldn't hear anything beyond the crunch-slide of pebbles beneath her feet and the faint melody of Norrin's cheerful whistling. Sound moved strangely here; the murky sky seemed to dull and swallow it, except for the tiny clanging of stones under her feet. Those sent shockwaves up through her bones and echoed in her skull.

"Okay, this island is weird, right? It's not just me?" Leeja asked as she finally reached Norrin.

He smiled and kissed the back of her hand. Immediately she forgot about the strangeness of the island; a primal urge to fuck raced through her.

Get it together, Leeja. This could be an actual life-or-death situation. This is not the time to be imagining what human cum tastes like.

"Swi'loor has...*special* properties you won't find anywhere else," Norrin said, helping her over a jagged boulder. "The island belongs to the sprites and nymphs and is deeply steeped in time magic."

Norrin and Leeja crested a second immense boulder. Leeja hoped she'd get a better lay of the land from up there, but all she could see stretching out in front of them was a dense canopy of trees.

"Aren't sprites extremely territorial and vindictive?" Leeja asked as they scrambled down the other side of the rock. "There's a guy who works on the docks who says that his cousin came over here once, and he accidentally stepped on a sprite's mushroom house, and then the sprite chased him down and bit him! In a few hours, his limbs started falling off one by one. He tried to row back to the big island, but by the time his boat bumped up against the dock, there was nothing inside but a squirming pile of parts!"

"I guess we'd better be careful where we step," said Norrin, smiling as he led Leeja between two giant white olive trees. Like all the white olive trees on Swi'loor, their ancient trunks twisted and bent around themselves, creating a complicated network of smooth, oblong chambers and tiny hiding places.

Leeja bent forward to peer into one of the many holes in the nearest tree, but thought better of it and retreated to the safety of Norrin's arm.

"The legend says," Norrin continued as he led Leeja further into the woods, "that many hundreds of years ago, trolls tried to establish a community here, the same as they did on the big island. They brought ships loaded with tools, weapons, provisions, and workers from their homeland."

His tone was mysterious, and Leeja felt a prickling sensation creeping up her neck. The further they walked from the shore, the more intense it got and the tighter she gripped Norrin's arm in both hands.

"The trolls worked for weeks, clearing boulders, cutting down trees, and building the first settlements. Eventually, the big ships left, taking most of the trolls back to the mainland for more supplies. And when they came back…"

Norrin paused dramatically.

"…all of their countrymen were gone, and everything they built had been leveled. Destroyed right down to the foundations."

"But trolls build with granite! And they lay their foundations eighteen feet deep!" Leeja's voice sounded strange to her; it was as if the sound only traveled a few inches from her mouth, and then it just...stopped. "Did someone raid the camps? It would take a massive army to destroy an entire troll settlement." She ducked under a branch and noticed the conspicuous lack of the sound of rustling leaves.

"That's what the trolls thought at first, that it was raiders. But when they inspected the remains, they found no evidence of fire or archers, no footprints! The only evidence there'd ever been trolls on this island at all was a fine layer of blue-grey sand over the ground where their buildings once stood and the granite foundations buried deep underground. It was as if some great force came along and crushed everything to a powder".

"What did the trolls do?" Leeja asked.

They were quite a ways away from the beach now, and Leeja was beginning to miss all those slippery little pebbles. The white olive trees gave way to sandarac trees, their straight ash-grey trunks stretched up at least twice as tall as Leeja, their wide, irregular crowns grew in thick, intertwining masses. The canopy of thin branches and spiny leaves seemed to grow closer and closer together, closing down on top of them. Despite the heavy forestation, there was no rustling of leaves, no calls of birds. Just their own blunted footfalls and voices whose sounds ceased the moment they were made.

"They left," Norrin said. "They left and swore never to return to this island."

"Well, that's not a very convincing story," Leeja said, loosening her grip a little. "You mean to tell me no one ever came back, and everyone has been afraid of the island ever since?"

"No *troll* ever came back," Norrin said smiling, "but when the elves conquered Th'myskôra a hundred years later, they ignored the warnings and sent their own scouting parties to Swi'loor."

Leeja gasped and clung to Norrin again.

If he wants to frighten me, I might as well enjoy myself. She breathed him in deeply. Sea air and warm, nutty musk. *Delicious.*

"The elves set up their tents on the beach. They built wooden lookout towers and equipped them with archers and warlocks. For a few weeks, it seemed like everything would be fine…"

"And then?"

"And *then* the elves left the beach." Norrin lowered his voice to a whisper, "They sent a scouting party inland to look for potable water. When the scouts didn't come back, the elves sent another party to find them."

Leeja crept along beside him. With each step, the thickening canopy of branches blocked out more of the sun.

"When the second party failed to return," Norrin continued, "the remaining elves ventured into the woods to find them. They searched for eight days and nights and couldn't find any of their comrades. So, they came back to the beach. But instead of their tents, huts, and watchtowers, all they found was…nothing. Just like with the trolls, everything they'd built was crushed to sawdust. The only thing left on the beach was one little dingy tied to a post."

"Please tell me they left!"

"You bet'cha they did. Those elves got in that dingy and rowed back to the big island as fast as they could, and no one has tried to build anything here since."

"Why then," started Leeja, sighing deeply, "did *we* come here?"

"For *this*," said Norrin grinning. He grabbed Leeja's hand and pulled her through a dense thicket. Leaves crunched soundlessly under her feet, and spindly branches scraped her shins and forearms. The pair ran deeper into the forest, leaping over large rocks and ducking to avoid low-hanging branches.

"Wait!" Norrin said, stopping abruptly. "Close your eyes."

Leeja did as she was told. With her eyes closed, she followed Norrin's prompts, groping and moving very slowly. After a few steps, the faint smell of honey drifted up, cutting through the pervasive smell of *him*. And she could hear the gentle, uneven bubbling and splashing of...*a waterfall?*

"That's far enough," he said. Leeja could feel his warmth against her back. Then he took her hand again, "Okay, you can open them now."

They were in a clearing. Soft, golden sunlight trickled in between the branches, and thick patches of soft clover carpeted the ground. Around the perimeter of the clearing were flowering bushes. Hummingbirds and brightly colored butterflies darted from blossom to blossom, it was the first life Leeja had seen since they arrived.

Directly across from them was a waterfall, tumbling down a cool grey cliff face and feeding a sparkling, emerald-green pond.

"Frank," Leeja gasped, "this place is wonderful."

"Worth risking the sprite's wrath?" he teased, setting down the basket.

"You can drop the act," she said, leaning in to kiss him on the cheek. "There aren't really any malevolent entities here, are there?"

"These woods are *absolutely* protected by a powerful cadre of unseen, magical beings who could easily rend our heads from our bodies." Norrin smiled. He took off his tunic and tossed it casually toward the basket. "But they don't mind day trippers. As long as we don't try to build anything, we'll be fine."

"So, the story about the cousin who came back home a wriggling stump...?"

"Completely fabricated." Norrin slid down his britches and stood before her in nothing but his smallclothes. His bulge was practically begging to be grabbed. Leeja allowed herself a long moment to stare at it and thought she saw it twitch under her scrutiny.

"But the rumors *have* ensured that this little oasis remains unpopulated," Norrin said, tucking a lock of Leeja's hair behind her ear, "and *we* get to have complete privacy."

He was gazing deeply into her eyes. Leeja didn't need any more prompting than that. She pulled him into herself and kissed him passionately, pawing at his smallclothes, wanting desperately to free that cock. Leeja could feel it thumping.

"Not yet," Norrin creaked out as he separated himself from her. "There are a couple more elements to this date. You wouldn't want to skip right to having sex in the mud and risk losing the bet, would you?"

"I assumed we'd fuck on the clover," Leeja said, and she heard the discreet sound of tinkling chimes; it almost sounded like laughter.

"The reason I brought you here," Norrin said, leading her to the pond's edge, "was to take you swimming."

"I don't swim," Leeja said, stepping back and wrapping her arms reflexively around her middle.

"But you *could*," said Norrin. "I saw how you looked at the crowd on the beach, and after what you told me the other night...I just thought...you know," he gestured around at the empty clearing, "If we had some privacy, you could really enjoy yourself."

Leeja was stunned. She blushed. Nobody had ever considered her like that before.

He remembered something about me and planned this whole outing so I would be comfortable? Is this what the girls meant about the men you date being kind to you? Because if it was, I'm not sure I'm going to be able to get used to it.

"I haven't even tried to swim since I was a kid," she said, trying to mask her overwhelm.

"We'd better start making up for lost time," Norrin smiled at her with that broad, inviting smile and backed slowly away from her into the pond. As the water saturated his smallclothes, they clung to his body, revealing more and more of his eager manhood.

"Fine, I'll come swimming if it'll make you happy." Leeja kicked off her booties and slid her britches down. Now, she was standing before Norrin in her bindings and oversized tunic. She took a couple of tentative steps into the pond. The warm water flowed over her toes.

In a little further.

The water was lapping at her ankles now.

"I'm an excellent rescue diver," Norrin was floating on his back a few yards out of her reach, "but I'd rather not *have* to save you today."

"If I were cute and tiny like you, I'd probably be comfortable with public nudity too." Leeja stuck her tongue out at him, and Norrin swam quickly up to her.

"I'm not *that* tiny, am I?" He stood inches from her, dripping from head to toe. His smallclothes had long ceased obscuring his cock and balls.

"Let's find out already!" Leeja lunged toward him, grabbing for his crotch again. But Norrin was too fast a swimmer. He propelled himself back to the center of the pond, where he tread water and smiled that infuriating smile at her, "If you want it, you'll have to come and get it!"

Leeja took a deep breath, closed her eyes, and tore her tunic off over her head. "I'll teach you to tease an orc!" she shouted before diving under the water and swimming toward him.

FOURTEEN

Leeja stretched out in the clover. Her muscles ached from the swim. Her long, damp hair was fanned out around her like a giant green palm frond. Her bindings and smallclothes were nearly dry now. She savored the flavor of lingonberry jam on her tongue. Leeja basked in the ever-present scent of honey in the clearing. The afternoon sun was baking her, and it felt terrific.

"I can't remember the last time I sunbathed," she murmured, stretching again and finding Norrin's face with her hand.

"So," he said into her palm, making no attempt to move her,

"I picked you up, we did an activity, we talked, we ate a meal... I'd say this was a very successful date."

"Does that mean you're finally ready to put out?" Leeja asked, sliding one finger along his top and then bottom lip.

"I could be convinced," Norrin said, sucking her finger into his mouth.

"That's the last straw, human!" she growled. In a second, Leeja had torn off her smallclothes and pinned Norrin underneath her. "Sex. Now."

Norrin smiled up at her, "You know what I want," he said, trailing a finger over the knot in her chest bindings.

"Fine." Leeja untied the bindings and worked quickly to remove them, unwinding the long strips of linen fabric. Before she removed the last layer, though, she paused.

He's been looking at my body for hours and seemed to enjoy it. But breasts are different. What if he thinks they're...weird? The last time I was naked in front of him, it was dark...this is the middle of the day.

"Hey," he said, interrupting her reverie. "You don't have to— "

"I-I want to. I want to want to, anyway..." Leeja took a deep breath and removed the bindings. Even though she'd barely been dressed before, the cool breeze on her breasts was a shock. Her nipples tightened as she tossed the bindings away. Leeja kept her eyes closed and focused on the smell of honey in the clearing, mixing with the smell of *him*. As her skin warmed in the sunlight, her sense of calm increased. Finally, she was able to open her eyes. Norrin was grinning up at her.

"You're perfect." he said, reaching one hand up to gently cup her breast.

Leeja moaned softly. She relaxed into his hand. Any prohibitive thoughts she'd had before were drowned out by the insistent pounding in her core. She mounted him and started to writhe, grinding against Norrin's bulge. He squirmed under her, removing his smallclothes between undulations.

Leeja felt his stiff cock spring up, smacking against her ass.

"I need you *now*," Norrin said, grabbing her ass firmly in both hands. He was trying to coax himself inside of her, but Leeja had the high ground,

"It's your turn to beg, human," she said, and spun around and pressed his shoulders into the ground with her knees. Her ass hovered a few short inches from his face, just out of reach of that greedy tongue.

"Not that I'm complaining," Norrin said, his breath warming Leeja's undercarriage, "but what are you doing?"

"Investigating," Leeja said running a finger gently along his thick, turgid cock. "I'd always heard that human penises were small and unremarkable. So, you can imagine my shock the other night when your fat cock bounced out of your small-clothes."

"Happy to disappoint," Norrin said, and his cock lurched in her hand.

Leeja took her time exploring it with her eager fingers. The cock was brown at its base, deep pink in the middle, and a frustrated, glistening purple at the head; it looked as though Norrin's dick wanted to get even longer, even harder than rock-solid, and it was angry that it couldn't.

"I've never seen a tri-colored dick before," Leeja whispered in genuine astonishment as she inspected her new toy carefully. A thick vein twisted and snaked along the length of the shaft; Leeja ran her finger along it and Norrin whimpered.

"Very sensitive, these human cocks," Leeja muttered, continuing her inspection. About two-thirds of the way up, a shiny, jagged scar stretched all the way around its circumference. "What is this? Were you injured?"

Norrin chuckled, "In a sense, I guess." Leeja was confused;

she felt compelled to run the pad of her finger around the scar in slow, gentle circles. "In Little Break," Norrin continued between moans, "where my parents are from, it's a tradition to remove the foreskin from male infants."

Leeja gasped and tore her hand away, "Your *parents* did this to you? Did it hurt? Does it hurt now? Don't you miss your foreskin?"

Norrin just laughed, "It probably hurt, but I don't remember. I was a baby, after all. And they didn't do it themselves; they had a healer do it. The procedure is commonly done and is completely safe."

Leeja moved her face close to the scar, observing its ragged, uneven edge. "It looks like it hurts."

"If you want to try and kiss it better, I won't stop you."

Leeja leaned in close so her mouth was only an inch or so away from the thick, pink monster. She pursed her lips and breathed a narrow stream of cool air onto Norrin's manhood. He shivered and let out a little moan. Leeja did it again, and the cock thumped against her lips. Then she kissed it softly, right on the scar, and Norrin moaned even louder, his dick bouncing against her mouth repeatedly before she pulled out of range.

"Don't stop now," Norrin groaned, groping fruitlessly at her torso.

Leeja was staring at Norrin again, and that's when she noticed his balls. Two large, egg-shaped masses encased in a stretchy skin sack. His balls were the same deep pink-brown as the base of his cock, and they were covered with coarse, curly blond hair. She ran a finger over them, and the balls jumped toward Norrin's body. The sack holding them wrinkled and contracted.

"Now *this* is interesting," Leeja cupped a warm hand around the sack, "*very* interesting." She squeezed Norrin's balls gently and rolled them between her thumb and middle finger. They were smooth; they felt delicate, a stark contrast to the thick, coarse skin that housed them. Norrin groaned in response to the pressure, and his cock began to buck for her again.

Leeja felt her own desire pooling between her legs; if she teased him much longer, she'd be dripping on his face. Leeja turned around, lining up his wild dick with her glistening pussy, and she started sliding her lower lips along its length, coating him in her slick from balls to head.

"Please," Norrin groaned, groping and pulling at her. He tried to move her hips, but Leeja would not be deterred.

"Please, what, human?" She asked, grinding her swollen clit against him.

He's not going to get inside this perfect pussy that easily.

"Please let me taste you," Norrin growled.

"Oh, is *that* what you want?" Leeja reached down and coated her fingers in her own juices. She slid her hand up to his nose, meaning to tease him, but he grabbed it and shoved her fingers into his mouth, sucking off every bit of her he could get.

"More!" Norrin was pulling her ass hard toward his face.

"I suppose we *could* do that again," said Leeja, "if you're sure it's what you *really* want..."

"I'm sure!"

Leeja crawled up Norrin's body slowly. Extracting every moan and whine he could muster.

Finally, her pussy hovered above his mouth. Leeja meant to stay there for a while, forcing him to smell her arousal, but he reached up and pulled her down onto his mouth.

He's stronger than he looks!

Now that his tongue was pressed against her clit, Leeja could think of nothing but the pleasure he sent through her. He applied gentle pressure, rolling his tongue around, setting off little electric shocks that sent white, hot pleasure coursing through her.

"Goddess!" Leeja cried out, closing her eyes and letting her head fall back. She was close, but to what she wasn't sure. There was a strange, exhilarating sensation stirring deep within her. She felt it faintly the first time she made love with Norrin. And it was stronger today, much stronger.

That's when Norrin sucked her clit into his mouth. The change in pressure pushed her over the edge. Leeja's orgasm sent her body into a series of quakes and spasms.

Norrin took advantage of her diminished state. He flipped her over onto her back and slammed his cock inside her still-quaking pussy.

Leeja came again, or was she still coming? The intense, new sensation was still building, like she was on her way to a different, more intense orgasm.

Her back arched, and she clawed at his forearms. Norrin showed no mercy. He pumped his throbbing cock deeper into her. His stroke was slow but forceful and unrelenting. With each push forward, he buried more of himself inside her.

Leeja gasped and moaned in between the tremors, "More! Pleeeeeaaaase!"

Norrin's pace increased, and his breath grew ragged.

Finally, he was buried to the hilt. Leeja gasped.

He's huge.

Norrin pumped his dick faster and faster now, slamming against her mound. He pulled his thick meat nearly entirely out and then back down into her, sending waves of pleasure that traveled up through her pussy to her pulsing clit. He grabbed one of Leeja's legs and slung it over his shoulder.

Leeja cursed. The adjusted position drove Norrin's cock even further inside of her. It was bashing up against her cervix.

Norrin must have been a big fan of the new position, too. He dug his fingertips into her thighs and expelled a guttural cry,

"I'm cuming!"

Leeja felt his cock thumping inside her as it spilled its sticky load, and then she came again with him. That same, strange sensation was still there, accompanying and enhancing her orgasm.

What is going on down there?

Leeja's body went slack and Norrin collapsed in a heap on top of her. She struggled to wrap her limp arms around his body, and Norrin nuzzled his face in her hair, murmuring contentedly for several, blissful minutes.

"I think I've found something we have in common," he breathed against her neck, "we both like fucking in the woods." Norrin rolled off of Leeja and stood on shaky legs to gather his clothes.

"Not so fast, human," Leeja said, springing to her feet and grabbing him by his still-somewhat-swollen cock, "I want to swim some more."

"Fine, fine," said Norrin, pulsing back to life in her hand. "Just let me get dressed first. Then we can swim as much as you want."

"You *have* got a lot to learn about orcs," Leeja said, walking backward into the water, her grip on his phallus firm. "For example, should the need arise, an orc can hold her breath for as many as eighteen minutes."

"I've always found that I learn best through experience." They were waist-deep in the emerald water now and still walking deeper.

"I'd be more than happy to demonstrate," Leeja said with a devious glint in her eye. She grabbed Norrin's hips and bobbed under the water. She opened her eyes and looked around in the murky green. Norrin was only a few inches from her face, but it was still difficult to make out the precise details of his strange, human dick...of *her* new favorite dick. Leeja blinked in the water, and her vision became more clear. She ran the flat of her tusk down its length, and the cock jumped in the water. Leeja remembered the humans from the Drowned Grim, how terrified they'd been at the idea of her tusks being anywhere near them.

She stood up slowly out of the water and backed away from Norrin, crossing her arms around her middle. "I'm sorry," Leeja muttered.

"What's wrong?" Norrin asked, stepping closer to her.

Leeja turned her head away as if she could make him forget the six-inch death blades jutting up the sides of her face, "I um...I didn't mean to hurt you," Leeja was stammering now; she wanted to flee from Norrin and her embarrassment but forced herself to stay and talk about it. "I forget how sharp they are sometimes...I never want to scare you."

Norrin stepped close to Leeja and took her face in both of his hands, "Do I seem scared?" He asked before kissing her gently, just once on the lips.

"No, you don't." Leeja took her time, taking several deep breaths before she opened her eyes and looked at Norrin's face. He was smiling warmly at her.

"Does *he* seem scared?" Norrin guided Leeja's hand down his sinewy body and wrapped it around his thick cock under the water.

It was rock hard and pulsing. "I don't know," Leeja shrugged. "I can't really see him from up here."

Norrin ran one thumb carefully along Leeja's tusk, smirking, "Maybe you should go down there and get a better look."

Leeja sucked in a huge breath and dove under the water, grinning. As the bubbles cleared, she was once again able to see that thick, pink human penis. It was aggressively hard, thumping into Norrin's abdomen every few seconds. His balls were tightly compacted against his body, braced against the cold water.

Leeja opened her mouth and seized upon her prize. She took the head of his cock into her mouth and began to work her tongue along its thick, impatient veins. She needed to feel the head of his cock ramming the back of her throat, but not as badly as she wanted to make Norrin squirm.

This is going to take a while.

Leeja worked her mouth lower down Norrin's massive dick and once again was shocked at his length. She'd seen his dick when he went down on her. She'd felt it filling up and stretching her pussy, but feeling his cock stuffed deep in her throat...that was a different kind of fullness. Leeja was desperate to feel more of him inside of her, but she forced herself to take it slow, only swallowing an inch more of him at a time.

Apparently, her teasing was paying off. Norrin started bucking and grinding his pelvis against her nose.

Leeja grabbed his hips and held him in place.

Not so fast.

Keeping his cock exactly where she wanted it as she slowly tightened her lips around his girth and rolled her tongue down toward the base. With each roll of her tongue, she worked herself a little further down his length. Finally, Leeja felt the blunt end of Norrin's massive cock pressed against the back of her throat.

Norrin started pulsing in her mouth, and Leeja knew he was close; his balls were pulsing rhythmically in her hand. Leeja slid several inches of cock out of her mouth. She wanted to catch Norrin's cum on her tongue, but she wasn't fast enough. The sudden movement caused Norrin to lose control. He coated the back of her throat and filled her mouth with his seed. Leeja swallowed the cum. She tightened her lips around his cock-head and continued to suck, demanding every last drop.

When his cock finally stopped bucking in her mouth, Leeja swallowed the remnants and bobbed up to the surface.

"So, were you keeping track of how long I held my breath?"

Norrin, in a state of what looked like shock and maybe partial paralysis, just shook his head slowly. He seemed unable to speak, but before Leeja could ask him about it, he grabbed her with both hands and pulled her close, kissing her deeply.

FIFTEEN

Leeja was still rubbing the sleep out of her eyes, as Rakka, the world's premier troll architect led her on a tour through the crumbling remains of a massive stone wall.

"This is best troll architecture anywhere," said Rakka, through his thick trollish accent.

"This is the Stronghold, right?" Leeja asked, eager to impress the ancient troll.

"You come here before, orc?"

"Yes!" Leeja blurted out, but then she remembered the reason for her last excursion into the Stronghold. The last time she was here, she was being run-through by both of Galdur's slithering members. "I mean,no...not really," Leeja said, blushing green.

Rakka raised an impatient eyebrow.

"That is," Leeja lied, "I've heard it's the most dangerous part of the island."

"You big, strong girl," Rakka said, slapping a heavy hand down on her shoulder, "you be alright." He was leading Leeja around the inside of the wall, looking for something. For each slow, belabored step he took, Leeja had to take two, and she was still lagging behind him.

"Here," he said, stopping at an intact stone block. It was tremendous, as wide as Leeja was long and at least twice as tall. "When Stronghold built, *every* brick like this." Rakka looked up into the sky and stretched his massive arms out in either direction.

I wish I could see what he sees. I wish I could have seen this place back in those days.

"This wall...sixty feet high, strongest wall ever build."

"How did it come to be broken?" Leeja asked timidly.

"Elves," Rakka sneered, "they soared above this place for twenty and days nights. Magical, liquid explosions rained down from them." Rakka turned to face Leeja; his tone became very matter-of-fact, "Very innovative."

"That's horrible," Leeja gasped.

"Stories of buildings and wars go hand in hand," Rakka shrugged. "Name this stone."

"Um...granite?"

"Very good," Rakka said, a smile twisting up one side of his huge, grizzled face. "Granite is best stone, strongest stone. We always use granite, yes?"

"Yes!" Leeja answered immediately.

We? Rakka, the Rakka just called me 'we'.

"Tell me," Rakka asked, stroking his matted beard and studying Leeja closely, "why is this place called Stronghold?"

"It was the first thing the trolls built on island," Leeja had learned that much from Arlynn. She scanned their surroundings for more clues, "They would have chosen this spot because it's centrally located and easily defensible..."

"Good, good. What else?"

Leeja climbed onto a broken section of wall to get a better look at the ruins around her. She saw the tower of Arlynn's favorite opium den, The Keep, and several other functional buildings tucked into the rubble. There, a variety of building styles and materials were used, not entirely unlike the patchwork of buildings in the Olde Magical Core.

If you ignore the fact that the streets are deserted, the mangled stone corpse of a once great city casts shadows everywhere you turn, and I haven't been able to shake the feeling that I'm being watched since we arrived...this is exactly *like the bustling, friendly mercantile district.*

"Most of these buildings are new," Leeja muttered to herself, "but *we* always use granite."

Leeja climbed higher onto the unbroken block. That's when she noticed it. The nearest granite remains were arranged in a hexagon. So were the next ones. All around the Stronghold were hexagonal structures in varying stages of disrepair. In fact, the wall around the Stronghold was one giant hexagon.

"Why hexagons?" She muttered to herself.

"Hexagon is best shape, strongest shape. We always use hexagons!"

Leeja looked out into the center of the Stronghold, trying to ignore the newer buildings and see only the troll's hexagons—only what was there before the ravages of war. Finally, she saw it: at the very center was one gigantic hexagonal granite foundation—a central building with smaller hexagons inside.

"It was a castle." She whispered.

"More." Said Rakka.

"A fortress? A city!" Leeja saw a pattern emerge from the rubble. All of the foundations were connected. "Everything is touching!" She called down to Rakka.

"Very good! Now you understand troll strength. We are strong together. We must touch, must push against each other. When we do, we can stand for one thousand years. No one can destroy our foundations!"

Leeja climbed down off the wall. "It's such a shame that this was all lost. I bet it was beautiful. I would have loved to have seen a great troll city right here on Th'myskôra."

"You will." Rakka coughed out in his husky, rumbling baritone. "Great builders of the past made foundations. We build something beautiful on top of them."

There's that 'we' again.

"You don't mean that *I* could help make the new Stronghold?"

"Why shouldn't you? Afraid of hard work?"

"No one's ever accused me of that," Leeja said proudly.

"Good. Now, you must simply create beauty."

Leeja shifted her weight nervously from one foot to the other.

Orcs aren't exactly known for their creative problem-solving...

"Don't worry, little one," Rakka said, pulling his lumpy face into a crooked smile. "There's beauty there," he poked her in the chest with his massive finger. "I can tell."

Leeja felt the green blush creeping up onto her cheeks. All her life, she'd wanted to make things. Permanent things that don't get washed away by the first heavy storm or crushed into the dust by the next raiding party. No one had ever recognized that desire in her before, let alone encouraged her. With that hard tap on the chest and his simple, no-nonsense statement,

Rakka had unleashed something inside of Leeja that she'd only barely been aware of herself. Something cracked inside her, and all of those girlhood dreams of permanence came bubbling up to the surface.

"Come," Rakka said flatly. He was already hoisting himself into his sturdy shrew-cart. The great two-toed shrews hitched to the cart hissed and chirped as Leeja approached, but Rakka cooed at them and they allowed her to board the cart without any more fuss.

"There is more to see," Rakka said as he cracked the reins and the shrews took off running, their snouts twitching at the ground.

Norrin woke up that morning with his signature boner. But now he had actual memories of Leeja to masturbate to, not just dreams.

"That woman's insatiable." Without realizing it, Norrin had started stroking himself. Wild images flashed across his mind of Leeja's tusks gently scraping against his abdomen as she sucked his brains out. Of her demanding that he tread water so she could wrap her legs around him and rock up and down on his cock.

Norrin looked down at his turgid dick. Faint, red half-circles were arranged in a neat circle around its length.

She bit me? When? It wasn't when she was going down on me in the pond, not with her mouth at all...

It was when she insisted that he fuck her bent over, from behind, half out of the water. Her pussy felt different then; something changed when she howled out those intoxicating words,

"I told you there would be consequences for making me wait, human," she'd growled back to him from the mud, "Now, cum in me!"

Norrin exploded all over himself, a poor substitute for the choking, biting suction of Leeja's greedy pussy. It would have to do for now.

Norrin cleaned himself up, got dressed, and went downstairs for breakfast.

THE SHREWS TRUDGED ON, and the old cart creaked. It was a beautiful summer day, and Leeja took her hair down, letting the breeze tug and pull it in all directions. Immediately, she was transported in her mind back to the muddy edge of the pond with Norrin. When he'd twisted his fingers in her hair and pulled. How she'd howled and bucked as he entered her from behind. The strange sensation deep inside her when she came around him.

Get ahold of yourself. An artistic genius is taking time out of his day to teach you about the island. Pay attention...and say something smart!

Rakka drove the shrews through the Stronghold and out of a different, smaller gate on the north face of the wall.

"I had no idea the wall had more than one entrance."

"Of course you didn't," said Rakka flatly, "that is point of tour."

"Of course."

Beyond the wall was a dirt path, just wide enough for the cart, winding up the side of a steep hill. On either side of the path was a vast forest of live oak trees.

Just like the ones on the way up to Norrin's special spot.

Leeja closed her eyes. The little cart rocked back and forth, and she was transported again. This time back to the clearing at the top of Norrin's secret hill, her head on his chest, being gently rocked back and forth by his deep, post-coital breathing. She listened for the rustling sounds of lizards through the hard leaves and remembered the crinkling, rustling sounds of the leaves under their bodies as they rolled on top of each other, switching positions over and over during their hours-long love-making escapade.

The shrews trudged on.

Leeja opened her eyes. They were very high now. The live oak trees had grown sparse, and she could see vast swaths of dried vegetation covering the rolling hills. Poking up between the brush were thousands of spiny green stalks, each covered with dozens of vivid yellow flowers. The flowers smelled lush and pungent. The earth smelled dry and clean. The whole hill-side seemed happy that Leeja was there.

"We are close now," Rakka said as the landscape changed for a third time.

"Close to what?" Leeja wondered out loud as she marveled

at the sea of trees that seemed to have sprung up around them in an instant. Tall, slender, silver-white trunks all standing perfectly straight, smooth, and unbent. Each one crowned with a beautiful crest of lush green. The leaves themselves were almost perfectly round, like the jingles on a tambourine and a hundred-thousand invisible fingers seemed to be playing them. The rustling, quaking, whirr coming from all directions was overwhelming, almost too much for Leeja's sensitive orc ears.

"This would be a great place to hide from orcs."

"From *anyone* with strong ears," said Rakka. He was wincing, but kept driving the cart up the hill.

"These trees are incredible." Leeja said, "I haven't seen anything else like them, not even on Swi'loor."

"Tree!" Rakka shouted. The closer they got to wherever they were going, the denser the trunks and the louder the leaves. They were hissing and crackling now.

"What?" Leeja was having a terrible time making Rakka's words out against the din.

"Only one tree! All of this is connected." Rakka raised his massive hand and pointed one gnarled finger down with finality, "Underground."

"How d—"

"Elves bring! This elf tree!"

The cart came to a stop in front of a particularly dense section of tree trunks blocking the path. Rakka stepped down out of the cart, rocking it wildly back and forth. With every step he took toward the roadblock, the noise in the trees got louder.

Their leaves quaked furiously taking on a metallic, clanging quality.

The giant shrews twittered and chirped nervously, bucking against their bridals.

Leeja clamped her hands over her ears.

Rakka kept walking.

The leaves were screeching now.

Rakka reached the roadblock. He thrust an arm between tightly packed trunks, and a moment later…silence fell over the hillside. Every one of the millions of angry, scraping, clanging leaves was completely still.

Leeja held her breath. Rakka stood a few yards away from her, frozen except for the slow, expansion of his massive back as he drew in a long low breath.

A moment later, the trunks slid elegantly, one by one, into the earth, revealing a dimly lit path.

Rakka tugged at the reins, and the cart rolled on, through the newly revealed opening in what Leeja finally recognized as a solid wall of trees.

"Where are we?" she marveled. The tree cover was so complete that it blocked out the sun. The only light came from thousands of glittering fireflies. The air was cool—like the most peaceful summer night. "How is it so dark here?"

"Elves do not like sunlight. They keep dark."

"You don't mean that this is If'aen Anor?" Leeja gasped. "I heard that the elves are so incredibly secretive that no non-elf has ever seen it! How did we get in? I don't think I've ever even seen an elf before today!"

"You will not see today either," Rakka laughed.

As Leeja's eyes adjusted to the dim light inside of the elf sanctuary, she saw that what she had assumed were simply more of the shimmering trees they'd seen on their way up the hill were actually structures—tall, elegant buildings made of intertwining tree trunks. Their silver-white exposed roots and trunks were twisted into elaborate living braids that stretched from the forest floor up into the twinkling, black sky.

Did the elves really abandon this place? Were they forced to leave like the trolls at the Stronghold?

"But everything here feels so alive," Leeja muttered.

"It is!" Rakka said in his gruff, thundering voice. "You will not see elves, but elves see you!"

Leeja looked around, uneasy. She could barely see in all this black, and she hadn't brought a weapon with her. In fact, she almost never carried her broad sword these days.

Stupid. I've gone soft living on this island for so long.

Leeja crouched. She scanned the air for sounds of footsteps.

Nothing. Only Rakka's labored breathing.

"Tell me, orc..." Rakka stroked his matted beard, "what have you heard about elves?"

"That they're violent. Merciless killers who hate outsiders. When they decide they want possession of a land, they swarm in, like locusts. They destroy everything and build their secret kingdoms. They think they deserve to rule over all other creatures."

"That is not *un*true," Rakka said thoughtfully, "but it is not the *only* truth. Today, we are here to see buildings. What do you see?"

"All of their buildings seem to be...carved out of living trees?"

Rakka laughed, "I thought so too the first time. Look closer."

Leeja approached the nearest building. She ran her hand carefully along a windowsill. There aren't any chisel marks, or nails." She examined the long, graceful door. "I can't see any place where the wood has been joined either. It's almost as if... the trees grew this way?"

"Tree. Only one tree. The same tree as outside."

"How can that be possible?"

"They bring clipping from mother tree. When elves find settlement site, they place clipping in dirt. All elves form circle, they give their magic to the clipping and to Architect. Architect stands in middle of circle. He pulls energy from other elves.

He directs clipping to grow down into the earth and spread. To shoot up from the ground fully formed, houses and bakeries and temples. Whatever elves need, he must make—no, he must feel."

"That's incredible. So... they could build anything *anywhere!*"

"Almost," Rakka said smugly. "They tried at Stronghold, after the city fell, but troll foundations too deep, too strong. Even elven magic is no match for troll masonry."

Leeja turned around slowly. Every building, hundreds of structures, all seemed to radiate from her exact position.

"This must have been where he did it. The elf who built this city. He stood right in this spot and imagined all of this beauty, and then it...it just was."

"Come, orc. We have one more building to see."

Leeja didn't want to leave If'aen Anor. She wasn't afraid of elves anymore, and she wanted to find one.

Such powerful magic they must have. I wonder if you can feel it just by touching them. What would happen if you slept with one? Would saplings sprout out of your nipples? If it's anything like the electric surge from fucking a human, it could be dangerous for the faint of heart...maybe I could talk Arlynn into trying it and reporting back. She's in excellent health.

"Come little orc!" Rakka was back in the shrew cart.

How does he keep doing that?

"We have one more building to see."

A LONG WHILE LATER, the little cart pulled up to a familiar sight, the six-sided temple to the goddess in the town square. Leeja walked past it nearly every morning on her way to the docks.

"You built this temple, right?" Leeja asked, finally feeling sure of something.

"I helped," Rakka said, shrugging and pushing the shimmering silver-white door open. "Have you been inside?"

"Oh, um… I'm not really very religious," Leeja was starting to blush. She followed Rakka into the dimly lit granite building. As her eyes adjusted, she saw not only fine troll masonry but also beautiful cascading buttresses and archways adorning and supporting the walls and ceiling, all made of the same living wood as If'aen Anor.

"After The Peace," Rakka said, lumbering around the perimeter of the central chamber lighting candles, "it was decided that master builder from each of the Three Realms would come here to Th'myskôra."

"All *three?*"

"We let the human do the floors."

Leeja looked down; now that the candles were lit, she could see an intricate mosaic, hundreds of thousands of tiny, glittering tiles depicting three armies hellbent on destroying each other. And in the middle the mayhem, and carnage— the goddess in a halo of golden light, compelling them all to lay down their arms.

"But...but how did you work with an elf? You're so different. And after what they did to the Stronghold! After everything the humans did in the war...I don't understand."

"People say elves ruthless and secretive. People say humans shortsighted, and dangerous. That may be true; I don't know all elves. I do know Il'daerian, my friend who lent his magic to help build temple. *And* I know, little orc, this place strong because we all build together."

CHAPTER
SIXTEEN

"Well, good afternoon, sleepyhead," said Glema, ladling a big helping of parrotfish stew into a wooden bowl. "I almost gave up on you."

"Don't keep the kids waiting on my account, Ma," Norrin said, kissing her on the cheek and sitting down at the kitchen table to eat.

"I've got a few minutes before class starts. What about you?"

"I'm only teaching on Saturdays for a while; I uh...wanted to spend more time helping Dad out."

She stepped back and admired her son, "My boy, teaching like his old ma...helping Dad build ships. You got so...grown up so fast...I still can't believe you're as tall as me..."

"Ma!" Norrin laughed so hard he nearly choked on his stew,

"I'm a twenty-nine-year-old man; six foot is a pretty standard height."

"Well you'll always be my little man!"

When Norrin was a boy, his mother was always taller than his friends' mothers and many of the fathers. She'd explained that her imposing height and long limbs were the reason she was the fastest rescue diver in the imperial navy. But Norrin liked to imagine she was secretly a mershifter. That would mean he was a merperson too!

"So," Glema said, sitting across from Norrin and savoring her tea, "tell me all about her..."

"Her who?" Norrin asked, innocently stuffing a chunk of rhubarb into his mouth. This opportunity to tease his mother was too great to pass up.

"You know precisely who, you brat!" And Glema threw a dishrag at him, laughing.

Norrin dodged it gleefully: "She's wonderful, Ma. She's strong, fun, and eager to learn and explore."

"Another one of your burly beauties, huh?"

Norrin smiled, "She's different. She always says exactly what she means. And she never lets me get away with anything. The first time I saw her, I tried to pick her up on the esplanade, and none of my usual lines had any effect. In fact, she practically tore my head off."

"Well, I've always said that you needed a strong hand."

"She's not just strong, Ma. When I'm with her, I feel...I dunno...happy, easy, like I've finally met my match."

"But what does she *do*?" asked his mother.

"This is Th'myskôra, not the imperial navy; we don't talk about people like that here."

"Oh, you know what I mean," Glema said, blushing, "How does she contribute? What does she enjoy?"

"Well," Norrin said, rocking back in his chair, "She's been

unloading ships for Bowen for the past few months. Of course, now, she's helping us with the repairs on the Flannery…Dad keeps trying to convince her to join a shoring crew and go full-time into shripwrighting."

"Your father is always trying to convince *everyone* to go into shipwrighting."

"Yeah," Norrin chuckled, "but I think she's a different kind of builder. She's always going on about the different styles of buildings on the island."

"An architect and a shipwright, hm?" Glema was silent for a moment, "A very promising match."

"I'm so glad you approve," Norrin said, getting up from the table.

"Oh!" said Glema, "I bet we could set her up with an apprenticeship with that troll builder…What's his name? You know who I mean…the one with the face!"

"His name is Rakka, and Dad already beat you to it," said Norrin, standing up from the table, "he's taking Leeja on a tour of the island as we speak."

Glema frowned.

"We've only been on two dates, Ma. Maybe you and dad could cool it just a tiny bit on the 'planning her whole life for her' front?"

"Fine," said Glema putting the stew away. "You bring her to dinner next week, and *then* we'll finalize that apprenticeship."

"Good*bye*, Mother," Norrin kissed her on the cheek again and hurried out the door.

. . .

"...AND THEN THORNE FELL IN!" Leeja cried out in between snorts.

"Wait," said Aengus, laughing. "Weren't you all still tied to each other?"

"Yes!" Leeja squealed, "First, the current took Thorne, and he pulled me in right after. Then the whole crew was in the water, splash, splash, splash, one right after another. Poor Phlip was the last one on the dock. He tried to resist; he even tried flying, but we were too heavy. Splash! He got pulled down with us, snatched right out of the air!"

Aengus and Leeja were roaring with laughter as Norrin reached the workbench.

"I hope I didn't miss anything important," he said, sliding up next to Leeja and placing a hand on the small of her back. Aengus gave him a knowing look.

"Just all the work," Leeja said, sticking her tongue out at him through her tusks. "Your father and I have been gluing and nailing patches into place all morning."

"There's still plenty to do," said Aengus, "There's sanding and painting and varnishing!"

"But as far as the rest of today...?" Leeja asked.

"Well, yes," said Aengus, "There's not much more we can do until the glue sets. Perhaps, Norrin, you'd like to make up for your late arrival to our dear Leeja. A cart ride, maybe?"

Norrin opened his mouth to answer but was interrupted by the unwelcome clacking of hooves.

Bowen.

"Leeja, I need you back on the dock!" he brayed across the dry docks.

"I know I agreed to let you have her 'till the job was done, and if this sets completion back, I understand," Bowen said, addressing Aengus, "but I just got a huge load in from Felft'halas. Everybody's down there working doubles just to try and get the dock cleared."

Aengus surreptitiously glanced at Norrin, raising an eyebrow as if to ask, 'What do you think?'

Norrin nodded in reply. The movement was so minute that no one else would have even noticed the exchange.

"That's alright, Bowen," Aengus said, smiling broadly. "Leeja's been a great help, but we're done with all the heavy lifting now; just cosmetic work left. We should have the Flannery finished by the end of the week."

A subtle look of terror flashed across Leeja's eyes.

"Don't worry," Norrin whispered in her ear. "We're gonna' have that third date and you'll win your bet. I *promise*."

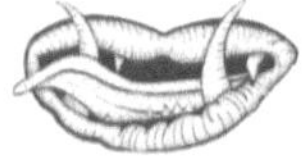

She'd only been gone a week, but it was long enough that Leeja felt out of place with her old work friends. She missed Aengus and his constant tidbits of information. She missed Norrin's lustful stares, the ones he thought she didn't notice. She missed the smell of him always lurking behind every corner. And she missed building the boat.

When Bowen had first told her she'd be doing repair work, she balked. She never considered herself a builder of anything. Still, there was something so gratifying about taking a formless plank of wood and shaping it to her vision. She loved learning the names and functions of all the tools, and she'd even started dreaming about coming up with her own design someday. She wasn't sure for what yet…but she knew there was a design inside of her, and she was going to get it out.

"Oof! Watch it, will ya!" Leeja stumbled back under the weight of a large crate.

"Don't tell me you forgot how to work on your little vacation." Greta grinned. She was at least twelve feet away from Leeja on the brigade and showed no hesitation about shouting her very strong opinions to Leeja in easy hearing range of everyone else working on the dock.

"Did *you* forget how to give a guy a heads-up?" Leeja asked, turning to lob the crate to Thorne, who was standing twelve feet from Leeja. Then he turned to throw it another twelve feet to Hubert.

"Relax, Leeja," Greta grunted. "Hhhup! I'm just razzin' ya a little."

"Oof!" Leeja huffed, "I missed you guys too."

"Hhhhup!" Greta launched the next crate into the air, "From what I hear, you didn't miss *all* of us…" She waggled her eyebrows in Thorne's direction.

"Oof!" Leeja looked around for a moment before catching on, "Oh, you mean Thorne? We fucked, but it wasn't a big deal…"

"You mean *it* wasn't a big deal? Hhhup!"

"Oof! Are you asking about his dick?" Leeja tried to whisper.

"Hhhup!" Greta giggled and wiggled her eyebrows again.

"Oof! There's nothing wrong with his dick. It's perfect-ly…" Leeja took a moment to find the right word, "fine."

"Ghu!" Thorne grunted, catching the large crate. "You talkin' about my dick, girly?"

"Hhhup! I've been informed that your dick is just fine." Greta shouted to Thorne over Leeja's head.

"Oof!" Leeja would have blushed if she weren't already bright green and sweaty from the work.

"Ghu! You ever feel like finding out for yourself, you know where to find me."

"Hhhup! I wouldn't want to step on anyone's toes," Greta shouted, indicating Leeja with a nod.

"Oof!" Leeja caught the next crate and sent it flying over to Thorne, "I told you, Greta, it didn't work out. Have at 'im!"

"Ghu! Yeah, the only reason Leeja slept with me was to try and prove to those human friends of hers that she's a human, too."

"Hhhup! Goddess, Leeja, is that true?"

"Oof! It sounds awful when you put it like that," said Leeja, blinking sweat out of her eyes.

"Ghu! Well, however it sounds, I'm glad you've got that human nonsense out of your head," shouted Thorne, tossing his crate along the brigade.

"What possessed you in the first place? Hhhup!"

"Oof!" Leeja didn't know what to say; she was still reeling.

"Ghu! Her human friends bet her she couldn't date like a human."

"And when it didn't work out, you just...quit? Hhhup! That doesn't sound like you, Leeja."

"Oof!" Leeja desperately wanted the conversation to shift, or maybe for the cracks in the boardwalk to widen and swallow her into some alternate dimension.

"Ghu! Like she said, it didn't work out."

"Hhhup!" Greta was still staring at Leeja, waiting for more explanation.

"Oof!" Leeja didn't explain.

"Ghu!"

"Hhhup!" Greta launched another crate.

"Oof! Actually...I *didn't* give up on the bet..." Leeja said.

"Ghu! You mean you dragged some other poor sap on a human *date* with you?"

"Who is it?" Asked Greta, "Someone from the Drowned Grim? Hhhup!"

"Oof!"

"Ghu!"

"Do we know him? Hhhup!" It was becoming clear that Greta was not in the mood to let things slide.

"Oof! You might..."

Why not just tell them? It's not like I've got anything to be ashamed of, and besides, it's a small island, they'll find out eventually.

"Ghu!" Now Thorne was staring suspiciously at her too.

"Hhhup!" Greta tossed another crate.

"Oof!" Leeja caught it and launched it towards Thorne. "It's Norrin. The shipwright."

"Ghu!" Thorne caught the crate and set it down on the ground. "Norrin? Of all the males on this island, you choose to 'date' *that* human? He's on permanent safari. He's a monster chaser."

"You don't know him like I do," said Leeja, "he's actually kind of charming. And I think he likes me... a lot."

"I have known that human for many years," said Thorne, "and he's only going along with your little bet because he couldn't stand the idea of *me* having something *he* couldn't!"

"This has nothing to do with you, Thorne," said Leeja, panting, "Norrin and I like each other, and that's all there is to it!"

"Then why did he wait until I bedded you before he made his move?" Thorne hissed.

"Uh, guys?" A distant voice called out. It was Hubert, "I need another crate!"

"Ghu!" Thorne threw his crate.

"Hhhhup!" Greta grinned as she resumed lobbing crates.

"Oof!" *Thorne is an idiot. Norrin likes me. He told me so on that first night, outside of the Spiced Goat.*

"Ghu!" Thorne looked so disappointed as he turned away to toss the crate.

"Hhhup!"

"Oof!" *He said that he'd never done anything like this before. He'd never felt anything like this before. He's not a monster chaser.*

"Ghu!"

"Hhhup"

"Oof!" *He practically begged me to choose him.*

"Ghu!" Thorne wasn't making eye contact with Leeja anymore.

"Hhhup!" Greta licked her lips.

"Oof!" *Begged me to choose him over* Thorne.

"Ghu!"

"Hhhup!"

"Oof!" *The last thing he said to me today was that we'd complete the bet.*

"Ghu!"

"Hhhup!"

"Oof!" *No. Thorne is wrong. Right?*

The dock crew carried on their work without any further attempts at conversation. All Leeja could think about was the moment she'd be able to get off that dock and back into Norrin's arms— the moment when he would make everything feel right again.

"FRANK! Hey, Frank, I need to talk to you about something." Norrin looked up from the tool chest he'd been packing to see a worried Leeja silhouetted by the setting sun.

"I thought you'd be toiling away for ol' Bowen all night."

"We're on dinner break, I have to be back in half an hour, but I need to talk to you."

"Talk?" Norrin scoffed, "I can think of at least two better uses of a nearly empty dry dock!" Leeja didn't smile.

Something's wrong.

Norrin closed the distance between them and wrapped Leeja in his arms. They were alone. Her body relaxed instantly. Norrin was sure he felt the tumult drain out of her as she tilted her head down to accept his mouth against hers.

Their hands explored each other's bodies, clawing, desperate to rediscover the pleasures they'd enjoyed at the pond, but things felt different today.

She's upset.

Norrin was overcome with the need to relieve her suffering, to once again send her screaming to orgasm and then to bask with her in post-coital bliss.

"I need you to be serious for a minute, Frank." Leeja pushed herself away from him, apparently with some effort, and held his gaze. "How's your um...I mean, after the lake yesterday..."

"My cock?" He asked, moving her hand to the bulge at the front of his britches, "He's very happy to see you."

"No, I mean... did I hurt it?"

"Please feel free to inspect him," Norrin untied his britches and forced his smallclothes down over his hips. His lengthy member sprung to attention the moment it was freed.

Leeja's eyes went wide.

"Do they hurt?" she asked, reaching out to touch the faint, half-moon marks that circled his member.

"Only a little. But if you're really feeling guilty, you could make it up to us. I, for one, wouldn't mind another display of your oral talents…"

Leeja grabbed each of his hips firmly and kneeled down, lowering her face to his manhood.

"No. Wait." She stopped herself and stood up. "This isn't what I came here for. I need to talk to you about the bet."

"Let's see," said Norrin, counting on his fingers. "Learn my name, check. Where I was born, check. One thing I am passionate about, check. One thing we have in common, double check.

"Sex on non-consecutive days, check. All that's left is for us to go on one more real date, and we'll have won."

Leeja looked over his shoulder, back toward the crew on the dock, "But what about after that?"

"After that, we'll be free from your friend's restrictions," he said, sliding a hand around her waist. "And I'll have wiped that smug look right off Thorne's face."

"But—" Leeja said, shifting her weight from one hip to the other. Her brow was furrowed again.

"No more worrying," Norrin said, scooping Leeja up and kissing her. "We're here, together, now. I want to get as much out of this moment as possible."

He dug his fingers into her ass and thighs, lifting her off the ground and carrying her a few feet to the back of the work cart.

Look at this big, powerful woman. My big, strong woman.

Norrin stood at the wagon's edge, carefully unlacing Leeja's leather boots and observing the prize before him.

"You're incredible," he murmured, kissing her newly freed ankle.

Leeja's eyes fluttered closed. Her hands shot up reflexively began to unlace her stays,

"MmmmHmmm," she groaned as Norrin's hands traveled up her leg, massaging her tight calf muscles.

He slid off the second boot with much less ceremony,

"I've got to have you. Right now!" Norrin barked, pulling her tight leather britches off and throwing them aside.

Leeja's eyes flew open, "What about Aengus?"

"Don't worry about him. Dad's gone to talk to Bowen." Norrin stood admiring Leeja, sprawled out on her back for him- just him.

How did I get so lucky?

"Talk to Bowen about what?" Leeja asked, a pout queering that pretty face.

"About you, of course," Norrin tried to crawl into the cart on top of Leeja, but she stopped him.

"Why should they be talking about me?" Leeja's nose was all wrinkled when she asked.

Adorable.

"The Flannery will be operational again soon. Dad wants Bowen to add you to the shoring crew. He's always trying to make a shipwright out of everyone."

"Oh," Leeja's hands started worrying the hem of her tunic. Norrin took advantage of her distraction and climbed into the cart with her. "Do you want me to leave, too?"

Norrin took one of her well-defined calves in each hand and began to massage them again,

"I think I'd better come clean, Leeja," Norrin said, sliding his hands up her thighs and back up to her hips. "It's no accident that Bowen sent you to help with the repairs."

"Oh, no?" Leeja was kissing Norrin's neck, biting and sucking at the skin there.

"When we first met on the esplanade, you rejected me, and that doesn't happen often," Norrin's hands were moving slowly up Leeja's body under her tunic.

Leeja moaned and wound her fingers through Norrin's thick, blond hair. "There she is."

Her body is so responsive. Gods, I hope I get to feel her second set of teeth again.

His fingers found her chest bindings and started untying them, "I asked the guys on the beach about you." Leeja's breasts were free now. They were huge, and soft in his hands. "Once I knew where you worked, it was easy. All I had to do was convince Dad to bump Bowen up the list."

"Wait," Leeja pulled back, startled, "isn't that, like...fraud?"

"Something like it, I suppose," Norrin said, pulling Leeja's tunic off over her head. "Having you was worth a little fraud."

He laid her down on the flat work cart, admiring her perfectly sculpted body in the shimmering golden light of the setting sun. "Now, stop worrying, and let me enjoy my dinner."

CHAPTER

SEVENTEEN

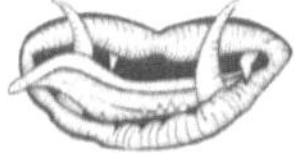

It was late at night when work was finally done at the dock, and Leeja dragged herself into the Drowned Grimoire for a *very* late dinner. She set herself up in the darkest corner of the tavern and ordered her favorite late-night snack, a piping hot basket of deep-fried man o' war. But as hungry as she'd been at work, Leeja couldn't bring herself to eat when the food arrived. Instead, she made slow circles with her finger in the small earthenware ramekin filled with sticky-sweet dipping sauce.

"I du' know which is more sour," said Brigid. The stout old

dwarf was bussing a nearby table, using her long orange beard to wipe down the tabletop, "the bluebottle 'er 'yer face."

"You don't think I'm trying to be a human, do you Bridgid?" Leeja asked, looking up from her dinner.

"'As someone been givin' you a hard time?"

Leeja only shrugged.

"Look, deary," Bridgid said, coming close and putting her small, meaty fists on Leeja's table to emphasize her point, "This is Th'myskôra. That means everyone here gets t' be friends with whomever they want. Everyone gets t' fuck whomever they want. Everyone gets t' do whatever work they want."

"But—"

"Do you really think," Bridgid interrupted her, "that I'd be allowed to run a tavern if I'd stayed in the Burrows at Alfotdrath?"

"No?" Leeja asked.

"No," Bridgid said with finality. "Back home, the men spend all day and night in the forges, crafting the finest axes in the Three Realms; and the women are only permitted t' battle and acquire treasure so that more axes can be forged." Bridgid's cheeks were going pink, "Work like this," she gestured around the tavern, "serving others, *helping others,* is forbidden. It's seen as frog work, unworthy of a dwarf. But do *you* think I'm any less a dwarf slinging ale than I was when I swung a battle axe?"

"No," said Leeja, more confidently now.

"Good. Now eat 'yer food and stop frowning up the joint. It's bad 'fer business."

"Two more ales, Bridgid?" It was Arlynn; Leeja had been so invested in Bridgid's speech that she hadn't even noticed her friends enter the tavern.

"My pleasure, girls," Bridgid said, winking at Leeja and sauntering back to the kitchens.

"Where have you *been* all day?" Arlynn asked as she and Imogen slid onto the wooden bench next to Leeja, "We waited for you in the apartment for hours."

"Well," Leeja started, gulping down some ale, "first I went on a tour of the island with Rakka the troll, then I was down at the dry docks fixing the Flannery with Aengus all morning, th—"

"Who is Aengus?" Imogen asked, "I thought you were working with Norrin."

"Aengus," Leeja continued, "is Norrin's father. The three of us have been working together on the ship. He's been teaching me a lot, and we were having a great time this morning, even though the work was hard."

Leeja stuffed a handful of man' o war into her mouth as if suddenly reminded of her biological need for food, "Finally, just in time for lunch, Norrin shows up, and before I get the chance to talk to him about any of the...unusual stuff from our date last night, Bowen comes trodding along sayin' they need me back at the fleet."

Leeja shoveled another man o' war into her mouth, "I never did get to eat lunch." She slugged down another mouthful of ale, "And before I knew what was happening, I was hurlin' crates with the Red Fleet for the next ten hours. The guys at work started asking me all these questions about Thorne, and Norrin, and the bet. The whole thing was very uncomfortable."

Leeja loaded in some more food and continued through a full mouth, "But it wasn't ten straight hours of work and inter-rogation. It was five hours and then a dinner break, which I decided to use to *try* to talk to Norrin about that weird thing that happened yesterday. But when I got there, Norrin didn't want to talk, he wanted to fuck."

Arlynn nodded approvingly while Imogen blinked, trying to keep up with Leeja's ever quickening pace.

"So we had sex instead. And *it* happened again. And *then* I had to go back to work for five more hours of dirty looks from Thorne and the other Titans. And I never even got to eat dinner! It's been a real three-hells-day."

"What *kinds* of questions were they asking about the bet?" asked Arlynn suspiciously.

"Oh, you know..." Leeja looked down at the table, she took her time answering now. She didn't want to hurt her friend's feelings, but they might as well know the truth, "Why do I care what a bunch of humans think of me? Am I too good for Titans...things like that."

"Oh no!" Imogen gasped, throwing an arm around Leeja's shoulders. "I'm sorry if we pushed you too far. It's just a stupid bet."

"You do know we don't think the human way is *better*, right?" Arlynn asked. "You just seemed unhappy, and we wanted you to try something new."

"You were right," Leeja admitted, smiling to herself. "I was really unhappy...for a really long time. I didn't realize just how unhappy until..." Leeja tugged at the end of her wild ponytail, hoping her friends didn't notice the green creeping up her neck and onto her cheeks.

Bridgid was back to drop off the ales, she gave Leeja an approving nod before returning to tidying the nearby tables.

"So," Imogen said, casting a conspiratorial glance around the table, "you like him, huh?

Leeja was sure she was blushing now; there was no hiding her excitement.

"Tell us about last night's date! We want to know everything!" demanded Arlynn. "Have you guys taken it to the 'next level' yet?" She wiggled her eyebrows at the end of her question.

"I think so?" said Leeja, she wasn't sure what all of the human levels of dating were. "Yesterday he told me a bit about his mom and his childhood; from what I can tell, he was a real brat."

"And you like that about him?" Imogen asked.

"I guess I do," said Leeja, blushing a more pronounced green. "It's more than that, though. When I'm around him, I feel like…I dunno," she closed her eyes and searched for the right words, "like anything is possible. Like I could really accomplish something."

"That's wonderful, Lee," said Arlynn, patting her on the arm, "but I meant the next level *sexually*?"

"Oh, Goddess," Leeja gulped as her face flushed green. With all the excitement of the day, she'd almost forgotten. "Last night," she whispered, leaning in, "something happened *down there* that's never happened before."

"Did you squirt?" Arlynn brayed, "Congratulations!"

"No," whispered Leeja, "and please keep your voice down. This is serious."

"Sorry, Leeja," said Imogen, "please go on." She shot Arlynn a warning look.

"It happened the first time last night by the lake and then again tonight at the Flannery. He was inside me, like any normal sex, but…when I started to cum, my pussy did a thing…"

"What kind of a thing?" Asked Imogen.

"It um..I, that is…my pussy…" Leeja struggled, "bit him?"

"You mean your vagina sprouted teeth and chomped on his dick???" Asked Arlynn.

"Essentially, yeah…"

"Has this ever happened before?" asked Imogen in a tone that made Leeja feel like a subject in one of her laboratory tests.

"Never."

"What did Norrin do?" Arlynn asked, biting her lip. She was hanging on Leeja's every word and digging her finger nails into the edge of the table.

"He yelped at first and tried to pull out, but it wouldn't let him go, so he just sort of...went with it."

"Is his penis...you know?" Arlynn dug her fingernails deeper into the wooden tabletop. Leeja was sure she'd leave a mark.

"It's fine. Eventually, after we both finished, the teeth retracted and he slid right out."

"So, he wasn't injured or frightened, and you guys are just *fine* still?" Asked Imogen.

"He was *a little* injured," Leeja admitted. "It left...teeth marks."

The girls squealed.

"And he, um...seemed very excited by them".

The girls shrieked with laughter.

"He said now that I marked his dick, I have to keep it."

"That is the single sexiest thing I've ever heard," said Arlynn looking off into the middle distance. "That dick belongs to you."

All three girls laughed, Leeja out of relief, "Thank the Goddess! I thought you guys would think I'm weird or gross or something."

"Weird?" Asked Arlynn, "I want you to teach me how you did it!"

"I don't think it works that way," said Leeja, smiling.

"She was teasing... I think," said Imogen.

"Oh," Leeja said, smiling. "Well, the problem now is...what do we do next? I mean...*after*. There's only one more date, and then it's all over."

"It doesn't *have* to be over," said Arlynn. "There are such things as long-term relationships, you know. Just look at Imogen and Keneth; they've been together for years, and it's going great!"

"Yes, great! Keneth is great, and we are great together," Imogen blurted out, nodding emphatically. "I mean… it certainly has been a very long time."

"I just don't know," Leeja said, pushing the last fried man o' war around in a puddle of thick, black sauce. "When I try to talk to him about the future, he always makes jokes."

"Typical man," Arlynn said, flipping her long, auburn hair. Leeja couldn't help noticing that she was still smiling, apparently enjoying the idea of owning *her* very own penis.

"I'm not much better," Leeja said, "The second I'm alone with him, my body takes over, and I become some kind of…sex monster. I can't keep my hands off him. Or my mouth. Or my crotch, for that matter."

"Is that why your libido has been on overdrive lately?" asked Imogen, her researcher persona back firmly in place. "Do you think your increased need for sex could have been in response to Norrin this whole time?"

"Yeah…maybe." Leeja had been trying to puzzle these changes out all week. "As long as I had sex once every five days or so, I've always been able to keep my head on straight." The girls nodded thoughtfully along. "But ever since I smelled Norrin that morning on the esplanade, it's like I can't get enough. I'd fuck him eight times a day if I could, maybe more. Hells, I'm swollen and dripping right now, just talking about him."

"Hot." said Arlynn.

"It's unimaginably hot, but what if that's all it is? What if I get all emotionally invested…*like you told me to*… and he ends up being the same kind of human …as you? No offense, of course."

"None taken." Arlynn was clearly proud of her many sexual exploits, "There's got to be some way to figure out what his intentions really are before you're in too deep." A silence fell over the table. Arlynn rolled her tongue back and forth across her top teeth, under her lip. Leeja knew this was her "thinking face." Imogen was staring down into her ale, and Leeja thought she saw a tear forming in the corner of her eye; she was about to ask about it when Arlynn piped up again, "I'm brilliant!"

"Congratulations," Leeja teased, rolling her eyes.

"No, listen. You *all* should go out on a double date!"

"Excuse me?" Imogen blurted out.

"The four of you—you and Keneth and Leeja and Norrin—it's perfect," Arlynn continued. "Think about it. Leeja still has to go on one more date with Norrin to prove she isn't a coward."

"Watch it, human," Leeja insisted quietly, fighting to keep her hands on the table and off her friend's throat.

"Then go on the date," Arlynn said, bringing her face dangerously close to Leeja's. "You can see what a good human relationship looks like up close. And it'll give Imogen a chance to size Norrin up. We've hardly spent any time with him, after all."

"I'm not sure this is a good idea," Imogen said.

"Of course it is." Arlynn had an exceptional talent for dismissing dissenting opinions when she was sure she was right. "You are a wonderful judge of character. You and Keneth can help Leeja find out how Norrin feels about her. And with dozens of witnesses around, she *should* be able to keep her teeth to herself."

Imogen still looked unconvinced.

"Look," Arlynn continued, "If you don't go, she'll probably just end things after the third date. Your good friend could spend the rest of her life wondering if she missed out on her one true, magical, special love."

"You don't believe in true love." Imogen rolled her eyes.

"But *you* do," Arlynn taunted back, "and Leeja *might*." Both humans turned their attention to Leeja, their eyes practically demanding an answer.

"I...um...I don't know." Leeja had never thought about it before. She wasn't even sure what 'true love' was. It certainly isn't a well-known concept back in Søgsund. Back home, in the horde, her mother never had fewer than a dozen mates. Were they all her true love? Clearly her father hadn't been, or it wouldn't have been so easy for him to leave. Would Norrin be like that? Make her pregnant and leave her alone to handle the mess?

"Well, I'd say it's time you figured out how you feel about it. "Arlynn said in that tone that said everything had already been decided, "Wouldn't you?"

"I don't know, this seems like...a big responsibility." If Imogen's eyebrows knitted any more tightly, they'd touch.

"If you're there, you can observe her...*condition* and get loads of data about the orc mating process," Arlynn goaded.

"I'll do it," Leeja said, ending the debate.

"Are you sure?" Imogen asked.

"I need to know if he's serious about me."

"Perfect!" Arlynn squealed, "Evening low tide at the Spiced Goat, day after tomorrow. I'll set everything up. Just stay away from Lover Boy until then."

Leeja groaned, "But I'm so horny, and he's *so* good at sex."

"You can suck it up for a couple days," Arlynn said dismissively. "Think of it as an investment in your future."

The three of them started to make their way outside. Leeja watched her friends scamper out onto the street. Imogen was excitedly deliberating what color gowns she and Leeja would wear on their date. Arlynn was very loudly composing a list of negative behaviors and attributes to be on the look out for. And Leeja quietly savored the scene. After so many years of trying and failing to mate, of never feeling like she had a place, things were finally starting to work out for her.

On Th'myskôra, Leeja had found two friends, desperately

committed to her happiness, and now she was bonding to a male who seemed very excited about the process.

If things go well on the double date, I'm going to stay on Th'myskôra and serve an apprenticeship with Rakka and make my horde. It might be a small, unusual horde...but I'm a small unusual orc.

Leeja pressed her palm against the Grim's heavy wooden door, but before she could join her friends out on the cobblestone, Bridgid grabbed her firmly by the wrist. The old dwarf palmed her a folded piece of parchment and whispered sternly in her ear,

"Meet me a' this address tomorrow night after the tide comes in. Come alone."

EIGHTEEN

It was a beautiful morning. The sun was shining, the birds were singing, the lizards were scurrying. Since Leeja had to go back to work for Bowen, Norrin didn't see much point hanging around the Flannery today. He decided to get up bright and early to accompany his mother to the shops.

"So, I was hoping you could pull some strings with the allocations committee, Ma. Maybe help push through my land use application?" Norrin looked up from his hands and saw the top of his mother's head. Glema, who was seated across from him at a little round table in the cozy, vine-encircled courtyard, was busy fussing with her ledger. She was checking and rechecking her shopping list and paying attention to little else. "You're still treating me like a child."

"Mmmhmm," Glema muttered, without looking up.

"I mean it, Ma, I'm really serious about this relationship. I think she's *the one.*"

"Thank you, d'Iehb," Glema said as the little blue grung slid two earthenware bowls onto the table. "I've got my big, handsome son with me today!"

d'Iehb inclined his head and made a little ribbit before hopping across the patio and back into the restaurant.

"Really, Ma???" Norrin asked, gesturing to the breakfast his mother had ordered for him.

"What?" Glema asked, "That's your favorite! You always get a Happy Creme Bastarde on Mamma's Helper Day."

Grinning up at Norrin from his bowl of thick custard was a face fashioned out of boiled blackberries and thin slices of candied June Pears.

"Have you been listening to me at all?" Norrin asked, pushing the bowl away. "I'm trying to have a serious conversation with you."

"Norrin, darling," his mother said, patting the back of his hand. "You're absolutely right. I've been preoccupied with my list. Now, please tell me what's on your mind."

Norrin took a deep breath, looked his mother square in the eye, and opened his mouth to speak.

"You have my complete attention, honey." Glema said, "Whenever you're ready..."

"Ma," Norrin sighed, "I have been trying to talk to you about Leeja..."

"Yes, the *mysterious* Leeja," Glema said, pouring Norrin some tea. "The one your father has spent so much time with, who I haven't even gotten to meet yet!"

Norrin buried his face in his hands as his mother continued.

"There was a time when you brought all your little friends to meet me right away, but I guess you're too grown up for that now..."

"Leeja isn't just one of my 'little friends,' Ma; she's special. But you can't just...make a proposition to a woman like that without something to offer her. Something material. That's why I came out with you today."

"Look who it is!" Glema shouted to someone over Norrin's head, "Thorne! Thorne, honey, come over here!"

Norrin swiveled around in his seat to see the burly cyclops striding across the street to meet her with his arms outstretched and a shit-eating grin plastered across his face.

"Ma!" Thorne boomed as he wrapped Glema up in a tight hug.

"It's wonderful to see you, Thorne!" Glema said, stepping back to get a good look at him, "My, how you've grown into such a handsome young man."

"Well, you look as lovely as the day we first met!"

"When you joined my children's swimming class? You couldn't have been any older than eight."

"A child of very discerning tastes," Thorne blinked his one huge eye at her and kissed the back of Glema's hand.

Glema blushed and giggled, "I have missed having you around the house. You two boys used to be so close. What happened?"

Norrin practically leaped up from his seat to stop Thorne from answering.

"I'm sure Thorne is very busy, Ma. We shouldn't keep him any longer."

"That's right," Thorne said, smiling even more broadly at Norrin.

He could tell her everything. Hells, Thorne could probably even make some stuff up, and Ma would believe him.

"I'm making some deliveries for Bowen. I'd better get back to it."

"Bowen the fawn?" Glema asked, gripping his forearm, eyes

wide, "So you must know this Leeja person; tell me, what's she like?"

"She's an orc, a Titan. She's strong, and beautiful, and determined."

"Well, that *does* sound like Norrin's type," said Glema.

"She's a little confused right now. Her father was a human, and moving to Th'myskôra has stirred up some...*curiosities* in her. She's got to do some more living...make some mistakes." Thorne looked right at Norrin for that last part. "I'm sure she'll make the right decisions in the end. After all, there are only so many places for a Titan to fit in here on our little island."

The two men stared into each other's eyes. Norrin could have ripped Thorne's head clean off that thick neck. If only his mother hadn't been standing there, he really would have given that one-eyed worm a piece of his mind.

"Personal growth and soul searching?" Glema asked, breaking the tension. "Maybe she's not the girl for you after all..."

Glema and Thorne both had a harty laugh at Norrin's expense. He could feel the heat crawling up his neck.

"I have it on outstanding authority," said Thorne, leaning in close to Glema's ear, "that the only reason she's seeing him is to win a bet. And *he* is only going along with it to spite an old lover."

"Now *that* sounds like our Norrin!" Glema proclaimed, and they laughed again while Norrin slammed back down onto his chair and began angrily shoveling heaping scoops of Happy Creme Bastarde into his mouth.

A rare summer storm was whipping the winds around the island into a frenzy. Trees shook violently, their branches creaking and threatening to snap. The lizards and bugs were all burrowed deeply in the earth. None of the regular night creatures were pawing at rubbish bins or creeping behind wagon wheels.

Leeja's hair had freed itself from its low ponytail and was whipping around violently, smacking her repeatedly in the face. It was a moonless night, and the wind had blown out most of the oil lamps. Still, Leeja trudged on toward the address from Brigid's note.

Finally, she reached Sagfair Street and turned right.

"Three hundred ninety-two, three hundred ninety-four, three hundred ninety-six!" Beyond that, there was not a house, only an overgrown garden and a narrow, dilapidated stone staircase stretching up the side of a steep hill and disappearing from view into the gloom of the night.

"Of course," Leeja grumbled as she began her ascent.

The wet stone stairs seemed completely vertical, and they shifted and crumbled slightly under each of Leeja's steps. The higher she climbed, though, the stranger the plants in the garden seemed to become. Spiky, twisted brambles jutted out across the path. Long vines with undulating flowers glowed silver in the darkness, lighting her way. A massive tree with shining daffodil-colored bark rained down a fresh spray of dense, glittering, magenta spheroids with every new gust of wind.

Finally, Leeja could see a little cottage perched on the hill above her. She was almost at the top.

"Step inta' the light so we can get a good look at you, deary," called a familiar, husky voice from deep inside the house.

Leeja ducked her head under the transom. She turned at the waist so her left shoulder passed through the vestibule before her right. Blinking in the bright light from a fireplace, Leeja unfolded herself in a cozy salon. Old women of various species sat in over-large wooden and leather chairs in a circle around the room.

A troll was seated closest to the entryway, a cyclops beside her, and then two goblins. Bridgid, the dwarf, was sitting on a long bench, holding hands with a dragonborn. Next to them, closest to the fire, was an imposing orc.

She must be ancient to have grown so large.

Her massive tusks curved up and out from her jaw, nearly scraping her forehead. Leeja stood staring at her. She was the largest female of all those assembled— even larger than the dragonborn Bridgid was canoodling with.

All this time, I thought I was the only orc on the island. Why didn't I smell her? Why hasn't she torn my head off? How have I lived on this island so long and never bumped into her?

"Come in and meet the crones, Leeja," Bridgid said.

Crones? That explains it; she must be out of the mating ages.

"Hello, umm...I'm Leeja?" Leeja said, settling into an empty wooden chair near the fireplace.

A low chuckle rumbled around the room.

"But I'm guessing you already know that," she continued, ringing her tunic out onto the polished stone floor. All the old women smiled and nodded at her...all except the great grey orc.

"You gonna tell me why I'm here, Bridgid?"

"You've made her sssweat enough, don't you think, darling?" The dragonborn hissed into Bridgid's ear.

The crones giggled again, except for the orc, whose grave expression remained unchanged.

"We've lived on this island a long time, Leeja," said Bridgid, motioning around the room. "Drixelorgen," Bridgid placed her tiny hand gently on the dragonborn's massive thigh, "has been here since before The Peace."

"Sssince the island was under the rule of elvesss," Drixelorgen said, picking up seamlessly where Bridgid left off. "In those days, it wasn't sssafe for d-...for anyone of mixed parentage, really... that's why I built this house here. Hidden high on this hill, deep in the brush. I was alone here for almost a century, but over the decades, governments and minds start to change." Drixelorgen placed her large, scaly hand on top of Bridgid's. "Eventually, different kinds of people sstarted coming to the island. And then one day, I met Bridgid. Sshe started living here in ssecret with me. We knew we wanted to live in a different world. A world where people like uss wouldn't have to hide anymore."

"Over the years," Bridgid continued, "we met more like-minded women. We started meeting here every month under the new moon. We used to joke that we were the council of old crones, but I suppose it's a pretty accurate description these days."

The crones giggled again.

"When my sister and I first got here," said one of the goblins, "we were terrified of being captured by elves. Every meeting was about safety. We were barely surviving in those days."

"But since The Peace," said the other goblin, "we get to meet and talk about happy things. To plan how we can shape the culture here, in this place. How we can make things better for our children and those who will come after them."

"But," the old orc grumbled from her chair. Her powerful voice demanded attention. It shook dust loose from the ceiling beams. "We must never get so optimistic that we forget the perils of the past."

All eyes were on the orc now. The air in the room had gone still and thin.

"This new peace is not guaranteed to last, and if the old dangers and pain should return, we need to be prepared. We must protect our own."

"So..." Leeja was now very aware of the thirteen eyes boring into her, "That's why I'm here? Am I in some danger?"

"A danger of a sort, yes," said Bridgid.

"Is war coming back to Th'myskôra?" Leeja was on high alert, ready to protect her friends.

Arlynn might not be so bad in a fight. But Imogen is too sweet even to protect herself, she'd be hopeless. And what about Norrin and his parents? These are sensitive people...artists...not warriors.

"Should we evacuate?" Leeja was addressing Bridgid directly. There was danger coming to the island and this dwarf was being intentionally cagey. Every second she didn't have answers, Leeja was angrier. More ready to attack.

"Quiet yourself, daughter," boomed the orc, "All will be explained."

"This is a personal danger...and it's only to you."

"Out with it, dwarf!" Leeja growled.

"Well," said Bridgid gently, "It's that human boy you've been seein'..."

"But *you* encouraged me to keep dating him!" Leeja was instantly and irrationally furious; her breath caught in her throat. "You practically talked me into it last night at the Grim!"

"I know, deary," Bridgid said, "but that was 'afore...ach... Jaania, you better explain."

The ancient orc rocked around in her seat opposite Leeja. Struggling under her own incredible weight, she propped herself up on one elbow so that she towered above all others assembled. Leeja gazed up into her hard eyes.

Just like Mother's. This isn't going to go well.

When the old orc opened her mouth to speak, a terrible rumbling sound filled the cottage. Like the crashing of an angry sea, punctuated by the occasional screech of contorted, splintering lumber.

"One of the chief functions of the Council of Crones is to protect future generations. When Brigid told me a young orc had moved to the island, I asked her to keep an ear out for certain... *warning signs* and to bring you here if you ever displayed any."

The crones all shuttered and tsked at the words "warning signs."

"Yeah, well, Bridgid knew about me and Norrin the whole time, and she never dragged me up here before. What changed between when you brought the girls their drinks and when we walked out of the tavern?"

Bridgid shook her head sheepishly, deferring to Jaania.

She's never held her tongue with me before. What is going on?

Suddenly, realization donned on Leeja.

"The teeth."

"The *dantų*" Jaania said. The fire cracked and leaped up, licking the front of the hearth as if to accentuate the danger.

"There are," Jaania began, "some perils inherent to inter-species...*couplings.* I would have warned you sooner, but I thought, with your being a halfbreed, that you might escape them."

"So you're telling me the teeth are normal?" Leeja was cheering up. "All orcs have them? That's great news! I was worried I'd contracted some kind of exotic virus."

"Don't rejoice too quickly," said one of the goblins, wrapping a comforting arm around her sister.

"The appearance of the *dantų*," Jaania continued, "Is normally cause for great celebration. They are triggered when an orc couples with a chemically compatible male. When two orcs are fully bonded, the male is marked. Each set of *dantų* is unique, if the bonding process is successful his penis will be known to all others as your property."

"That's good, isn't it?" Leeja interrupted, "Norrin and I like each other a lot. Knowing that we're chemically compatible is... comforting, I guess."

Jaania sighed, and all the other crones clicked their tongues, "It *would* be good if you were coupling with an orc or another Titan, maybe even an imp...but *humans* are different."

"I know Norrin's different," Leeja said, closing her arms around her chest, "I'm different too; you called me a halfbreed not two minutes ago."

"If you have the *dantų*, then you're more orc than you real-ize, and you had better heed my warning, girl!" Jaania was breathing heavily now, and the green of her skin was deepening.

"Girl? I'm thirty-five," Leeja muttered.

She's beginning to remind me of Mother.

"Precisely the age at which you should be assembling your horde," Jaania snapped.

"But I don't want a horde! Isn't that what you've all been going on and on about?" Leeja asked, turning back to Bridgid with pleading eyes. "That's the whole point of old lady club! You do what you want and look out for each other, right? So why are you prescribing something different for *me*?"

"It doesn't matter what you *want*," said Jaania with an air of finality that subdued the room. "The dantų have chosen for you. If you continue to bed this human, you will be mated to him. For life."

"I don't understand…"

"Every time an orc adds a male to her horde, she is bonded to him for life," Jaania explained. "She will take his needs as her own. His joy is her joy. His accomplishments lift her up. His failures, his pain, are visited tenfold upon her. It is true with every male in her horde. Once a female has bonded, she must be in communion with her male. If he is taken from her, the pain of their physical distance is excruciating."

"I had no idea the bond was so intense," Leeja was wide-eyed and gobsmacked. "Mother never spoke of it…I always thought she just really liked sex."

"The burden of mating is incredible," said the old orc. "The heights of pleasure and depths of desperation cannot be comprehended by those who have not experienced it."

"So…" Leeja started timidly, "when my father left her?"

"Your mother's soul was fractured. A piece of her was ripped out and stolen away. She bares a wound that can never heal. No matter how many lovers she takes, no matter what joy she receives from her remaining horde, there will always be a raw, infected hole in the center of herself."

"If she hadn't had the rest of her horde to look after," the old cyclops added, "the pain of separation probably would have killed her."

Leeja shivered as the words rippled through her body, the hairs on her arms prickled and stood on end. "Is it the same for all Titans?" She looked around the room at the somber faces of her elders.

"Every sspecies of Titan has its own version of bonding," said Drixelorgen, "Ssome bonds *can* be amended."

"But humans don't experience a bonding of any kind," said the larger goblin, her sister looking as if she might cry. "For them, mating is always a decision...a whim. Human mating is often intense but always temporary."

"Serial monogamy, they call it," added the cyclops.

"When we mate with each new partner," said Jaania, staring a warning into Leeja's eyes, "we mate for life. When an orc takes a male, he is her responsibility forever. Humans take one mate at a time, lavish them with affection for a few months or years, grow bored, and then depart to find a new temporary mate."

The younger goblin cried out softly at these words.

"Even if a human were somehow to remain a faithful partner," said the cyclops wistfully, "they live such short, fragile lives. Your human will die many decades before you fall, and you will be left here utterly alone. Begging the goddess to take you and end your suffering."

"They don't do it to be cruel, deary," said Bridgid. "It's simply their nature. They cannuh' help themselves. Humans cannuh' love us the way we love them."

"You must not see this human again," said Jaania. "Leave

the island at once, before the bond is complete. It's your only chance to avoid a lifetime of pain."

NINETEEN

L eeja looked down at her own defined pectoral muscles, well-built shoulders, and sharp clavicle peeking out of her new lapis lazuli colored gown.

What am I doing in this restaurant? Why am I still on this island?

When Jagluk, the tailor, had first presented her with it, the low wide V of the portrait neckline made her feel extraordinarily curvaceous and feminine. She couldn't wait to see the look on Norrin's face when he first saw her in it.

It would have been a crime to skip town and let all of Jagluk's hard work go to waste.

Now, she was seated across the table from Imogen in *her* new gown: icy blue with a sweet horseshoe neckline. She was radiant, nothing improved Imogen's mood like having new gowns made.

It would have been cruel to leave Imogen alone. We already agreed to wear our matching blue gowns tonight. An orc always keeps her promise.

Imogen's inviting, wiry, golden curls were plated in a crown around her head, except for a few tightly wound, expertly placed ringlets around her face. Leeja's wild green hair was parted in the center of her head and gathered in a complex mass of braids and twists at the base of her neck. They both had several dozen pearls placed painstakingly in their up-dos by Arlynn earlier that day.

It was worth the risk of staying, to get to spend the day with my friends. And who knows, maybe Norrin isn't as dangerous as those crones think.

Seated to Leeja's right at the elegant, round table was Norrin. She hadn't seen (or smelled) him in days, and having him so close to her now was intoxicating. She breathed deeply and filled her lungs with him. All the usual smells were there: brine, musk, and the unmistakable smell of human male. But tonight, there was something else, a subtle, fresh scent like the breeze after a spring rain.

Norrin must have paid a visit to the apothecary and gotten himself some elvish perfume.

Norrin looked extremely put together this evening. He was wearing a well-tailored, golden brocade tunic with elaborate sleeves. The tunic ended in a row of neat, meticulously implemented pleats just below his plump ass. Under that was a pair of skin-tight green woolen hose that left little to the imagination. Leeja could feel the dantu stirring in her core.

I've never seen Norrin so dressed up before. He really put a lot of effort into this date, maybe it's as important to him as it is to me. At the very least, he wants to make a good impression with Imogen… that's got to count for something.

Leeja forced her eyes shut.

If I keep looking at him, I will mount him right here in this restaurant!

She turned her head so that when she opened her eyes, she'd be forced to look at Imogen's boyfriend, Keneth. And what a sight he was! Stringy black hair, greasy skin, and a patchy, uneven goatee…if you could even call it that. He wore a stained, oversized linen tunic over a pair of old brown linen britches. And he smelled sour, like something about to die….and liquor. Leeja's nose wrinkled, she tried to focus on the smell of roasting goat wafting out from the kitchen. But Keneth kept demanding her attention.

Perhaps it's only customary for humans in new relationships to attend to their appearances. But why then would Imogen put so much effort into her appearance? She's been with Keneth as long as he's been with her. Perhaps it's a matter of personal preference and Norrin will continue to look and smell appealing after we are bonded.

Leeja looked around the elegant, dimly-lit dining room. Most of the human women were dressed in a fashion similar to Imogen and herself. The human men varied a little more in their appearance, although none were quite so dressed down as Keneth. And none of them burned the insides of her nostrils as sharply either.

Perhaps finery is a marker of human status. In any case, Imogen wouldn't have stayed with Keneth all these years for no reason. I've got to figure out what is so special about their relationship.

"Let's have another pitcher of wine for the table, sweetheart!" Keneth bellowed, slapping a passing barmaid on the ass.

She rounded on him, opening her mouth to speak. But when Imogen flashed her an apologetic, wide-eyed, pleading look, the server returned to the kitchen without further comment.

"This is the first time I've ever been to the Spiced Goat," Imogen said, turning back to the group with an exaggerated cheeriness in her voice, "What about you, Norrin?"

"I came a few times when they first opened," Norrin hadn't said anything in several minutes. The soothing, baritone rumble of his voice sent prickles of excitement up and down Leeja's spine, "it is the only fancy restaurant on the island, after all." Norrin flashed Leeja a knowing smile, "This is the first time I've been here since the remodel, though. The ceiling wasn't so...pretty the last time I was here."

"That's called beaming!" Leeja was so excited to talk about architecture that she almost forgot how horny she was. "I talked to the owner the last time I was here. The beams were part of the original design, but a couple of years ago, a painter came in from Diocleatianopolis! He painted the beams in those contrasting colors and added flourishes and gilding. It really brings out the detail in the woodwork, don't you think?"

Norrin leaned excitedly toward Leeja as if he meant to answer, but Keneth inserted himself loudly into the conversation,

"Speaking of gilding, Norrin," he said, shoving a considerable chunk of bread into his mouth, "Gold. Bullion. It's the future." Bits of wet bread shot out of his mouth in all directions as he spoke. "And I can get it for you. I've got a guy back in Brilansis who's got a buddy who's about to open a mine. In a few months, we're all going to be rolling in it."

"Aside from a few obscure spells and for certain aesthetic projects, gold is largely useless here on Th'myskôra," Imogen said, her face still flushed from the encounter with the waitress.

"Give us a minute here, would ya', sweetheart?" Keneth said, plastering the side of Imogen's face with flecks of bread and spit, "This is man talk."

Norrin smiled, "And what, precisely, would you need from me? How do I get in?"

Leeja stared across the table at her friend. Imogen's normally cheery face was constrained as if there were something she was trying very hard not to say out loud.

"Just a few ships," Keneth said.

Norrin laughed into his wine, causing it to bubble up slightly onto his face.

"Is that all?"

"Four of your father's fastest should do it," Keneth laced his fingers behind his head and leaned back, pushing the finely engraved hardwood chair back onto just two legs.

Imogen, avoiding eye contact with both Leeja and Norrin, spoke again, "To get even *one* ship built, you'd have to submit a proposal to the allocations committee. Even if you got approval, you'd be placed on a *very* long waiting list. We've been over all of this before."

Keneth slammed his chair back down on all fours and turned in his seat. He was facing Imogen directly, "You never support me," he said between gritted teeth. "The real world isn't like your precious academy, with rules, and graphs, and facts or whatever. In the *real* world," Keneth pulled his face back up into a smile and turned to once again address Norrin, "You get what you can take."

"What do you say, Norrin," Keneth reached his dirty hand across the table, "Are you ready to take everything you want from this world."

"I'm still not sure how gold helps me accomplish that," Norrin said, fighting a smile.

Keneth rubbed both temples and closed his eyes. He spoke slowly, as if to a child. "Gold is shiny. People like it. When we have lots of gold, we can trade it for extra food, clothing, women, anything we want."

Extra women? So that is *the human goal, after all. The crones were right!*

"I'm tellin' ya, Norrin, this whole island is one huge unrealized opportunity. Once we introduce gold, it will be exactly like Brilansis, and men like us can own it all!"

"If Brilansis is so wonderful," Imogen asked, a hint of sarcasm sneaking into her voice, "then why did you come to live on Th'myskôra?"

"Because I was poor in Brilansis".

"Poor?" Leeja interrupted, "I'm sorry, I don't think I know this word."

"It's a human word," Imogen said curtly. "It means that you are denied access to some or all of the necessities of life, like food, housing, medicine, leisure time, meaningful work, and reproduction."

Leeja was shocked, "There is nothing like 'poor' on Titan. Who denies these things?"

"The rich," said Imogen bitterly. "People who take more than they need. They amass piles of food that rot in their stores. They steal magical objects that they can't even wield and hide them away where no one will ever see them or get any use out of them. They force the poor to perform dangerous and humiliating labor for many hours every day, and then they hand out table scraps. Just enough food to keep their workers alive."

"Why don't the poor just kill the rich and take what they need?" Leeja was truly confused; orcs would never stand for such conditions.

"Because," Keneth huffed and rolled his eyes, "the rich hire private forces. They recruit some dumb, strong men and give them the best weapons and a little money. If the poor ever try to steal or damage something that belongs to the rich, they kill them."

"I had no idea humans were so...barbaric."

"We're not," said Norrin, easing Leeja's fears with his familiar, gentle smile, "not anymore. Nowadays, most human city-states are very similar to Th'myskôra. Individuals work for the good of the community, and the community meets the needs of the individual. Brilansis is...a *special* situation."

"Brilansis is a stain," Imogen practically spat the words out. Leeja had never seen sweet Imogen so angry before. She watched her friend become increasingly agitated as the evening wore on.

"It wouldn't be like that," Keneth said, returning his attention to Norrin. "The problem with Brilansis is bad men are in charge. They just got too carnivorous. But Th'myskôra is a blank slate waiting for good men with vision to help its people realize their full potential."

"Hmmmm...yes, very interesting," Norrin said, taking another drink of his wine and flashing another smile at Leeja before returning his attention to Keneth.

Why is he saying cruel things and smiling at me? Does he think that I want to be a rich? Has he been cruel the whole time, and I didn't recognize it because I don't know human words? This is the man I'm ignoring the advice of the crones for? A man who agrees with Keneth?

"We could be those good men," Keneth was gulping down wine and slurring his speech, but somehow Norrin just kept smiling at him, hanging on his every word.

"The one thing Brilansis never had is a strong king," Keneth slammed his goblet down on the table and stood slowly, staring off into the middle distance.

"*I* could be that king! Here, I will rule jus'ly over the fine pipple of Th'myskôra. And *you!*" He bent down and slapped Norrin hard on the shoulder,

"You will be my most cherished advisor. You can be the minister of excellent ships!" Keneth was practically kneeling on top of Imogen now so he could 'whisper' into Norrin's ear,

"And don't forget...the minister of very nice boats gets to have as many women as he wants! Almost as many women as the king!"

Norrin guffawed into his goblet, sending droplets of wine up onto his face again. Imogen was blushing deep red; she tugged Keneth's arm until he finally returned to a seated position mumbling to himself.

Leeja could see that her friend was in pain. She knew enough about human socializing to know that a change of subject would be considered kind,

"Your new gown is really quite becoming, Imogen."

"Thank you," Imogen said, mustering a weak smile. "Jagluk has really outdone himself this time."

"On both counts," said Norrin, lifting Leeja's hand slowly to his lips.

Leeja blushed, and Imogen giggled.

Maybe Norrin's not so bad after all...

"We can't give Jagluk *all* the credit," said Leeja, "it was Imogen's suggestion that we have gowns made to match our birthstones."

"In that case, I must also extend my compliments to you." Norrin's gaze lingered on the plunging neckline of Leeja's gown before he lifted his glass to toast the ladies.

"Now, Imogen," he continued, raising an eyebrow, "Leeja

tells me you're doing some research into the mating habits of orcs?"

"N-not exactly," Imogen sputtered.

It's working! Everyone is ignoring Keneth, and the conversation has moved on to more pleasant topics. Imogen is even smiling again.

"My work is primarily focused on finding new practical applications for previously uncatalogued magical abilities."

"That sounds fascinating," Norrin said, taking another sip of wine.

He's so charming.

Imogen's face was returning to its customary color. Nothing improved her mood like getting to explain her research to someone new.

"Oh, it is! Until very recently, the Three Realms kept the secrets of their magics closely guarded. But since The Peace, practitioners are increasingly willing to share their knowledge." Imogen took a quick sip of wine. "My research partner is out in the field, and he sends back the most incredible data for me to analyze in the laboratory!"

"Research partner? More like...freak-search partner," Keneth groaned, rejoining the conversation. "That little shrimp has blue skin and a *tail*! But not a shrimp's tail! He's got a pointy devil tail! In the new Th'myskôra, there won't be any pointy tails allowed. Right, Norrin? As soon as we get all the gold, the only weirdo blue-skinned people will be the sexy sweethearts crawling all over us!"

Before anyone could respond, the barmaid arrived with a vast, steaming platter that nearly covered the entire table.

"Dining for four," she said, placing half a barbecued goat and several pounds of roasted vegetables before them. "Is there anything else I can get you?"

"I wouldn't mind another squeeze of that tight ass," Keneth

murmured, perhaps under the impression that he could not be heard.

"We'd like to use your washroom." Leeja stood up and grabbed Imogen's hand. Leading her in the direction indicated by the server. Before they left the dining room, her half-orc ears distinctly heard Keneth say, "So, what's it like...humpin' the beast? She grindin' your bone to make her bread, or what?"

Leeja also distinctly heard Norrin laugh.

"A GENTLEMAN NEVER KISSES AND TELLS," Norrin said with a wink, raising his glass.

Norrin saw red, but his charming, friendly demeanor never faltered. Charm had always been his weapon of choice.

Just get through this dinner, Norrin. In a couple of hours, Leeja will be in your bed, and you'll never have to see this idiot again.

"How about you and Imogen?" he asked. Norrin wasn't willing to spoil the evening by getting into a brawl, but that didn't mean he was going to listen to Keneth badmouth Leeja.

"She's alright," Keneth slurred between gulps of wine. "...finally started putting out again."

Norrin set his goblet carefully on the table.

Leeja likes me in this tunic. She practically purred when she saw me in it. I'm not about to spill wine all over it.

"It was so long since we banged, I thought for sure there'd be cobwebs on my dick when I pulled it out!"

"Wow, that is...really hard to listen to," Norrin gritted his teeth.

Does Imogen know he talks about her like this? If not, somebody's got to tell her, preferably somebody other than me.

"Haha! Yeah, man." Keneth was smiling like an idiot. "Imagine how hard it was to *live* through."

"You must have been in agony."

"Don't get me wrong, now," Keneth leaned back in his chair and hooked his thumbs under his arms. "There's always plenty of girls willing to pull up the slack. It's just so much more convenient when I don't have to go looking for it, ya' know?"

"Sure, sure..." Norrin nodded and smiled along.

How much deeper is this asshole going to dig this hole? He's got to know that I'm going to tell Leeja everything he says...

"Yeah, I never thought of myself as the commitment type, but there's really something to be said for getting a boner in the middle of the night, and getting it polished off right there and then in your own bed. In your own place..."

"*Your* place? I thought you and Imogen lived in academy housing..."

"Uh—wha?" Keneth stammered, finally it was his turn to blush, "Well, I guess *technically* we have the place because of Imogen's position, but every man is the king of his castle, right buddy?"

"Sure, sure." Norrin was still smiling pleasantly.

I can keep this up as long as you can, dipshit.

"And that brings me back to those ships!" Keneth shouted so loudly that several other patrons of the restaurant turned to look for the source of the commotion, "And our gold! By this time next year, you and me are gonna' be kings!" Keneth snatched up his goblet, saw that it was empty, and grabbed Imogen's. He held it out, toasting no one.

"Here's to unmitable genius. To becoming the masters of all

we see. To me not having to settle for one priggish girl just to have some place to live, and to you never having to climb that ugly green mountain again!"

Norrin was furious, hot rage boiled up inside of him. Instead of reaching across the table and squeezing the life from Keneth's throat, he laughed politely and took another sip of his wine.

Praise the gods Leeja didn't hear any of that.

"Boy, that Keneth sure is something," Norrin kept his voice down even though the couples had parted at the fork in the road.

"I can't believe what happened in there," Leeja said, shivering in the breeze, "Imogen has been with him for so long, I was sure..."

"*Too* long, if you ask me," Norrin draped his cloak over Leeja's shoulders.

"I wasn't aware there was a time limit on love."

"Love?" Norrin scoffed, "I'm not sure that's the right word for what we just witnessed. Keneth is a complete asshole. He's obviously just using Imogen until something better comes along. That girl's got to get some self-respect..."

"You happen to be talking about one of my very best

friends," Leeja said, stopping dead in her tracks, "I won't have you badmouthing her!"

"Lighten up, sweetheart," Norrin leaned in to kiss her, "this is not a matter of life and death."

Leeja recoiled at the word 'sweetheart'. "Are you going to start grabbing other girls' asses too? I thought it usually took humans a couple of years to lose interest."

"Some relationships are just not worth saving," Norrin shrugged. "She could do a lot better."

"So it's true," Leeja said, her voice getting louder with every trembling sentence, "humans just couple up with whomever, use them for a while, and then abandon the relationship when something better comes along. We saw one bad night, and you think they should both give up and move on. Everyone said humans were flippant about love, at least *now* you're being honest about it."

"Are you comparing *me* to Keneth?" Norrin's jovial demeanor finally faltered. "Please tell me you aren't comparing us to *that.*"

"Why shouldn't I?" Leeja barked, "You're going into business with him. It's only a matter of time before you're treating me the way he treats Imogen."

"Leeja, look at me." Norrin held her forearms firmly. "I would never, under any circumstance, treat you like that."

"Why not?" Leeja's eyes were puffy and red and pleading. Norrin knew what she wanted him to say.

"Because I...I'm not like him. I thought you understood, I was just having some fun in there."

"Oh, I understand you perfectly, Norrin," Leeja said pointing to her ears, "These aren't just for show, you know. I heard you both while Imogen and I were in the other room."

"You didn't hear what you thought you heard."

"Are you saying I *didn't* hear you laughing at all of his jokes!"

"Yes, I was laughing, but that's just what you have to do with guys like that. I didn't mean it."

"You *had* to laugh while he insulted me?" Leeja looked down at Norrin, angry tears threatened to spill down her face. She wrapped his cloak tightly around herself. "I don't know why I'm surprised, you're both..."

"Human?" Norrin felt his features harden. "I've had just about enough of this human bashing. I'm not Keneth... and I'm not your father!"

"How dare you?" Leeja wasn't yelling anymore. Her eyes were wide, her nostrils flared, and she spoke so quietly that Norrin had to strain to hear her.

That got her.

Leeja removed Norrin's cloak and extended a powerful, trembling arm for him to take it.

"No need for melodrama," he said, trying to push the cloak back to her, but Leeja was too strong. Her arm would not be bent. "Leeja, you're being unreasonable and spoiling the evening. Now, would you please just put the cloak back on so we can get home?"

"*We?*" Leeja asked, arm still outstretched, "*We* are not going anywhere. This was the third date. There is no more 'we'. I won my bet, and you got to take something away from Thorne." She shoved the cloak more insistently toward him. "We both got what we wanted."

"Leeja, don't talk like that; you're being ridiculous."

She didn't answer. Instead, Leeja released her grip, letting his cloak land with a wet thud on the muddy road, and walked away, leaving Norrin alone and confused in the night.

"LOUSY, DECEITFUL, OPPORTUNISTIC HUMAN," Leeja mumbled as she paced up and down the alley.

She'd been stomping around all night arguing with herself. She was meant to go home with Norrin after the date. She should be eating fruit tarts with his parents at their kitchen table right now. Instead, she was wandering the streets, sweaty and disheveled, still wearing last night's gown.

"I should go home and change."

Home! Home to Arlynn and her condescending smile. I wouldn't even be in this mess if it weren't for her.

"Why don't you try *real dating*? The kind with *feelings*?"

There's no home for me on Th'myskôra if I can't trust Norrin.

Leeja's core was crying out for him. Her body had expected to be mated last night and was bitterly disappointed. But Leeja's pain was so much worse than that. When she'd walked away from him last night, it felt like she'd reached down her own throat and pulled her guts out.

"How is it possible to miss a person this much?"

Leeja hoisted herself up onto a large barrel behind the pickle emporium. She drew her knees close to her chest and, exhausted, finally did what she'd needed to do all night: she cried.

As the tears and snot poured out of her head, some clarity sneaked back in.

"Maybe I *have* been too hard on him. After all, Norrin wasn't actually making the lewd comments last night. And it isn't his fault I've started bonding with him. He doesn't even know what the dantụ mean."

How could he? He's only ever dated humans before.

Leeja took a steadying breath and hopped down off the barrel.

Maybe I will go home and wash up. I'll wash up and get something to eat, then I can go talk to Norrin. I'll give him one last chance.

"And if it doesn't work out, I can catch a ferry ride back to Søgsund. I'll fuck every orc in sight until the dantụ choose someone else to bond to."

Who am I kidding? I can't go back to Søgsund, I'll be killed.

"I'll figure all that out when the time comes. Right now I don't even know if I have to leave. And I won't know until I get to the bottom of Norrin's intentions."

Leeja took a deep breath, and strode down the alley, her purpose renewed.

It's amazing what a little crying will do for your mental state.

Before she could turn onto the street, however, she was struck by a familiar voice.

"Well, that makes another successful safari for Norrin the big game hunter!" It was Thorne, entertaining what sounded like a rather sizable group of 'concerned' creatures. Leeja crept closer. She wanted to see their faces,

What in three hells is a big game hunter?

"We all knew he wouldn't stay happy with pixies and tieflings forever," said a raspy male voice Leeja didn't recognize. A chorus of grunted consensus and stamping hooves rose up in response.

"Now that he's bagged the half-orc, whaddaya reckon he'll move onto next?" asked another strange voice. "An ogress?"

"Perhaps a dragonborn. Or a *cyclops*?" asked Martel the griffin. Leeja could practically hear him sneering.

"He's already had a cyclops," said Thorne, "He'll want to move onto some new 'adventure' when he's done with this one. Maybe a griffin?" There was a rustle of feathers and a disgruntled hiss in response.

Leeja stepped out from the alley, "I'd like to have a word with Thorne alone if you gentlemen wouldn't mind."

The other creatures exchanged guilty looks. Some doffed their caps and mumbled apologies as they scurried off, leaving Thorne to face Leeja alone.

"Good morning, Leeja," said Thorne bitterly, "you look... used."

"*This* is how you spend your free time?" Leeja said, snarling and bearing her tusks. "Gossiping about innocent people?"

Thorne threw his head back, roaring with unamused laughter, "Innocent? Norrin?" He laughed again and fixed his over-large blue eye on Leeja. Then, sneering, he added, "The Klesukroq Casanova strikes again."

"Stop talking about him like that!" Leeja was enraged, angrier than she'd been on the street with Norrin last night, even angrier than at dinner with Keneth. Something precious was being threatened, and a biological need to protect it crawled up her throat.

"I tried to warn you before, girly. It's not my fault you didn't listen." Thorne was mocking her. Leeja was sure of it. "Your little human is notorious on this island for lovin' and leavin' every monster he can get those nimble hands on."

"Stop lying!" Leeja spat. "He's only ever been with humans before, he told me himself."

"I'm not the one who's been lying." Thorne clicked his tongue and shook his head slowly in a display of pretend disappointment. "...that's a new low, even for *him*."

Leeja let out an ear-splitting growl, and Thorne dropped his artificial smile. He sank down into his stance and raised his claws for a fight.

Leeja lost control of herself. The ringing in her ears and red haze over her vision demanded action.

She lunged at Thorne, ready to bite through his throat.

He caught her before she could strike him and held her tightly to his chest. Leeja squirmed and thrashed in Thorne's arms but couldn't break free.

"If this gown weren't so tight," she growled, "you wouldn't stand a chance. You'd be dead where you stand!"

"Calm down, girly," he said gently in her ear. "We're friends, remember? It's your old buddy Thorne."

Leeja bucked and thrashed against the cyclops' bare, sculpted chest for at least another minute before regaining some of her senses.

You're not going to beat him, not today, so get ahold of your breathing and find out what this cheese-eating turd-pile is on about.

Finally, Leeja's heart rate slowed, and she stopped struggling in Thorne's arms. He released her, and Leeja staggered forward a few steps. She turned to face him, trying desperately to regain control of herself. As her vision returned to normal, Leeja noticed Thorne sniffing the air.

Is he scenting me?

"I'm so sorry. Leeja, I didn't know." There was nothing in Thorne's eye now but pity. He sat down heavily on the wooden stoop of the pickle emporium, and Leeja joined him, exhausted.

"What do you smell?" she asked, terrified of the answer.

"A mated orc," Thorne said bluntly.

Leeja buried her face in her hands. "I thought I had more time," she croaked. "Okay, so maybe he lied about sleeping with non-humans before, but you were exaggerating, right? It might not be *that* bad."

"It isn't just sleeping around," Thorne said, "I've known Norrin a long time, and he's a lot of fun...at first. But he doesn't understand that his actions have consequences. He can't handle the responsibility of being mated." Thorne took a deep breath and closed his eye, "He's just not a very serious person."

"But you can't *know* that," Leeja said, desperately trying to convince herself. It's not like anyone has ever mated to him before..."

Thorne shifted in his seat, gazing off into the distance as if he were watching a scene play out in front of him.

"What is it, Thorne? What aren't you telling me?"

He sighed and turned to her, "Norrin and I were kids together. We practically grew up at each other's houses."

Whenever Thorne came up in conversation, Norrin brushed him off with a joke, sometimes a bitter joke. Leeja had assumed they'd had a long-standing rivalry; she never would have guessed they'd been friends.

"Well, when we got a little older, our friendship got a little closer...a lot closer, actually."

"I don't..."

"We were each other's...*firsts*."

"First, what?" Leeja asked, panic once again rising in her.

Thorne took a steadying breath, "First love, first lover, first..."

"Mate?" Leeja asked.

Thorne nodded.

He lied. Not only am I not his first non-human, I'm not even his first Titan.

"We were young, too young to know what we were doing. We were eighteen and twenty. We'd both fooled around with people before, but nothing like that. It was an incredible summer. We spent every moment together. We were already close, but one night, we were up in his bedroom, and he kissed me. Everything changed after that."

Thorne smiled despite himself. Leeja's head was swimming. She was dizzy and disoriented.

Goddess, please let this be a joke.

"We spent every day together that summer. We hunted and wrestled and made love under the stars. We'd paddle out to Swi'loor and make believe the pixies were after us; we chased each other until one caught the other and we came crashing down into each other's arms."

Why would he take me there? To their *special place?*

"I think I'm going to be sick," Leeja said bracing herself against the stoop.

"We swam behind the waterfall and confessed our love to each other. And that was when I decided to bond myself to him."

Leeja was confused, bewildered. She shook her head wordlessly at Thorne.

"Mating is a little different for cyclopses; we have to opt into the bond, but once we do, it is...*challenging* to break."

"So, what happened?"

"The summer ended," Thorne said, sitting up straight and filling up his chest. He leaned his head back, and looked very nonchalant, but the tremor in his voice was unmistakable. It was the same tremor Leeja felt when she thought about leaving Norrin.

"He started an apprenticeship with his father. I was working for a fishing outfit, and we saw less and less of each other as the months wore on. Of course, I spent every second I could with him, but he started to make less of an effort to see me. Our lovemaking was brief and impersonal. We'd be walking down the esplanade hand in hand, and Norrin would drop mine when a pretty female walked by."

Leeja cringed, thinking of how Norrin had first approached *her* on the esplanade.

How often does he pick up women there?

"Eventually," Thorne continued, "I flat out asked him, 'Do you still love me?' What do you think he said?"

Leeja shook her head again; she could feel tears welling up behind her eyes.

"He laughed at me. That son of a bitch laughed." Thorne's voice was brittle now, "I'll always remember those words, 'Don't take everything so seriously. We're just having fun.'"

"So," Leeja stammered, "you're *still* mated to him?"

"Thank the goddess, no," Thorne's shoulders relaxed a little, and he turned to face Leeja again. There is a ceremony a cyclops can undergo that will break the bond. It is excruciating and must be completed in the old caves on Saetabis. I spent a whole year waiting for Norrin to return to me, wishing things would go back to how they were, but after another summer passed...I finally told my parents what I'd done."

Thorne's eye was red, one colossal tear rolled down his chiseled face. "Look, Leeja," he said, taking her hands between his, "I don't know exactly how mating works with orcs, but if your bond to Norrin isn't complete yet, if there's any way you can escape this human, do it now."

Norrin stomped down the stairs and through the kitchen.

"Ready for some lunch, little man?" his mother asked. "And

where's your friend Leeja? We didn't hear you two come in last night."

"Not now, Ma," Norrin said without stopping. He was headed straight into town.

Glema leaned over to ask Aengus, in not-so-quite a whisper, "You don't think they've broken up already?"

"That would be a new record," Aengus chuckled.

"I'll show *you* a new record," Norrin muttered as the kitchen door slammed shut behind him.

He marched quickly down the hill, his feet nearly getting away from him, "Call *me* a human, will she?!"

Norrin stalked past the workshop, "Toss *my* best cloak in the mud!?"

He stormed up the esplanade, ignoring the boaters and sunbathers, some of whom called out greetings to him, "There's no 'we' anymore," he huffed, "Why? Just because *she* said so?"

Norrin was so angry his vision was starting to blur; even still, he could see the Drowned Grimoire up ahead,

"If that stubborn, short-sighted orc thinks she can make me fall in—into *feeling* feelings with her and then toss me aside, she's got another thing coming."

Norrin threw open the heavy wooden doors and charged up to Leeja's favorite table, where he saw Imogen, Arlynn, Bridgid, and...*Thorne* all assembled and looking sour.

"Fantastic," he snarled, "the committee's all here."

Imogen sniffled and dabbed her nose with her sleeve, Thorne rolled his eye, and Bridgid pressed her round, meaty fists deeper into her hips, staring daggers at Norrin.

"Well?" Norrin demanded, "Isn't anyone going to tell me where she is?"

"She's gone!" Arlynn wailed, unable to restrain the torrent of tears any longer. "She left town forever, and it's all my fault — me and my stupid bet. If I'd known, I never would have..."

Imogen wrapped her arms around her friend, "There's no way you could have; you were trying to help. Leeja knows that; she doesn't blame you."

"Donnah' blame yerself, deary. Even the crones weren't sure Leeja had the dantu," said Bridgid, patting Arlynn's shoulder. "Even if we did, there's no guarantee this disaster could have been avoided. The orc matin' urge is nearly impossible t' overcome."

"Um, *hello*?" Norrin interrupted. "Is anybody gonna catch me up? The last thing that happened was my girlfriend and I got into a little fight, and now you're all acting like it's the end of the world or something."

"A little fight, he says," Thorne was sneering, as usual. "We can always count on Norrin to miss the plot."

"You stay out of this," Norrin raised his voice and rounded on Thorne. He was angry and confused; getting a few good punches in on Thorne's big, stupid head might just make him feel better.

"Oh, put 'yer dukes down, boys," Bridgid said, stepping between them. Thorne flashed a bratty smile at Norrin, and Bridgid led him to a seat. "'E needs to know what's going on if only to spare the next orc he stumbles upon."

"There's not going to be a 'next orc.' I'm with Leeja. I only *want* Leeja!" Norrin was dangerously close to losing his patience with this old dwarf.

"Sure, you *want* her..." Thorne said dismissively.

"Leeja's begun bonding to you," Bridgid said, ignoring their squabbling.

Norrin was struck dumb. He stared around the room, a goofy smile creeping onto his face.

I can't believe my luck!

"Because she was not living among orcs," Imogen said, finally providing some information, "there was no one to warn her of the...physical manifestations of her growing attachment."

"Physical manifestations?" Norrin's hand slid down the front of his britches, "You mean the teeth? You *all* know about the teeth?"

Bridgid nodded, "I understand that the bondin' process was in the advanced stages?"

Norrin shrugged and shook his head, "She, um, didn't really mention it."

"And since you've proved yourself an unworthy mate..." Bridgid continued.

"Excuse me?"

"It has been decided that Leeja must leave town, ne'er t' return. Or to stay away until her body has decided to mate with at least two or three *other* males."

"Or until you die." Thorne offered brightly, "That would soften the blow of your betrayal."

"What is your problem with me?" Norrin demanded.

Thorne scoffed, "as if you don't know."

Arlynn and Imogen started crying again, and Norrin turned his attention towards them, "She's *your* friend! You didn't try to stop her? To talk some sense into her?"

"Of course we did," Arlynn snapped, "What do you think that double date was about?"

"I never should have agreed to it," Imogen whimpered, "I just wanted to prove that human men are capable of being good mates. But, but...she was right, they're all trash!"

Thorne had that shit-eating grin on his face again.

"Where is she?" Norrin demanded, getting aggressive again, "As much fun as you all seem to be having sitting around deciding what is best for everyone else, I would like to speak to Leeja before final decisions are made about *our* relationship."

"I'm sure you think you could make her happy, dearie,"

Bridgid said gently, "but orcish love is forever. Can you know that you'll feel the same way in sixty years? Or a hundred?"

"Where is she?" Norrin shouted, getting to his feet so violently that his chair slammed into and scraped across the stone floor.

"You're too late, sleeping beauty," Thorne's lip curled. "She left on the Flannery two hours ago."

"She..." Norrin staggered, bracing himself against the wall. "She never even said goodbye."

CHAPTER

TWENTY-ONE

L eeja stood at one end of her private cabin, naked from the waist down, waiting very impatiently to be fucked. Kidrish, the siren, stood at the other end of the cabin, completely naked and taking his sweet time. His broad shoulders nearly touched the walls of her cramped cabin. The top of his carefully coiffed blonde hairdo scraped the ceiling every time the ship bobbed and dipped in the water.

He's more muscular than Norrin, but they're both blondes and about the same height. Norrin was clean-shaven, and Kidrish has a well-maintained beard. The smell's not quite right, but he has that smile.

Leeja's favorite thing about Kidrish was his welcoming, honest smile; it reminded Leeja of...home.

Kidrish was very comfortable being naked (another quality that reminded her of Norrin). His half-hard cock bounced along with the ship looking just as happy-go-lucky as its owner. In its present state, it was only about a foot long, and it was pink!

If I squint, it almost looks human. If I ignore the suction cups, that is...

The Flannery rocked hard to port, and Leeja was tossed across her cabin and onto the cot.

"Outstanding!" Kidrish proclaimed, resting his fists on his narrow hips and tossing his head back like a bull sea lion. He laughed heartily.

Kidrish did everything heartily. Now that Leeja was on the bed, his mating arm grew rapidly to its full length and girth.

"The time has come, fair Leeja, to plunge headlong into adventure!"

Leeja rolled her eyes.

It's just fucking.

In the two weeks since she'd set sail from Th'myskôra, Leeja'd gone to bed with practically every male who would have her hoping to activate the dantų and forget about Norrin once and for all. So far, she hadn't had a single bite. She started with the males who were the *least* like Norrin: an angry grung, a nihilistic ibis, a sentimental dwarf. This time, she tried to tempt the dantų into mating by going to bed with the closest Norrin replica she could find.

Kidrish sauntered across the tiny cabin toward her. He reached the cot and put one webbed foot up next to Leeja's hip.

The men on deck were enjoying their dance hour. The sounds of accordion, tambourine, and heavy footfalls permeated the cabin. And, of course, Kidrish started singing along with their bawdy shanty.

"She heaved herself into the sea
Screaming, 'Come on boys, come and rescue me.'"
They sing this same song every day.

His hips rocked and undulated along with the music. His mating arm was now fully engorged. It was practically long enough to be a third leg! Because of Kidrish's unique anatomy, his tentacle did not become erect; instead it snaked and bobbed around excitedly, only a few inches from Leeja's face. Its many suckers were plump and quivering. Each was individually focused on her. As Kidrish's dancing caused his cock to bob and swing slightly from side to side, the suction cups turned, each one remained focused on its goal.

"Giving the crew the old 'Aye oh.'
She wants a lifeboatman."
Again, with the singing?

Leeja reached a tentative hand up and wrapped it around the tip of Kidrish's squirming cock. Immediately, she felt the persistent, sucking pressure of its tube feet. She gave the cock a little squeeze, and a viscous, green fluid, oozed out from its surface.

"So are you gonna' save me, Lifeboat Man? Or are we gonna sing all night?" Leeja squeezed again, and the ooze coated her hand.

"Lassie," Kidrish groaned, giving her a warning look, "once you've known the pleasures of the briny deep, no other man will satisfy ye."

"I'll consider myself warned," Leeja said, pulling her hand away from the hungry suction cups. A dozen pops sounded in quick succession as she freed herself. Leeja looked down at her hand and arm; dozens of mint green circles now dotted her skin where the suckers had pulled her blood to the surface. Kidrish's ooze coated her arm clear up to the elbow. It was getting everywhere.

The siren lowered himself down on top of her. The incredible weight of his chiseled body was too much for her to resist; Leeja had to lay back on the cot.

I supposed Kidrish is actually a lot more muscular than Norrin.

He held himself up over her on straightened arms, humming along with the men on deck. Leeja wrapped a leg around his waist. She dug her heel into his ass, trying to hasten his entry, but Kidrish was too strong to be rushed.

"So eager," he said in his customary jovial sing-song voice before flopping his heavy cock down on top of her. Its thick base was pressed up against her ass. Its pink, fleshy length ran up her slit, grinding into the flesh of her clitoral hood and applying significant pressure to her mound. The end of the cock had snaked its way up inside Leeja's tunic and was groping at her large, round breasts and suckling at her tight, green nipples.

Finally, we're getting somewhere.

The little suction cups at the cock's base went to work, groping and pulling, sucking at her flesh and pubic hair.

"Well?" Kidrish asked, clearly impressed with himself.

The suction against Leeja's delicate skin was intense and a little uncomfortable at first. But after a few moments, each suction cup found its place, and they all started working in concert. They applied and released pressure in steady waves along her opening and on the top of her mound. Each time the suckers pulled at her lower lips, Leeja felt herself becoming wetter. When they pressed hard into the mass of her pubic hair, Leeja felt an electric jolt shoot out from her swollen clit in all directions.

"I could get used to this," Leeja sighed between waves of pleasure.

"Outstanding!" Kidrish proclaimed. He was kneeling on the cot between her legs. His fists were perched on his hips as if he were having a heroic portrait painted. "Are you sufficiently prepared for intercourse?"

"Slide it on in!" Leeja forced herself to say out loud. She had to close her eyes to keep from rolling them at him.

Kidrish used both hands to heft his massive, wriggling member off of Leeja and line it up with her pussy. This time when the suckers were removed from her skin, a little burst of pain accompanied each pop.

He stood at the foot of the cot, giving the slimy, squirmy thing room to work.

"Brace yer'self, Lassy!" Kidrish called out as he approached.

His mating arm wriggled and writhed; its tapered tip desperate to plunge inside Leeja's warmth.

Finally, it made proper contact with her lower lips. The smallest suction cups spread Leeja open, and the ones that followed gripped her tender, internal skin. All of the suckers worked together, sucking and pulling to embed the cock further and further inside her.

The sensation was exhilarating. Leeja's breaths were shallow. Her eyes watered. The pleasure was unlike anything she'd ever experienced before.

Every few seconds, a sucker would latch onto Leeja's clit momentarily, and she'd let out a surprised little yip.

Kidrish's cock continued to work its way inside Leeja, crawling like a starving beast. As it bunched up and leaned out again, Leeja felt intense fullness and pressure pulsing through her core. The robust and flexible cock sucked and pushed and throbbed against sensitive spots inside her that Leeja had never felt before.

"Ha-*ha!*" Kidrish brayed triumphantly, "I'd say that's plenty for your first time."

He was still standing near the cot. Leeja was full to bursting with his coiled, writhing cock, but there was still more he was holding back from her.

A satisfied smile spread across Kidrish's face as he closed his eyes and resumed singing along with the men on deck.

"Then the lifeboat sailed from north to south
And the crew all gave her mouth to mouth..."
Nooo! I was so close; why is he singing again?

"Fuck me!" Leeja demanded, flailing her hands fruitlessly out toward Kidrish's hips.

Kidrish kept singing,

"...and they puffed and preened for to win her hand,"

But he did start pumping his hips slowly, dragging his knotted, twisting tentacle across her g-spot. The movement caused the suckers to gently pull and push her clit.

Leeja's eyelids fluttered, and her eyes rolled back.

Thank the Goddess. Now, if only he would stop singing.
"Giving the crew the old 'Aye oh.'
She wants a lifeboatman."

Leeja kept her eyes closed. She tried to focus on the sex, grinding her ass against the cot and squeezing her pussy to trigger an orgasm. But the singing was too distracting. It kept pulling her back from the brink of ecstasy.

Sexy thoughts. Sexy thoughts. Think sexy thoughts.

Suddenly, images of Norrin came rushing into her mind. The two of them were naked, sitting in his favorite spot, looking out over the bay. His warm arm was wrapped around her. As they both looked out at the night sky, blanketed in twinkling stars and its perfect reflection in the rippling, black ocean waters, Leeja felt so small. Norrin dragged his nose gently up her arm and kissed her on the shoulder. She felt protected and cherished. Norrin kissed her on the lips and slid his hand up to her breast.

Her pussy jolted back to life.

Back in the cabin with Kidrish, Leeja ran her hands up her torso and began squeezing her own breasts. She ran a thumb over her erect nipple and whispered a single word, "Norrin."

Her back arched and her breath caught in her throat. Her pussy clenched and released around the undulating tentacle sending uncontrollable tremors of pleasure through her body in wave after wave.

Leeja heard a deep, guttural voice croak and wheeze from deep in her own chest.

Waves of fluid rushed out of her, and she screamed soundlessly as her body shook and jerked uncontrollably.

Finally, the pressure ended. Leeja's back fell into the cot, her hands lay lifeless at her sides. She could breathe again. She was limp, struggling to catch her breath.

"Orgasm achieved!" Kidrish said before slipping his cock swiftly out of her.

The action caused Leeja to orgasm again, just an aftershock this time. She grunted as the renewed fluttering in her pussy sucked the air out of her lungs.

Leeja reached down to her opening. Immediately, her fingers were coated in a mixture of fluids.

She slid a tentative finger inside of herself, "No teeth."

"Time to get back on the great, two-toed shrew," Norrin took a deep breath and pulled open the heavy wooden doors of the Drowned Grim.

The Grim was decorated with thick garlands of red and golden leaves. Vast piles of apples were arranged in all manner of artistic presentations. The band was in full swing. A raucous crowd drank and danced, and the familiar smell of spices and treats hung thick in the air.

Norrin shouldered through the crowd and took a seat at the bar.

"Good Harvest!" Bridgid said, sliding a tankard of hot, spiced cider into his hand. "No hard feelings, then?"

"Good Harvest!" Norrin said, raising his drink to her and smiling, "I'm glad to see you."

He really was. Norrin had spent most of his time lately hiding away in his father's workshop. It was good to be around people again.

Norrin swiveled around on his stool and watched the revelers swirling around the tavern. Beautiful bodies of all shapes, sizes, and colors decked out in harvest-themed duds pranced, drank, and danced with each other. At least two dozen pairs of charming breasts were peeking out over the tops of low-cut gowns, and there were bulging, eager crotches every-where he looked. Best of all, everyone was smiling. The whole place was happy.

Norrin drained his tankard, and a squat, blue barback almost instantly replaced it with a full one.

Just like old times.

Norrin savored his cider as he carefully looked over his options, considering each one.

Before he could make a selection, Norrin was jostled by a couple of inebriated girls. He nearly fell off his stool but maintained his winning smile and recovered quickly.

"Oh, sorry," said a bright female voice.

Norrin turned to see a lovely red faun steadying a very drunk human girl.

"No apologies are necessary," Norrin said, smiling as he stood up and helped the faun slide her friend onto his stool. "It wouldn't be a proper harvest festival if someone didn't overdo it on the cider."

The faun giggled a little. It was a musical sound, like tinkling bells.

Norrin took a step back to observe her more fully. She was lithe and sinewy. She wore a thick, woolen gown of emerald green with red, orange, and gold apples embroidered along the hems that perfectly complimented her warm red coat. The gown was extremely low cut, revealing her shoulders. Norrin could make out her lean musculature just under her fur. The fur on her hands was cream colored; it transitioned to deeper and deeper shades the higher on her arm he looked. She had a cream-colored stripe from her face, down the middle of her exposed chest, and cute little cream-colored spots peeked out from behind her high, independently mobile ears and spread down either side of her neck.

"My name is Eláfee, by the way," the faun said, offering her hand.

Norrin took it in his, "I'm Norrin," he said, kissing it gently. "I hope it's not too forward to say that I love your spots."

"Thank you," Eláfee giggled, "they go all the way down."

He leaned in and said, "I'd very much like to see that someday."

"Today could be someday," Eláfee said, giggling again. The musical sound filled Norrin's head; he felt giddy and light.

Is it the cider, or is this girl bewitching me?

"What about your friend?" Norrin indicated the human on the bar stool behind them.

"Oh, um…" Eláfee looked around the crowded tavern, "Our other friends are just over there. Will you watch her for a minute while I get them?"

"I will guard her with my life," Norrin made a little bow.

Eláfee curtsied, giggling again before disappearing, engulfed by the churning crowd.

Norrin heard a low, grumbling moan coming from behind him. It was the human girl, still sitting on the bar stool, but now with her forehead plastered to the bar top,

"More cider," she croaked out.

"I think you've had enough for one night," Norrin laughed as he waved down the barback. Before he could ask for it, a tankard of cool water was on the bar before him, and the little amphibian had hopped along to the next patron.

"Try to drink some of this," Norrin said, wrapping the human girl's hand around the tankard.

She pushed herself up and steadied her elbows on the bar. With what looked like considerable effort, the human girl took the heavy tankard in both hands and started taking little sips of water.

"Where's Elee? And Fivï? We need to do Good Harvest," the drunk girl looked like she might cry. Norrin put a steadying hand on her shoulder,

"They'll be back soon, don't worry."

"This is my first Good Harvest," the human girl slurred.

"I can tell," Norrin said, laughing gently, "you're doing great. Just keep drinking that water."

"All right, *Norrin*! Baggin' 'em young!" A familiar voice shouted over the music and merrymaking.

Norrin turned to see Keneth, his little pot belly pressed against the bar. Norrin scanned the tavern for Imogen or Arlynn but didn't see either of Leeja's human friends.

"You here alone tonight, Keneth?"

"C'mon, man," Keneth said, leaning too close and shouting in Norrin's face, "You don't bring a girl *to* the harvest festival; you take a girl *from* the harvest festival!" Keneth laughed loudly at his own joke. His breath stank like rotting teeth. "Too bad for me, you already got the drunkest girl here!"

"What? No, I'm just—" Norrin stammered, but Keneth plowed on before he could finish his sentence.

"Congratulations on getting rid of the giantess," Keneth turned away again, trying to get the barback's attention, "I mean, I'm sure she was a great workout, but my god...you two looked ridiculous together. I mean, she's *huge*. She's got bigger muscles than me, and I'm no slouch, am I?" Keneth pulled up his sleeve and flexed his unimpressive bicep. "No slouch at all!"

The barback placed two tankards in front of Keneth, who turned to pick them up. "Anyway, that orc was gross. This girl here is way more your standing." With that, Keneth disappeared back into the crowd.

"Moira, you are a mess!" said a tall, lanky woman with an eagle's head. Eláfee was back with three other girls who all started fussing over the very drunk human Norrin had been watching.

"I think I like cider too much, you guys," said the human as her friends helped her to her feet, "I'm sorry."

"I think it's time to get you to bed," said Eláfee.

"Oh no, Fee. I'm so sorry," the human girl started to cry. "The handsome man! You won't get to go with the handsome man now because I'm too drunk."

Norrin smiled.

Oh, to be young and unable to hold one's liquor.

"Don't worry, Moira," Eláfee said conspiratorially, "the girls are going to take *you* home, and the handsome man is going to take *me* home."

"Oh good," Moira said, then, turning to slap Norrin on the shoulder, "You better do a real good sex day, handsome man!"

"I'll do my best," Norrin chuckled.

Then Eláfee laced her fingers between Norrin's and gently tugged him toward the door. Her fur was impossibly soft; it sent a shiver up Norrin's spine.

As the two made their way through the bawdy crowd, revelers bumped and jostled them about. A gargoyle telling a loud story stumbled backward, knocking Eláfee hard into Norrin. He felt her ass against his crotch, and his cock thumped.

Easy, boy, it won't be long.

Norrin steadied Eláfee, and they both smiled.

"I'll lead you to safety, fair maiden," Norrin said in his most gallant voice, moving her swiftly behind his body and holding her tight to him as he navigated them through the crowd.

"My hero!" Eláfee squealed, giggling and kissing him on the back of the neck.

Norrin bobbed and weaved through all manner of drunken festival goers, dodging hooves, horns, and axes. He made a big show of it all, to the delight of the ever-giggling Eláfee.

When Norrin reached the door, one final obstacle blocked his path: a scraggly human male with stringy hair colored an unnatural shade of black and stretched across a large bald spot on the top of his head.

"Keneth," Norrin said wearily, "would you excuse us a minute, buddy?" He put a hand on Keneth's shoulder.

Keneth spun around. He was unsteady on his feet and had a crazed look in his eyes. "Who wants to start a fricas with me?" he demanded.

When he recognized Norrin, Keneth's body relaxed, and he put back on his customary, slimy smile. "Woah!" he said, looking Eláfee up and down, "Nice score! This one looks... *pliable.*"

Norrin forced a polite smile and held the door open for Eláfee, but before he could follow her out onto the street, Keneth grabbed his arm,

"Congrats on the upgrade, man," he said, then, pulling Norrin's face uncomfortably close to his, Keneth asked, "Does this mean you won't be needing that little human girl tonight?"

"She's pretty sick, man," Norrin said struggling not to grimace. "I think her friends are gonna take her home."

"Oh, gross! I can't get puke on these shoes, that stuff never washes out. Thanks for the heads up."

Norrin nodded and made his escape.

On the street, the night air was brisk. Norrin took Eláfee in his arms; they encircled her easily. Her body was soft and warm against his.

Eláfee rocked up onto the tips of her hooves and kissed Norrin gently on the mouth. Her lips were slight and soft, covered with a fine layer of downy fur. He felt her cold, wet nose brush against his. Eláfee opened her mouth slightly, and Norrin accepted her invitation, sliding his tongue inside and tasting her. She wound her fingers up into his thick blond hair and let out a little moan, another sound that sent an electrifying shiver down Norrin's spine.

When he finally broke off the kiss, Norrin leaned back and gazed at Eláfee in the lamplight. Her big, doe eyes practically glowed. Tiny gold flecks shown and glimmered back at him. They were beautiful eyes, but they were the wrong eyes.

Eláfee took Norrin's hand again and tugged at it, "My place is just up here," she said eagerly.

But Norrin didn't move. He closed his eyes and imagined what it would be like to make love with her. The feeling of her delicate fingers intertwined with his. Her small, pert breasts pressed against his mouth. Her delicate body writhing under his. How fragile she would feel in his arms.

"I'm sorry, Eláfee, but I think you'd better go back inside to your friends."

"What's wrong?" she asked, "Did I do something?"

"No, not at all," Norrin said quickly. You're great, better than great! I just...I need to go home and figure some things out."

TWENTY-TWO

"SCREEEEEE!" The ear-splitting cry of the man-eating beast of Wildomire ricocheted off the canyon walls, leaving Leeja's ears ringing.

She hiked her skirts up above her knees and took off running south toward the canyon's mouth.

Anything worth having is worth working for, she reminded herself.

Powerful gusts of wind barreled down the canyon, overtaking Leeja and nearly knocking her off her feet. It was the beast, flapping his great, terrible wings. Toying with her.

Leeja steadied herself. She was sure he'd take her soon, but she couldn't give up, couldn't stop running. The canyon floor was rocky and uneven. Leeja jumped over a boulder, nearly clearing it in one leap, but catching her bare foot on its jagged edge.

Injured and bleeding, she ran on. Each time the pad of her foot struck the hard ground, sharp, bright pain shot up her shin.

Leeja sensed another air pressure shift and scrambled into a shallow hole, crouching down and covering her head with her arms. His feathers brushed against her as he flew past.

Goddess, I haven't run like this since I was a kid in Søgsund.

Leeja forced herself back onto her feet with a wicked grin. She was bruised, bloodied, and exhausted, but she forced herself to run.

He's circling back for another pass.

The wings of the Beast of Wildomire are nearly silent, even to orc ears, but Leeja had learned what to listen for over the past week; she knew he was ready.

Alright, Leeja, better make this look good.

She summoned as much strength as possible and broke into a full sprint. She couldn't have been more than fifty feet from the canyon's mouth and the dense forest just beyond. If she made it under the canopy, she'd be hidden.

The ground under Leeja's feet grew damp, the earth was softer. She was nearly there. She reached out her hand, and she ran. She could feel the cool air of the forest drawing her in.

Then, crunch.

His talons sank into the flesh of her shoulders, and they were airborne.

I wonder what he's broken this time, Leeja laughed to herself as she drifted off to sleep, secure in the grip of the beast, soaring higher and higher up into the clouds.

LEEJA blinked awake to the familiar sight of bones and half-rotted carcasses strewn about a tremendous cliffside nest. Her skirts were pulled up past her waist, and she felt the air, thin and freezing, on her exposed genitals.

"You're awake," said the beast of Wildomire, a towering hawk-man hybrid with a powerful golden beak, razor-sharp talons, and enormous glassy black pupils.

Leeja grunted affirmatively, still too tired to move.

"Thank you for running," said the beast.

"My pleasure," Leeja said, mustering a smile and starting to push herself up onto her feet.

"No!" said the Beast, rushing over to stop her, "Stay down. Look broken." His movements were quick and choppy. His head jerked around constantly; it was as if he thought some other predator might swoop down at any second and make off with his prize.

"Alright," Leeja said in her most soothing tone, laying back down in a crumpled heap.

The Beast made an excited, trilling noise at the back of his throat, and he began scratching around at the nest excitedly, moving closer and closer to Leeja.

"Stop!" she said, throwing up her arm. The beast stood confused, cocking his head sharply from one side to the other. "I thought we could talk a little first this time."

The beast only blinked his gigantic round eyes at her.

"What's your name, for example?" she asked him, "I mean, you're *given* name? What do your people call you?"

"It would be impossible for you to pronounce," said the beast.

"Well, what are you passionate about? What interests you?" Leeja asked.

"Hunting. Catching. Mating."

"Alright," said Leeja, groping around desperately in her mind for some question she could ask, some trick that would make it work this time. "How about your father? Do you get along with him?"

"Many eggs are knocked out of the nest by breeding males and are dashed on the rocks below. Mine was not." The beast blinked his empty eyes at Leeja a few more times before asking, "Is mating permitted now?"

"Sure," Leeja said, crawling over to and draping herself over a large rock.

That excited trill rippled up through the beast again, and the feathers on the back of his neck stood on end as he approached her.

A small slit opened up in the feathers of his pelvis, then his huge, milky-white corkscrew cock snaked its way out into view. Leeja was slick as soon as she saw it.

The next moment, the beast was on top of her, nipping at the back of her neck, sending warm green blood dribbling down her back.

She felt his blunt eager cock pressed up against her opening. *Good thing I don't need much foreplay.*

The beast was ramming into her over and over, desperate to breech her opening. With each strike, Leeja's pussy grew wetter.

He won't last long once he's in; I better concentrate.

She closed her eyes, and memories of Norrin flooded her mind. The gentle way he explored her body with his calloused hands. His soft lips and eager tongue working their way down her bare torso.

"Fuck!" Leeja shouted, digging her fingers into the boulder and causing little bits of rock to break off. The beast was inside of her now, stretching her cunt to its limits.

The beast was squawking and flapping wildly behind her.

It won't be long now.

The downy feathers around his crotch tickled her lower back and ass crack. The firm, smooth feathers of his wings, nearly silent when he'd hunted her, were rubbing against each other wildly now, causing a cacophony of rustling, fluttering, and susurrus all around her.

Leeja concentrated on the memory of Norrin at the pond, the first time the dantų appeared. He had her from behind then, too. They'd been laughing, talking, and kissing all day. At that moment, he buried his strong fingers in her hips and bit her ear as she bucked backward against him. When Norrin came, she felt his cock thumping inside of her, and her own orgasm was unleashed.

Back in the nest, in the present moment, Leeja started to orgasm around the beast's cock. Her inner walls squeezed and fluttered, drawing out every drip of his cum.

"Thank you," Leeja whispered as the beast's monstrous, spent dick slid out of her, leaving a glistening trail in its wake.

Leeja lay shaking on the rock, as residual ecstasy crashed over her in wave after wave.

I've got to get into better shape. I should start running again.

Leeja was able to fight off sleep for a few minutes. Her body calmed, and she watched the sun sink lower and lower on the horizon; her eyelids sank with it. She had just enough strength left to slide a finger inside her sore and slippery pussy.

"Nothing."

IT WAS late in the harvest season. Each day was shorter than the last. Norrin toiled away in the workshop from before first light until exhaustion forced him to his bed. On more than one occasion, it was the sound of the plane (or some other tool) slipping out of his unconscious hand and clattering to the floor that signaled the end of Norrin's workday.

"Time to eat," said Aengus, setting a big bowl of stew on the drafting bench.

When did he get here?

Norrin grumbled something unintelligible.

"Your mother insists," Aengus slid a spoon into his son's hand.

Norrin ladled in a wet mouthful of turnip and cabbage. It was wonderful. He hadn't realized how cold and hungry he'd been until the elegant fish broth slid down his throat, warming him from the inside.

"You've been taking a lot of meals out here lately," Aengus said, lighting the various candles and lamps around the room.

"You know how it is when a design grabs ahold of you," Norrin said around a full mouth. He was shoveling the stew in now.

"A man possessed, eh?" Aengus ran a practiced hand along the ship's hull. "She'll be fast as the dickens...maybe your fastest yet. But why so big? Planning on racing with a four-man team?"

"I was thinking more like two people on a long-term voyage." Norrin said, excited to share the improvements he'd made to the classic design. "When she's finished, she'll have an ample cabin with a full-sized bed. And down here," he said, directing his father's attention to the hold, "we'll be able to fit enough supplies for a three-month excursion, maybe even longer!"

"*Will* we?" Aengus asked, "Which two people did you have in mind?"

"I, um..." Norrin's cheeks flushed, "I'm still not sure if I want to go with a wheel or a tiller. What do you think?"

"I think a wheel is going to be more accessible for a novice sailor, don't you?" Aengus was smirking now. Norrin tilted up his stew bowl, slurping some broth and breaking eye contact with his father.

"By the way," Aengus continued nonchalantly, "I saw Bowen in town today."

"Oh?" Norrin asked, trying and failing to match his father's easy tone, "How's uh...how's the Flannery doing? Repairs holding up well?"

"The old girl is doing fine; she's docked at the Wildomire Bluffs for three weeks. I imagine the crew is enjoying some much-needed shore leave." Aengus turned back to the ship again. "I bet a fast ship like this, skillfully piloted, could make it to Wildomire inside of three weeks."

Norrin dropped his bowl and ran over to the drafting bench, where he started frantically flipping through large stacks of parchment. "But she's not ready!" His voice was shaky and panicked."Even if I work non-stop, she won't even be seaworthy in three weeks!" He kept checking and rechecking his plans as if he might find some calculation or some hidden trick that would make the work go faster.

Aengus put a steadying hand on his son's shoulder. "If you let your old man help you, you could be back with Leeja in no time at all."

Norrin dropped his papers. He hadn't heard her name spoken aloud in months, and it crushed him.

"I don't even know what I'm doing here," he said, turning to his father with pleading, watery eyes. "Building her this boat... that's just..."

Aengus wrapped his arms around his son and squeezed him hard. And Norrin cried. It was the first time he'd let himself cry over Leeja, and all of his frustration, and loss, and anger came spilling out onto his father's shoulder.

"Son," Aengus said, "I love you. I love the easy way you move through life; it's the same way you move through the waves when you're out there racing. You never work too hard, you never try to force an outcome, you see which way the wind is blowing and you go with the flow. And most of the time things work out pretty well for you, you usually win. But there comes a time in a man's life—"

"She *left* me, Dad!" Norrin interrupted, "She left, and she didn't even tell me she was going, and now it's over. I know it's time to move on...so why can't I stop thinking about her?"

After several long moments, Aengus spoke again, "Sounds like you really care about this girl a lot."

Norrin took a deep, steadying breath, "Dad, I think I love her."

"Before The Peace, I was living on Little Break. I was an apprentice shipwright, working for your grandfather. My interest in ships was merely academic. I loved the idea that man, through ingenuity and will, could approximate the perfect design of the great beasts of the sea. That we could, if we just tried hard enough, move great distances with the speed and elegance of the gods...I say 'we', but I was a terrible sailor."

"Was?" Norrin joked, though his stuffy nose.

"As I was saying," Aengus chuckled, "my interest was academic, theoretical, maybe even spiritual, but not practical. I made the ships, but I was more than happy to stay in my safe, familiar harbor in Little Break. But all of that changed when the Imperial Navy showed up recruiting."

"Mom..."

"Norrin, she was magnificent," Aengus' focus softened, he stared out the window as if he were watching Glema for the first time all over again. A wave of adoration washed over him.

"She was standing on top of this steep, craggy cliff face ready to dive into the water below. We called the place Widow's Court because nobody made it off that cliff alive. The whole town was gathered around watching. Everyone was sure she'd chicken out or be mangled in the waves below.

"But your mother just turned to the crowd and she shouted down, 'The Imperial Navy trained me to be a rescue diver and the Imperial Navy can train you to be great too!'

"Her demonstration partner was below her, bobbing around on the waves. It was a two-hundred foot-drop, at least. Glema turned back to the water, she raised her arms over her head and...I swear to the gods she glowed.

"She leapt into the air. Everyone gasped. She twisted and spun. Old women covered their eyes. She plummeted toward the sea. Children shrieked. She kept her focus. We were all terrified, but Glema kept her cool. She was in charge. I was sure she'd be killed.

"And then... she made contact. She broke the water's surface and disappeared from view with barely a splash.

"She was under there for what felt like an hour. And then... and then she just bobbed back up to the surface. Not only was she alive, but she could swim! She grabbed her demonstration partner around the ribs and started haulin' his ass back to shore.

"She made it back in record time, and this guy, the man she was dragging, he must've weighed at least three hundred pounds. Not that you would have known from looking at Glema. Your mom pulled him through the water like he weighed nothing at all.

"When I saw her standing, victorious, on the beach, I knew what I had to do.

"I know," said Norrin smiling. He'd heard this story a thousand times but would never dream of interrupting it. "That's the moment you decided to join the Imperial Navy.

"That was my moment. The moment that I knew what I wanted from life," said Aengus, "and I decided I would do whatever it took to get it. So," Aengus turned his gaze back at his son, "what will you decide to do with *your* moment?"

TWENTY-THREE

"Bonny Leeja," Kidrish called in his familiar, welcoming sing-song manner from across the Double Gentlewoman Inn. "Come 'ave a dance with us!" The crew of the Flannery had taken over the little tavern every night for the last eighteen nights straight.

The Double Gentlewoman was an enchanted inn and tavern; every task, the needs of all the guests were attended to by unseen magical forces. In all of the many days and nights Leeja had spent there since their shore leave began, she had never seen a single worker anywhere on the premises. Still, the fire in the hearth never went out, and the gigantic cast-iron pot that hung above it filled with a hearty stew thrice daily. A fresh pile of warm bread and a stack of clean bowls were always on the inexplicably tidy fireside table.

She'd decided to stay in a room at the inn, and every morning, as soon as she stood up out of bed, the sheets and pillow shook themselves out and then laid back down neatly in their places. At first, Leeja found it all very charming. She'd used the magical novelty of the place to try and convince herself that Wildomire was going to be her next start. That she'd finally be able to find a new male to mate with. But as the days wore on, she was no closer to her goal. The magic of the Double Gentlewoman no longer inspired hope and wonder. Leeja was actually starting to resent the easy, anonymous service. She missed *her* tavern. She missed Bridgid always bustling about, gossiping and minding everyone's business but her own. She missed her well-meaning, ill-informed human friends.

If it weren't for these stupid teeth, I never would have had to leave home.

After eighteen days and a dozen dead-end lovers, Leeja had begun to resent everything about the Double Gentlewoman.

Kidrish was still staring at her from across the room. Dancing jauntily and waiting for her reply.

"No thanks," Leeja barked over her shoulder. She had no intention of leaving her stool tonight.

No workers meant no band, which is probably why the crew of the Flannery always insisted on taking their shore leave here. Every night, those musically inclined crew members would take turns on the bandstand, playing into the wee hours to entertain their fellow crew members and delight unsuspecting lodgers.

Tonight, Yenaria the harpy flew in wide, easy circles around the vaulted ceiling playing a bladder pipe. Violent Mathias (Leeja's mentor on the shoring crew) used all four of his arms to play a very complicated hurdy-gurdy. And, of course, Kidrish joined them to sing along with every ballad. He even had his own devotees. Half a dozen human women showed up to the Double Gentlewoman every night, attracted by the siren's call. They swooned at his feet, and (if he sang too many songs in a row) they would even start fighting each other to decide who got to stand closest to him.

It's too bad orcs are immune to siren songs. Otherwise, my dantų might have activated by now.

"Ale, please," she called out in an even, steady tone. A fresh tankard full of cold, frothy ale appeared on the bar before her.

"That's a neat trick," said a voice Leeja didn't recognize a little further down the bar.

It was a human male, a rare sight in Wildomire. He was very muscular and swarthy. A little shorter than Leeja with a broad, welcoming smile. He had jet-black hair except at the temples where it had silvered, and he wore a matching, dazzling silver goatee.

The practiced hands of an older lover would be a welcome change of pace after the last two weeks in the beast's nest.

Leeja flared her nostrils and pulled the human's scent inside of herself. He smelled just like any other human.

This guy won't trigger my dantų. He doesn't smell anything like Norrin.

"If only everything were as easy," Leeja said, drinking from her magical tankard.

"In my experience," said the human, "it's people who make things complicated."

"And I'll just bet that you could show me some of life's simple pleasures," Leeja said, honey dripping from every word.

So this human isn't a potential mate. Maybe it's okay if I sleep with him for fun. You know, the way sex used to be, before I was forced to take up this impossible love quest.

"Not at all, boss," said the human, making a little bow, "I

just thought we could both benefit from some friendly conversation."

Leeja shook her head, laughing a bitter, raspy laugh, "Save your 'boss,' human, I've got no horde."

"Oh," said the human, "lost your lover?"

Perceptive little human, aren't you?

"He lost me, actually," Leeja huffed.

"What did he say when you broke it off?"

"Nothing," Leeja said, guilty, taking another swig. "I left town without saying goodbye."

"So, for all you know, he's moping around some other tavern at this very moment," the human said.

Leeja had spent considerable energy refusing to imagine what Norrin might be up to at any given moment and she didn't really want to start now.

"Ha!" she spat. "It's been three months. Norrin's probably fallen in and out of love with half a dozen *monsters* by now. That's the human way, isn't it? Serial monogamy?"

"Human's might not be quite as simple as you think," said the man before assertively stating, "Ale, please." When he grabbed the newly arrived tankard, Leeja saw a weathered gold ring on his fourth finger. It was his only adornment and stood in stark contrast to his understated attire.

"That's a human marriage symbol, isn't it?" Leeja asked, remembering the pewter rings Aengus and Glema wore.

The human smiled, "That it is."

"Does your wife know you're out in the taverns chatting up dangerous, young orcs?" Leeja was still teasing him.

If this human was determined to break his wedding vows tonight, it might as well be with me.

"She's no longer with us," said the human, his smile faltering.

Leeja shrugged at him; she was not well-versed in human euphemisms.

"The boss died twenty-two years ago this winter," said the human. Then the smile spread back across his face, all the way up to his sparkling lavender eyes as he looked around the tavern at the rowdy sailors. "She would have loved this place. She loved dancing."

"How long were you together?" Leeja asked.

"We just celebrated our thirty-fifth anniversary," the human puffed up with pride.

"But she—", Leeja started.

"The boss and me are forever," said the human, tapping his ring.

"You'll never remarry then?" Leeja asked.

"Never," said the human smiling.

"So, you just roam from tavern to tavern looking for meaningless, anonymous sex?"

Finally, something I understand.

The human laughed gently, shaking his head, "I meant it when I said I was just looking for conversation."

"I didn't think humans were capable of that kind of devotion," said Leeja.

"There's a saying in the north, 'If you've met one human, you've met one human.'" He chuckled, "Your young man, did he prove himself unfaithful to you?"

"Not exactly," Leeja stammered.

"So, why did you leave town?"

"He...we weren't a good match." Leeja swirled her ale around her half-empty tankard. "I left to find someone else to bond to."

The human smiled a knowing smile, "Have any luck yet?"

"No!" Leeja slammed her fist down on the bar, "And I've spent every free moment trying. It doesn't matter what position we use, or what he smells like, or how many times I have sex with the same male. I just can't make the dantų appear." Leeja settled back down into her seat, defeated. "It was so easy with Norrin; I don't know what I'm doing wrong."

"It was easy with me and the boss too," the human smiled.

"And now that she's gone, what are you doing with the rest of your life... you'll just...?"

"I'll wait, and I'll love her," said the human. "We were each other's only love. I know that wherever she is, she's waiting for me too."

"I, um," Leeja was stammering again, the room was starting to spin. "I need to step outside and get some air."

"Hardtack, smoked fish, lemons, cider, *and* dried figs! Is that everything?" Glema called up from the hold.

"Sounds great, Ma!" Norrin shouted back before returning his attention to Bowen. The two of them were cross-referencing the Flannery's itinerary with star charts, maps of the trade routes, and the latest storm prognostication.

"You'll have missed them at The Bluffs," Bowen said; Norrin could have kicked himself.

Leeja had been in the same port city for three weeks, and he hadn't managed to meet her there. If only he'd brought Aengus in on the build sooner, the ship could have been finished *weeks* ago. Leeja could be in his arms right now. But he'd chosen to pout, and now she was out there somewhere hating him, or worse, maybe she'd moved on entirely.

"If the wind is kind," the ruddy satyr continued, "you could catch up around, Smoghelm. But if you want to be safe, I'd say sail straight to Dar Guruhm and wait for her to dock there."

"I don't have time to be safe, Bowen," Norrin said. "For all I know, Leeja'll leave the crew in Smoghelm to start a horde there. Come to think of it, she may decide to stay behind in Wildomire..."

"I haven't gotten any rumblings of discontent among the crew in any of the Flannery's correspondences," Bowen snorted. "It's rough sailing from here to Smoghelm. Sail to Dar Guruhm, get a nice room at the inn, and wait for her there."

"I've done too much waiting," Norrin said, "I've got to see her now."

"Come have a look at this, son!" Aengus was making some last-minute adjustments to the sails, "I know we were considering a square rig, but I think the lateen sails are going to give you a slight speed advantage, and every second counts, right?"

"Getting to Leeja fast is the only thing that matters," said Norrin eagerly, admiring his father's handiwork.

"Speed isn't the *only* thing that matters, kiddo," Aengus said. "You'll be getting increased speed and maneuverability, sure, but you're giving up some stability. I want you to promise me that you'll be careful. We don't need you capsizing out in the open sea."

"C'mon, Papa," said Norrin, "you're looking at the paragon of nautical safety!"

"I'm serious, boyo," Aengus waggled his long finger. "Promise you'll avoid rough waters!"

"I...um..." Norrin was starting to lie when he was interrupted by a couple of familiar voices.

"Norrin! Hey, Norrin! Can we talk to you a minute?" It was Leeja's human friends, Arlynn and Imogen, calling out to him from the boardwalk.

"I gotta go see what they're on about, Dad," Norrin said, scurrying away from the question and hopping down to meet the girls.

"We heard you were going to go find Leeja," said a teary-eyed Imogen.

"Don't try and stop m—" Before Norrin could finish, Arlynn grabbed him hard around the waist.

"We never should have let her leave!" she sobbed.

Imogen forced a soft bundle of brown paper into Norrin's hands. "It's a warm winter dress. It's got a fox fur lining; we had Jagluk make it to match the exact green of her eyes."

"I thought you girls didn't approve of my seeing her..." Norrin said suspiciously.

"We were trying to protect her because we saw her falling in love with you," said Arlynn, "but we shouldn't have meddled. We chased her away to try and protect her, and we think... *I* think you might really love her."

Norrin looked at them both; he made sure they saw the sincerity in his eyes before he spoke, "Leeja is more important to me than anything else in the Three Realms. You don't have to worry about protecting her from me. And once I get her back," he added reassuringly, "I'll never let her go again."

Both girls threw their arms around Norrin in a big, weepy group hug, "Bring her back to us, please," Imogen said.

"Norrin!" Bowen shouted from the deck, "If you're shoving off today, now's the time while you still have the tide!"

"Don't worry," Norrin told the girls, "Leeja and I will be back home in no time." He turned towards the gangplank but was stopped by a burly, red cyclops.

"You can't just let her live in peace, can you?" Thorne

boomed. He was standing between Norrin and his ship, between Norrin and his happily ever after with Leeja. "She left you. What is so hard for you to understand about that? You don't just get everything you want the second you want it. Sometimes, *you're* the one who gets left alone."

Norrin took a steadying breath, determined not to fight with Thorne today. He would not be bated. "Look, Thorne, you and I were kids when we were together; it was puppy love. You've got to let that go."

"Puppy love?" Thorne roared, "I...I bonded to you! Do you know what it takes to break a cyclops mating bond? The physical and emotional pain? The *shame* you put me through?"

Norrin was stunned. "I never knew, you...you never told me."

"Would it have changed anything if I had?"

"I don't know," said Norrin softly, "I'd like to think I would have been a little nicer...if I knew *why* you've been such a jerk all these years."

Thorne chuckled, and rolled his eye.

"Thorne, I'm sorry I hurt you." Norrin said gently, looking into his eye. "You have every right to be angry with me."

Some of the fire faded from Thorne's eye, and his posture softened. It was almost as if Norrin was looking at his childhood friend again, the old Thorne. "I never thought I'd hear you apologize for that. I was starting to think you didn't know how."

"This is my first time," Norrin joked, "how am I doing?"

"Not bad...for a human." Thorne said, "you're gonna have to do better than that to win Leeja back, though."

"Thanks for letting me practice on you. It was long overdue." Norrin wrapped his arm around Thorne. The two of them hugged for the first time in over a decade. "I am sorry, Thorne. I've missed you, ya' know. I've missed us, the way we used to be. We were friends longer than we were enemies, maybe we could get back to the old us, to being friends like before."

Thorne smiled, a rare sight these days, "If you manage to bring Leeja home, I'll consider it."

Norrin breathed a sigh of relief and made his way back onto the boat where his parents and well-wishers were rushing around, all trying to make a last-minute adjustment or improvement.

"Are you sure we can't come with you, dear?" Glema asked as Norrin tried to shoo the last stragglers back onto the dock. "Your father's an excellent sailor, and having a master rescue diver onboard could be very helpful in rough waters..."

"For the last time, no." Norrin said, kissing his mother on the forehead, "I have to do this on my own."

Norrin stood on his little ship, gripping a long sturdy pole. He made contact with the dock, and pushed against it with all his might. Aengus and Bowen had poles of their own and they heaved against the ship from the dock. Little by little, the ship was freed. The ends of Aengus' and Bowen's poles splashed into the water and Norrin was able to straighten out and raise the sail.

She caught the wind. Finally, Norrin was alone on his little ship, heading out on the most important race of his life.

As the dock and its inhabitants shrank smaller and smaller in the distance, Bowen called out, "What's her name? The ship? What're you calling her?"

"The Leeja!" Norrin called back.

TWENTY-FOUR

"All hands! All hands, man battle stations!" Chaotic shouts, clanging bells, and the scraping of iron against wood seemed suddenly to be coming from every direction.

Leeja grabbed her heavy leather tool belt and bounded up to the deck. "What's going on?" she shouted, moving through the crowd, desperate to find Violent Mathias, or anyone from the shoring crew, for that matter.

"We're under attack, woman!" Violent Mathias said, grabbing Leeja by the arm, "Help me get these cannon balls into position."

Leeja nudged Violent Mathias out of the way and easily dragged a pallet of cannonballs over to the Flannery's broadside.

"Is it pirates?" Leeja asked the gunner as she helped load a cannonball and then heft the cannon back towards the incoming vessel.

"Not sure yet, miss," said the gunner, taking careful aim. "She's not flying any flag, far as we can tell."

"Should we really be shooting at her then?"

The gunner was lighting the fuse, "Cap'n doesn't want to take any chances. I'd cover those orc ears if I was you, miss."

Leeja clamped her hands over her ears as hard as she could, pinning them to her head, and took several quick steps away from the cannon. Squinting, she tried to make out some identifying mark on the tiny ship in the distance.

"Looks small for a pirate ship!" It was too late; the cannonball shot across the sky and landed a few short feet from the unknown vessel, rocking her violently from side to side.

"Don't worry, miss," the gunner shouted over the chaos. "Cap'n's ordered us to fire only warnin' shots."

Another warning shot was fired at the little ship from a nearby cannon. It struck a cliff, sending rocky debris raining down. Leeja clambered up to the quarterdeck, desperate to put as much distance between her very sensitive ears and the persistent cannon fire as possible.

"Just a moment, Captain," said the calm voice of Martel, the griffin. He had the sharpest eyes on the crew and so served as the lookout. "Someone is flapping his arms on the deck of that ship. I think they're trying to tell us something."

"Hold yer fire, boys!" the captain cried out over the din of explosions. "How many are there? Are they armed?" the captain asked.

"Looks like just one, Captain," the griffin answered, "I'd like permission to fly over there and get a closer look."

"Could be a trap," said the captain, stroking his luxurious ginger beard, "What do you think, Leeja?"

"Me, Sir?" Leeja was stunned. She hadn't realized the captain even saw her there.

"A good captain values a second opinion, lass."

"It could be someone who needs our help," Leeja said tentatively, "If we blow her out of the water, we'll never know for sure."

"Alright," huffed the captain, "but go armed." He thrust an arquebus toward the griffin's chest, but Martel scoffed at the wooden long gun, presenting his razor-sharp claws.

"I'm *always* armed."

"Fine, fine," the captain grumbled, "but if I get even a whiff that something on that ship isn't right, I'll blast 'er to smithereens!"

As Martel flapped his massive wings and rose slowly above the Flannery, the captain roared to the crew, "Gunners, reload! Take direct aim at the unknown ship and be ready to fire on my mark!"

Leeja held her breath as the griffin approached the ship.

When Martel was just a tiny dot in the distance, circling the ship in a holding pattern. The captain turned back to Leeja, "What do you hear over there, orc?"

"Just a lot of bawking and screeching," Leeja said, craning her neck, "I can't make the words out, but he doesn't sound angry."

"Steady, men!" called the captain as the yellow dot that was Martel grew larger and larger. "He's coming back! Hold yer fire. Martel is coming back!"

Finally, Martel was touching back down on the quarterdeck

with what almost looked like a grin spread across his avian face.

"Well?" demanded the captain, "Be they friend or foe?"

"That depends," Martel bawked, "on what *she* says."

Martel and the captain both turned their attention to Leeja, "What? I? I don't..."

"It's that human," the griffin said, he was practically purring now, "the one you ran away from. Norrin, was it?"

At the sound of his name, a shiver shot through Leeja's entire body. She was dizzy and flushed. Her breath caught in her throat. She wanted nothing more than to be held by him... well, *almost* nothing.

"I'll have no member of my crew crimped by some rapacious human," said the captain, bristling. "You didn't confirm she was aboard, did you?"

"No," Martel's dulcet voice rolled around Leeja's ears like mead, "but I don't think he means to steal her."

"Then what *does* he want?" the captain demanded. He and Martel were staring at Leeja again.

"*I* don't know what he wants," she muttered. "I thought I'd never see him again." The captain looked uneasy, so Leeja quickly added, "He isn't violent, though. He builds ships. As a matter of fact, he helped with the repairs to the Flannery. His whole family is good friends with Bowen..."

"Is something the matter with the ship?" the captain asked.

"He didn't say," the griffin was swinging his long golden tail in a lazy, snaking figure eight. He was definitely purring now. "All he would say is that he needs to speak to Leeja."

"Look here, girl," the captain was red in the face and addressing Leeja again, "if this ship is in danger, I need to know about it."

"Of course, Captain."

"Does that mean you'll speak to him?" Martel asked, licking his beak.

"I um…" Leeja blushed bright green, "I can't be near him anymore. It could be…dangerous for me if he gets too close."

"The crew will protect you, Leeja," said the captain, "but *you* have to protect us."

"Alright," Leeja took a deep breath, "as long as you promise he won't get too close, I'll do my part."

The griffin made an excited little chirp and took off again. Leeja held her breath as Martel shrank into the distance, circled Norrin's ship a few times, and then flew back to join the Flannery.

Norrin's ship changed course and was now barreling toward the Flannery. Norrin was barreling back toward Leeja.

What could he possibly want? He must hate me after the way I left him. I would hate me.

Martel landed again, and the captain rushed up to him, "Well? What did he say?"

"Not much," said Martel, smirking, "but when I confirmed Leeja was aboard and willing to speak with him, his eyes went wild, like those of a man possessed."

Leeja tried to swallow, but her mouth had gone dry.

"I'd be more than happy to deliver another message for you while we wait," the griffin tilted his head, indicating the impending ship. It was coming into focus, but still quite a ways off.

"Um…sure…I, I mean yes!" Leeja was still trying to impress the captain, "Please tell Norrin that as a member of the shoring crew, I am more than happy to meet with him and discuss any potential repairs the Flannery may need."

Martel threw back his head and roared with laughter before taking flight again, "Can't wait to hear how he takes *that*!" He crowed before winking at the captain and flying off to meet Norrin.

The captain frowned and rolled his eyes, "Stow the munitions, boys!" he shouted down to the crew. Leeja thought she heard a tinge of disappointment in his voice. "There'll be no battle today."

Leeja made to leave the quarterdeck and get to work, but the captain grabbed her by the arm. "Not you, girl. You're staying right here where I can see you."

Leeja watched Martel touch down on Norrin's ship. She strained fruitlessly to hear their conversation, "Are they whispering?"

After what seemed like an eternity, Martel was finally back aboard the Flannery. "I delivered your message."

"And?" Leeja thought she might faint.

There's nothing wrong with the Flannery; I'm sure of it. Aengus would never sign off on a project that was anything less than perfect. So, what could Norrin possibly have chased me halfway across the Equiloam Sea to say?

"He seemed...*distressed*," the griffin oozed, "to put it mildly."

With the threat of conflict behind them, the attitude amongst the crew shifted from agitated to curious, nosy even. A crowd was forming around the quarterdeck. Everyone wanted to know what Martel and the human had discussed. Several wild theories were being developed by the crew.

"Maybe she owes him a life debt, and he's come collecting," suggested Steven The Goblin.

"I'll bet he's been hexed, and now he's got toes growing out of his face, and he needs a lock of her hair to make an antidote," said Yenaria.

"I bet," said Kyg'n'owr, a kraken, joining in on the fun, "she implanted her fertilized eggs in his abdominal cavity and skipped town. And soon, the young will gnaw their way out into the cruel world, motherless and abandoned…human males gestate the eggs, right?"

Leeja buried her face in her hands, "Maybe he's come to demand a duel," she muttered.

"From what I understand of the situation," purred Martel, "he'd be well within his rights to run you through."

"For the last time," said the captain, "no one is dying on my ship today!"

"Alright, laddies!" Kidrish sang out over the clatter, weaving through the crowd, making marks on a long piece of parchment. "Last chance to place yer bets! The human is nearly upon us!"

Leeja gazed out over the broadside of the Flannery. Fewer than one hundred yards away, Norrin, in a ship she'd never seen, was dropping anchor.

"Ahoy, human vessel." The captain had made his way down to the deck and was hailing Norrin, "This is Captain Mirtaruk Gloryeye of the Flannery: fifth ship in the Red Fleet; what is yer business?"

"Ahoy, Captain Gloryeye!" Norrin shouted back. Leeja's knees betrayed her. She crumpled on the spot and sat, helpless, shielded from view by the pulsing, undulating mob of her crew.

Why did his voice have to be so beautiful?

"I am Norrin Galanou, son of Aengus and Glema of Th'myskôra; I have business with Leeja, the half-orc!"

Whistles and hoots spread through the eager crew. There was also some noticeable clanging of broadswords as some in the crew were convinced Norrin had nefarious intentions.

Leeja had never felt so visible in her life. Every single person on the ship had involved themselves in this spectacle. She wished she could melt into the ship, disappear into the grain of the wood, or at least not be able to hear every one of their conversations and whispers in such precise detail.

"What business do you have with her?" the captain asked.

"With all due respect, Captain," Norrin shouted from the deck of the little ship, "my business is my own. I must speak with Leeja privately."

Up on the quarterdeck, Martel was still stationed at Leeja's side. He was lying on the floor licking his claws now, and each time Leeja groaned or shifted uncomfortably, the griffin made a delighted little chirp.

"It is not customary for sea captains to serve up members of their crew to any human who sails by and demands them without explanation," the captain shouted back.

There was a long, quiet pause— quiet except for the deafening thumping of Leeja's own heartbeat against the inside of her skull.

"Fine!" Norrin finally shouted back, "Will you please tell her that I've come to take her back home? Tell her everyone misses her, and things haven't been the same since she left."

"This ship is due back in Th'myskôra in three months," shouted the captain. "Why should she leave with you now, human?"

"Because," Norrin hesitated for a moment, "because I love her. Every day we spend apart is agony for me."

There was an eruption of chattering gossip among the crew.

"Well, we can rule out face-hex and sabotage," Kidrish sang out merrily as he crossed out the corresponding entries on his parchment.

"I told you the ship was fine," Leeja muttered, and Martel threw his head back, roaring with laughter again.

"Well, Leeja," the griffin purred, "what say you?"

"Sure, he loves me *now*," Leeja said, sitting up straight, "what happens to me when the season changes?" She was asking herself more than anyone else, "Will I end up like that human in the tavern at Wildomire? Or like the little goblin back home?"

Martel flew up into the air and screeched.

"Stop!" Leeja whispered, terrified, as she lunged toward the griffin's paws. She was too late. He was airborne and making a proclamation on her behalf, "The fickle cruelty of human lovers is legendary; why should she trust you?"

Several confirmative "Yars!" rang out from among the crew.

"Tell her...tell her not all humans are the same. Tell her that I'm not like Keneth." Norrin shouted, "I don't like Keneth or think he's funny, and I was never going to go into business with him. And I only played along that night in the Spiced Goat because it was easier than arguing. But I know now I was wrong. I should have stood up for her. And tell her that if she comes back home with me, nothing like that will ever happen again."

Leeja's heart melted.

Does he mean he's going to fight for me? No one's ever done that before.

An incredible twinge of guilt and desire tore at her insides. "He's wonderful," Leeja said quietly behind the assembled crew members. "I wish I could...but what about Thorne? How can I know he won't cast me aside the same way?"

Violent Mathias shoved his way from the back of the crowd, near Leeja, up to the captain's side, "Cap'n," he said, "Leeja is havin' difficulty trustin' the veracity of these claims, seein' as this human once broke the 'art of that cyclops."

"They call 'im a 'Monster Hunter' back on Th'myskôra, Cap'an!" added Steven The Goblin.

"That's a good point," said the captain, "Your reputation isn't exactly sterlin', human."

Leeja cringed in her hiding place, "You know, you can all

stop interfering in this conversation at any time. I really wouldn't mind."

"Leeja!" Norrin shouted, trying desperately to make out her face among the crew crowded around the quarterdeck, "Please come out here and talk to me!"

"Stow 'yer shrews, young man," the captain said, "I have a responsibility to the safety of my crew, a responsibility I take very seriously; answer the question. Can you promise that Leeja will be in no danger if she goes with you?"

Norrin turned and shouted toward the crowd, "Thorne and I were kids together! I was a dumb kid and I made dumb mistakes with him. But what I feel for you is...it's totally different. And I'm different now too. I'm a man now and I want to be a good man. You make me want to be a better man, Leeja!" She could hear his voice trembling; she wanted to comfort him. To run into his arms. "I go to sleep every night dreaming of the life we'll build together; I wake every morning remembering those perfect moments spent making love to you."

"Awwww," several crew members cooed altogether.

"But I can't promise you'll never get hurt if you come with me. I can't promise we'll always agree on where to live or how to raise our kids. I can't promise that the sex we have when we're eighty will be as acrobatic as when we first met. The only thing I can promise you, Leeja, is that I love you."

She couldn't hide from Norrin any longer. Leeja had to see him. She got down to the deck and started pushing her way through the crowd, almost involuntarily. Her body needed Norrin, and it was calling the shots now.

"Leeja, I promise," Norrin was still shouting into the crowd, "that I will choose you every day for as long as I live. I promise that no matter what happens, I will always work toward your best interests; even if you decide to form a whole horde, you will always be my forever."

"Alrighty, young man," the captain started, "your message has been received, and we'll relay it. You best be pulling up anchor and heading back home now."

Norrin didn't say anything back. Leeja could hear her crew talking amongst themselves, moving around the deck, and in the distance...splashing? Chains being dragged across a wooden deck?

He's not really going home, is he?

"Wait!" she shouted breathlessly, shoving her way through the crowd and rushing to the ship's edge. "Norrin, don't go! I love you too! I've tried to deny it since we met, but you were made for me. You're all I've thought about since I left."

Norrin released the anchor chain and beamed up at her.

"I know you might hurt me someday," Leeja continued, "but I'm going to have to take that risk. I'm yours, Norrin Galanou! I have been since you first stalked me down the esplanade!"

Norrin, crying and grinning, shouted back, "Well, get down here, Leeja! I wanna marry you!"

The crew went wild, wolf-whistling and clapping and collecting on bets.

"Permission to leave the ship, Captain?" Leeja asked.

The captain stroked his beard and hummed, "I don't know... our contract is for three more months..."

Angry shouts erupted from the crew, "Cap'ain, 'ave a heart!"

"Oh, alright," he finally sighed, winking at Leeja, "permission granted."

And before he could give the order to lower the rope ladder, Leeja was overboard and swimming toward Norrin.

The crew erupted into cheers, applause, and arquebus fire, cheering Leeja on.

He pulled her out of the water, and in one swift motion, Leeja was back home in Norrin's arms. She crushed her body against his; Leeja could feel his cock growing hard against her, that beautiful human cock, the only one she'd ever bite again. Her hands searched the familiar shapes of his shoulders, back, and ass. It was impossible to touch him enough.

"Norrin, I'm so sorry I never sh—"

Before she could finish, Norrin's fingers were twisting through her wild, green hair, tugging just hard enough to command her attention. Then he pulled her face close to his and kissed her deeply, ravenously, like a starving man.

CHAPTER
TWENTY-FIVE

Below the deck of the little ship, Leeja stood dripping wet in front of her horde. In front of Norrin. She lunged at him, pushing him onto on the oversized down mattress and scrambling for his britches, trying to untie them, but he stopped her,

"Please, I want to look at you".

"It's not wise to keep an orc waiting, human."

"A few more minutes won't kill me." Norrin was grinning at her.

Leeja smiled, "My tunic must be soaked through."

"It is," Norrin took in a ragged breath. Leeja could see his cock struggling in his britches.

She bent down, peeled off her leather booties, and tossed them aside in a wet thud.

Norrin's hand moved to the front of his britches. He started stroking his cock.

Leeja walked slowly around the cabin, examining her surroundings. Her body ached for Norrin, but if he wanted to play games, then she was going to win them.

She turned her back on him, slowly running her hand over the woodwork. She knew he was staring at the muscles beneath the translucent linen.

Norrin groaned.

"This ship is beautiful," Leeja said bending down slowly to examine a built-in cabinet. It was low, and long, nearly the length of the cabin. More importantly, Leeja knew the shapes her ass was making in her skintight, leather britches. She stood back up and hooked her thumbs into her waistband.

"I'm glad you like it," Norrin croaked. It was practically a whisper.

She turned slowly to the side and arched her back as she carefully slid her britches down to the floor, being careful to keep her wet linen smallclothes in place,

"I don't remember seeing this one around the docks, when did you make it?"

Of course Norrin made it. The smell of him emanated from every plank of wood. Leeja slid her finger across the exposed head of a nail. The moment she touched it, the nail he'd selected and driven into place, her desire for him came flooding up to the surface. She closed her eyes and was transported back to her many nights without him. The nights she lay awake in her bed trying to convince herself that she didn't need him.

That she didn't need to be selected and handled and pounded by him. By Norrin, her mate.

"Recently," Norrin said.

"Oh?" Leeja tried to act nonchalant, they were still playing, after all. She kept her eyes closed. She knew that if she looked at him, she wouldn't be able to resist the incredible sexual draw of him. "I don't remember seeing it in your father's workshop either."

Leeja grabbed ahold of her tunic, bunching it in her fists, as if she were going to take it off, "When did you start building it?"

"The day you left." Norrin was inching closer and closer to the edge of the bed.

Leeja turned her back on him again. She pulled her tunic off over her head and dropped it onto the wooden floor.

"Fuck," Norrin croaked.

Leeja's sex clenched.

He made this ship for me.

Leeja slid her thumbs into the waistband of her small-clothes.

"Now why would you do a thing like that?" She shifted her weight from one hip to the other, showing off her round, sculpted ass. An ass she knew he loved to look at.

"I couldn't stand being apart from you."

"But there are so many beautiful people on Th'myskôra," Leeja's breath caught momentarily in her throat, "you couldn't have been *that* lonely."

A sudden red haze blurred out Leeja's vision.

I have no right to be jealous. After all, I've had a dozen partners since I left...

But Leeja *was* jealous. Her heart raced as she tried desperately to force images of echidnas and centaurs groping at the soft, suntanned skin of her mate.

"There's no one else in the world for me, Leeja. I've been drowning since you left me. I haven't

thought of anything but seeing you again."

Leeja's breathing returned to normal, "And now that you see me?"

"I need to see more!"

Leeja looked over her shoulder and saw Norrin on the bed, desperate, panting, clawing at the sheets.

She slid off her smallclothes and turned to face him. The air was cold against her wet skin. Leeja felt gentle rays of sunshine dance across her flesh. As she looked into Norrin's eyes, she saw an expression she'd only seen on a few faces, and never directed at her.

Reverence.

"You're glowing..."

Norrin slid off the bed and onto his knees. He grabbed Leeja's ass and pressed his face into her center. His mouth was greedily searching, kissing and licking through her pubic hair to find its prize.

"Are you sure you won't get tired of me someday?" Leeja rested her hand on top of Norrin's head.

Norrin looked up at her from the floor, eyes smiling, "There's no one else in the world for me. You and me are forever, Leeja." He slid his tongue through her folds and made contact with her clit. An electric shock shot through her body, wracking her with pleasure. Leeja's head lolled back and her eyes fluttered closed. Norrin slid his hand up between her thighs, gently spreading them.

That was it, the feeling she'd been chasing all this time. She was back in Norrin's arms; his warmth surrounded her and his scent permeated every part of her.

He slid two familiar fingers inside of her, and Leeja moaned.

She tightened her fingers in his hair as the tension of her pleasure and desire mounted.

Norrin kept lapping at her swollen clit, working his fingers in and out of her desperate pussy. He slid his free hand up her back, gently caressing every bulge and divot of her flesh.

Leeja shivered as Norrin dragged his careful fingers around to her breast, squeezing it and applying gentle, tugging pressure to her erect nipple.

"Now!" she roared. "I need to make love now!"

In a flash, Norrin was on his feet, completely naked, fully erect, and dripping precum.

"Lay back on the bed," he said, and Leeja quickly complied. The sheets were soft and smooth against her bare skin, a striking contrast to the rough linens onboard the Flannery.

Norrin climbed on the bed. He knelt before her, placing one of her knees over his shoulder, lifting her ass and tugging her body down the bed to meet his.

He reached down, wrapping his hand around his thick, bucking cock, and pressed it against her slick outer lips.

"I just realized something," Leeja said, a wicked grin spreading across her face. "This'll be our first time having sex in a bed."

"Don't worry, we won't make a habit out of it."

Norrin slammed his cock inside of Leeja. A primal, guttural moan escaped his throat as he closed his eyes and started pumping deeper and deeper into her.

Leeja's back arched, her lungs betrayed her as her mouth stretched open over and over again in a series of ever more intense, voiceless screams.

Norrin's pace quickened. Now each stroke plunged his cock inside her to its full depth. Leeja's vision whited out. Her sex clenched and released in waves of pleasure so powerful, nothing else existed for her. There was no sea, no sunshine, no ships. Only Norrin's perfect cock and wave after wave of debilitating, quaking pleasure.

Then she heard it, Norrin yelped, a sound that was half pleasure, half pain. Leeja's orgasm was winding down. She was still pulsating, and leaking, but it was less intense; she could breathe again and her vision cleared. When she opened her eyes, she saw Norrin looking down at her. He was sweaty, red in the face, and grinning, "You bit me."

Leeja took her leg down off Norrin's shoulder. She tried to scoot up the bed, to remove Norrin from her and check for damage. But when she moved, he was pulled up the bed with her,

"You're stuck!" Leeja was horrified, she squirmed and wriggled, trying to free Norrin's cock from the danty.

"If you keep that up," he croaked out, "I'm going to explode."

"You...like this?"

Norrin shuttered. His breathing was labored as he slowly nodded his head.

"In that case," Leeja said wrapping a leg around his hip, "get ready to explode."

Leeja used one leg to push her pelvis up from the bed, and the other to keep Norrin's crotch firmly in place next to hers. She ground against him, rubbing her swollen clit on him. With each undulation, Norrin's arms shook more violently, his breath grew more ragged, and his face more desperate.

He was completely at the mercy of her throbbing, biting, cunt. Leeja could feel her own pleasure mounting again, her sex was tightening. She was going to cum again.

"I love you, Norrin," her words sent him over the edge. Leeja felt Norrin's cock thumping and spirting inside of her. She felt the warm rush of their combined fluids tumble out of her. Norrin was dripping down her ass crack. It pushed Leeja to another earth-shattering orgasm. She clenched and spasmed. She pulled Norrin down hard on top of her. And they both lay in the bed, clinging desperately to each other. Pleasure pulsed in waves through them both as each of their bodies heightened and prolonged the other's climax.

Finally, the shaking and moaning stopped. Leeja's breathing slowed and returned to normal and Norrin's spent cock slid out of her before he rolled over to lie next to her and hold her.

Leeja sat up to inspect the damage to Norrin's dick. She carefully ran her finger across the fresh red, teeth marks.

"They go all the way around," Norrin smiled inspecting the new markings, "you can't back out now, you gave me a ring! We're official."

Leeja stretched out her arm and admired her left hand, "You know, I think I might want a ring of my own."

TWENTY-SIX

Leeja had been awake for several minutes but, wasn't yet ready to open her eyes. She lay warm and contented in her bed, rocked lovingly by the Equiloam Sea.

"It's time to get up!" Norrin called cheerily into the cabin.

"No, thank you." Leeja pulled the covers over her head and rolled onto her other side.

"Everyone is expecting us."

"Everyone is stupid. I only love the bed."

The covers began to move gently over Leeja's feet and up her legs. Before she could protest, his solid and practiced hands rubbed the tight muscles of her sizable calves.

"Not fair," Leeja groaned, adjusting her legs to give him better access.

"Should I stop?" Norrin's hands moved up her thighs and eventually dug into the near-permanent knot in her hip.

"You don't get to stop," Leeja managed through moans, "I wouldn't be in this mess if it weren't for you."

"Alright, roll over, and I'll get the other side."

"I'm too big to roll," Leeja said, bunching the covers even tighter around her head and rolling to the other side.

"You'll never be too big for me," Norrin said, leaning down and kissing her round, pregnant belly.

Leeja hummed softly, stretching out as long as she could in the bed and wiggling her fingers and toes.

Norrin pulled the covers up a little higher, exposing her swollen breasts, "I never would have thought they could get *bigger*." Leeja rolled onto her back, and Norrin worked his way up her body, rubbing and kissing her in all of her tight, aching places. He took special care to be gentle with her tender breasts, and Leeja was extremely grateful. He kissed her chest and slowly made his way up to the bunched-up blanket still covering her face. He gently kissed her up and down her neck, dragging his nose along to tickle her most sensitive spots.

Leeja let out a long, satisfied sigh, finally pulled the blankets down over her head, and blinked the early morning sunlight out of her eyes.

Norrin's soft, gentle lips were pressing against hers immediately, bringing a rush of warmth to her face, invigorating her. Leeja grabbed Norrin by the back of the head and pulled him closer, deepening the kiss. They explored each others' mouths with the same eager passion they'd had that first night on top of the hill more than two years ago.

Norrin broke off the kiss. He pulled back and gazed adoringly down at his bride, "Good morning, boss."

"Good morning, horde," she smiled up at him. "You don't really want me to cover all of this body up with *clothes*, do you?"

Norrin shook his head and chuckled, "If it were up to me, you'd never wear clothes again. In fact," he said, turning his head to side-eye her, "if you want to stay here and make love all day, I'm sure the crew would be fine breaking ground without us."

"You'd like that, wouldn't you, human," Leeja grumbled as she wobbled out of bed and around the cabin, hastily getting dressed.

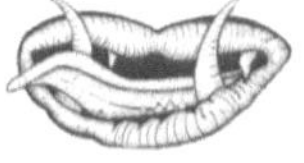

Springtime had once again come to Th'myskôra; the ground was soft enough to begin construction on a new little cottage.

Leeja and Rakka pored over the house plans, triple-checking that no detail had been omitted.

"The main bedroom will overlook the sea, right?" Norrin asked for the third time today.

"Don't worry," said Rakka, slapping a tremendous hand down on his shoulder, "you and small woman will wake up every morning with sea air slapping your face from the tide."

"And the baby's room is…"

"Right next to ours," Leeja assured him. "We'll hear every peep."

"But what about—"

"Don't worry so much, Frank!" Leeja kissed him softly on the nose. "It's a baby, not a mephit. It's not going to explode."

"I know, I know. The baby will be perfect. It's just...this spot, *my* spot; there's no other place like it in the Three Realms."

"Leeja is significant student, house will be perfect." Rakka turned his back to Norrin, blocking his view of the plans. Trolls, after all, are not known for their patience.

Norrin accepted defeat and joined Aengus, who was already hard at work digging a trench for the house's foundation...a perfect hexagon.

"When exactly does this 'working with your hands' get fun?" Arlynn asked, struggling with her shovel at the far end of the trench.

"When you start sweating," Leeja laughed. "In fact, the sweatier you get, the more fun you have."

"Look at me!" Imogen yelled. She was stumbling back and forth with a huge, grey hunk of granite. With a great deal of effort, she managed to heave it atop a pile of similar stones being gathered for the construction project. "I'm so strong! Did you see me, Leeja?"

"Careful," Arlynn teased her, "you might get a callous on those dainty researcher hands."

"You're both doing great!" Leeja laughed again.

"Hey, everyone! We brought snacks!" Norrin's mother, Glema stepped out into the clearing with Bridgid and Thorne.

"Oh, my! That's a steep hike," Bridgid huffed, setting down a large basket of fish sandwiches and ale. "No wonder this spot was yer secret for so long!"

"Well, it's not a secret anymore," Norrin said, taking a sandwich. "Once this house is built, we're going to have you all over for dinner at least once a week! Isn't that right, dear?"

"Oh, sure," Leeja said, joining them, "you and all the crones are expected at the baby shower.

"Jaania can't wait to meet your little one," Bridgid beamed, placing her meaty hand gently on Leeja's belly. "It's all she talks about lately!"

"Have you decided on a name yet?" Thorne asked around a mouthful of sandwich, "You know, Thorne works weather the baby is a boy *or* a girl."

"Let's just concentrate on getting this house finished," Norrin said smiling, "then you can all argue about baby names and dinner parties, okay?"

"A dinner party is a wonderful idea," Arlynn said cheerily, "Imogen can even bring her new beau, to meet us all, if he can fit us into his busy schedule, that is."

"I'm sure that can be arranged," Imogen said, blushing a deep red and avoiding her friend's gaze. "And maybe *Arlynn* will have someone to bring along soon too?"

"Don't you go trying to drag me into domestic bliss. I'm perfectly happy as I am!"

"I've heard *that* before," said Leeja, and she stood with her husband, her new parents, and her very best friends in the whole world. They all looked out over the bay at Norrin's favorite view on the island. The view he shared with her the first night they made love. The view she would wake up to every morning for the rest of her life.

ACKNOWLEDGMENTS

I would like to extend my most heartfelt thanks to my long-suffering husband and alpha reader. And to my beta readers MC Newstead, Audrey Ruff, and Kylie Welch who really helped my sand down a lot of the book's rough spots. And, of course, the hugest 'thank you' to the members of the Princess Cafe: Sarai, Joey and Lady Perbert whose opinions and emotional support are invaluable.

THE SIREN'S PACT

Enjoy The Human Bet? Get The Siren's Pact for free!

Set one hundred years before the Equiloam Romance series: War between the Humans and the Elves is inevitable, but when true love arrives in the form of a dashing Siren, Jumana will have to decide if her loyalties lie with humanity...or with her heart.

ABOUT THE AUTHOR

Mona Howell is just a forty-year-old girl who enjoys writing silly-fun books for the monster smut girlies. She lives in Huntington Beach, CA with her husband and ten stone fruit trees.

(If you liked Imogen, good news! In the next book she meets the man, well...*incubus,* of her dreams)